Primal Hunger

When the sun goes down, passion is unleashed.

Kennedy Beaumont loves her bartending job, even if her spirited nature sometimes gets her in trouble. Like threatening to hose down one of Pendragon's co-owners. When it comes to Tristan, she could use a good hosing down herself—maybe it'll help her stop casting him as the star of her wickedest dreams. Since he goes out of his way to avoid her, it ought to be easy to put him out of her head—until he reluctantly offers her a ride home.

Gargoyle shape-shifter Tristan Callaghan hasn't had time for anything other than recovering the mystical dagger that was used to permanently lock his brother in a prison of stone. The cat inside him should have stopped craving Kennedy's touch long ago, but now that she's sitting next to him in his car, his very human need for her is sharper than ever.

The distraction is costly. In a split second, Kennedy finds herself thrust into a dangerous, millennia-old hunt for Excalibur. A hunt that marks her for death—and leaves Tristan with a painful choice—sacrifice his family, his quest...or the one woman meant to be his.

Warning: There's nothing tame about this alpha male hell-bent on claiming his mate. Featuring bone-melting explicit sex, graphic language, violence and a little harmless bite...or two.

Primal Attraction

He'll stop at nothing to claim her... If she doesn't kill him first.

A lethal huntress, Sorcha lives to track and eliminate rogue immortals—until her latest assignment turns out to be a sexy, gargoyle shape-shifter. From the start she's shaken by the lust his touch awakens inside her. Not only that, but the cat is convinced she's his mate, and for the first time, she's unable to kill her target.

Still mourning the loss of his mate, Cale is stunned to find Sorcha alive. Yet the woman he aches to possess doesn't recognize him and is after the only thing that will save his brother—a mystical weapon that will lead to Excalibur.

Determined to protect his family and reclaim his mate, Cale ruthlessly takes advantage of Sorcha's one weakness—her desire for him. Desire that could unlock their past...or cause him to lose her all over again.

Warning: Featuring a sarcastic, ass-kicking heroine going toe-to-toe with the stubborn shifter who's dead set on reclaiming his mate. Also contains graphic violence, death-threat foreplay and scorching sex that will make you roll over and purr.

Look for these titles by
Sydney Somers

Now Available:

Shadow Destroyers
Unbreakable
Stripped Away
Storm Warning
Dark Obsession

Spellbound
Say You're Mine
Don't Let Go
Whatever It Takes

Pendragon Gargoyles
Primal Hunger
Primal Attraction
Primal Pleasure

Enslaved
Waitin' on a Hero
Call Me Cupid
Talons: Caged Desire
Trust Me

Print Anthology
Talons
Night Spell
Primal Seduction

Primal Seduction

Sydney Somers

Samhain Publishing, Ltd.
577 Mulberry Street, Suite 1520
Macon, GA 31201
www.samhainpublishing.com

Primal Seduction
Print ISBN: 978-1-60504-941-0

Editing by Lindsey Faber
Cover by Kanaxa

Primal Hunger, ISBN 978-1-60504-669-3
First Samhain Publishing, Ltd. electronic publication: September 2009
Primal Attraction, ISBN 978-1-60504-881-9
First Samhain Publishing, Ltd. electronic publication: January 2010
First Samhain Publishing, Ltd. print publication: December 2010

Contents

Primal Hunger

Chapter One

"What are you going to do, fire me?"

Bold words for a woman who adored her job, even if she was the one holding the hose, and Kennedy Beaumont knew it.

Drops of water from the warning shot she'd fired glistened on the bar between her and the two men who looked ready to tear each other's throats out. Despite the pounding beat of music—courtesy of the house band—more than a few heads had swiveled in her direction the second she'd snatched the hose from beneath the counter and promised to drench the pair if they didn't knock it off.

Not that the threat would have been a problem if both men were drunk or hassling her. Unfortunately, the quiet regular with dark blond hair and a wicked-looking scar that curved from the corner of his mouth to his ear had never uttered a disrespectful word to her, never even needed to be cut off and dumped in a cab.

The other guy was her boss—sort of.

Tristan Callaghan ran a hand through his dark hair as though she'd actually gotten him wet. Intimidating on a good day and downright feral looking when pissed off—like now—his piercing blue eyes routinely locked her feet to the floor. But grinning, furious or indifferent, his heavy gaze never failed to unleash a slow curl of warmth that wrapped around her backbone. Never failed to make it impossible to fully satisfy the hot ache that pulsed between her thighs.

But not even her body's predictable response to Tristan's presence swayed her to lower the hose. Not when he looked just wild enough to jump the bar and take it from her if she showed the slightest weakness.

In her six months working at Pendragon's she'd learned the only thing the bar's patrons respected was a steel-edged spine and the guts to back it up. Backing down from a fight—hell, even breaking eye contact too quickly—often caused more trouble than holding your ground.

That alone kept her arm up, her fingers poised on the trigger. "Well?"

A ghost of a smile caught the regular's mouth, and Tristan scowled at him. For a moment she thought she might have to carry through on her threat, then he turned and vanished into the sea of bodies crowded around the bar.

Kennedy stared after him, not really surprised he hadn't said a word. He never had much to say to her, not even after his month-long absence. More than once she'd caught herself envying the other waitresses he regularly flirted with and teased. But not her. Never her.

"I think you can lower your weapon now."

She gave the regular, Dolan, a dirty look. "No thanks to you."

He shrugged and reached for his beer, studying her over the rim of his glass. Unlike half the men, whose attention strayed to her chest at least twice while ordering a drink, she'd never caught him looking at anything but her face.

She finally replaced the hose, sweeping the area to be sure Tristan didn't plan to finish what the pair had started the second her back was turned. Pendragon's was packed again tonight, the crowd just hitting its drinking stride. Between filling orders and cleaning up after sloppy drinkers there wasn't much time for chatting and even less for her usual people watching.

And in a place like this there was never a shortage of interesting people coming and going. Half the time it seemed like the bouncers only let in the most unusual people lined up outside. Many of regulars acted more like animals than human beings, and that was before they consumed amounts of alcohol that should have landed at least half of them in the hospital with alcohol poisoning.

As long as the bouncers ran a tight ship and her tip jar continued to fill, she didn't worry about it. Much.

Wiping down the counter, she allowed herself a quick breather, wondering if Tristan had already left for the night. The whisper of awareness across the back of her neck said no, but she hadn't spotted him a while.

"What do you see in him?"

Kennedy glanced behind her. "Who?"

Dolan arched a brow. "The cat."

She frowned.

He rolled his eyes. "Tristan." He forced it out as if the name curdled on his tongue like sour milk.

Cat? More than once she'd compared Tristan to a sleek predator, usually when he managed to sneak up on her or the few times she'd walked into the office as he came slowly awake, stretching. She hadn't imagined anyone else, least of all a *guy,* making the same ridiculous comparison.

"Well?" he prodded when she remained silent.

"He's my boss." She turned away long enough to pour a glass of draft for another customer.

"You're attracted to him."

She shrugged. "He's easy on the eyes." Very easy. "But then so are at least half a dozen overpaid actors. Doesn't mean anything."

"He's different." Dolan's brows drew together as though he couldn't possibly figure out why that was.

It was Kennedy's turn to roll her eyes. "Not that it's any of your business, but there is nothing going on between me and Tristan."

He cocked his head thoughtfully, his gaze far too probing. "But you've thought about it."

Too many times to count. Her attraction to Tristan hummed under her skin like a fever that wouldn't break. The month he'd been away should have been plenty of time to get over the waste-of-time crush. But the second she'd turned around to find him standing on the opposite side of the counter tonight that same hot awareness had burrowed straight through her stomach.

It didn't help that he was the only one she fantasized about these days. She'd never been one to shy away from what she wanted when it came to sex or taking care of her own needs. That she couldn't achieve that same intense pleasure without imagining him there with her—his hands trailing across her skin, his mouth slowly devouring her—left her increasingly frustrated.

"Need a refill?" She nodded to Dolan's empty glass without answering his question.

He shook his head, an oddly resigned expression falling over his face.

For some reason Kennedy suspected the look had nothing to do with passing on another beer. Thankfully, the pace picked back up and she didn't have time to think about their unusual conversation, or wonder where Tristan had vanished.

"So what was that about?"

Tristan cursed under his breath and straightened from the catwalk that looked out over the crowded bar. He didn't glance in his brother's direction, knowing nothing short of a serious brawl or a threat to one of their own drew Cale from his office. "Nothing."

"When Kennedy reaches for that hose, she usually has a damn good reason for it."

"She's crazy?" Tristan offered.

Cale snorted. "You just think that because she's one of the few who actually stands up to you."

"One of these days that's going to get her into trouble." Maybe not with him, but sooner or later she'd piss off the wrong immortal and wind up hurt.

"So then why didn't you take the hose from her?"

Tristan didn't answer. It was far wiser to keep his mouth shut than admit he hadn't gotten over his fascination with the human. He was pretty damn sure if he'd gotten close enough to touch her, he wouldn't have stopped at prying the hose out of her hand.

Not when her deep brown eyes soothed the wildest parts of him and at the same time unleashed a hunger he didn't know how to satisfy. The second he'd entered the bar and caught her scent, the cat inside him growled possessively. Only when he'd felt the pull of her, the animal prowling restlessly inside him, did he realize how much he'd missed her.

He'd left town to hunt down a lead as much as to let his craving for the human's touch pass. One look from Kennedy tonight, one stubborn arch of her brow as she pointed that hose at him, and he'd wanted to grin at the challenge she presented. Wanted to feel her fingers wrapped around more than that makeshift weapon.

Cale nodded below. "Any problem with Dolan that I should know about?"

"We just had a little disagreement."

"One that involved Kennedy."

"The Fae was...watching her," he finished lamely.

"He wouldn't be the first." Cale studied him carefully.

Tristan shrugged. He wasn't in the mood for one of Cale's infamous "don't screw the staff" talks. Admitting he'd allowed the Fae to provoke him with vague comments about Kennedy wouldn't go over so well with his brother. It wasn't going over so well with *him*.

Hell, he wasn't even sure why he'd let Dolan get to him at all. The bar was packed with attractive females and more than one had crooked her finger at him tonight. Instead, he continually caught his gaze sliding back to the spirited blonde behind the bar.

Below, Kennedy smiled at a guy at the counter—a damn dragon—who tried impressing her with some smoke and mirrors trick as dull as Avalon's barren region. A moment later she laughed and leaned forward to whisper something in his ear. The dragon's hand came up to catch her shoulder, holding her close as he whispered something back.

Tristan nearly snarled. Tangling with the dragon would be a hell of a lot more interesting than the Fae. The Fae who chose that moment to turn in his chair. It took Dolan only a second to pick Tristan out above and grin at him.

Bastard.

"Where's the dagger?"

If Cale noticed his attention had strayed back to Kennedy, he didn't let it show. Relieved his brother was letting the subject drop, Tristan brought his beer to his mouth. "In the vault at your place."

He hadn't wanted to carry around the enchanted weapon any longer than necessary. Too many immortals coveted the six daggers, which when united would reveal Excalibur's resting place, to risk bringing it here. It didn't matter which side of the covenant the immortals below intended to honor, Tristan knew where his own clan's loyalties lay—with Arthur.

While some awaited Arthur's return, others wanted to make sure Morgana, his half-sister, remained in power. Without Excalibur the sorceress's reign might be limited to the kingdom of Camelot, but all of Avalon would be at her mercy if she got her hands on Arthur's sword.

"Any trouble acquiring it?"

"Not this time." He'd expected the fledgling sorceress who had used the mystical weapon to curse their brother would be ready to fight him for it. Instead, Tristan had found her lair eerily deserted. Twice before he'd come close to tracking her and the dagger, only to lose her trail and have to start over.

"He doesn't blame you."

"And you would know that how?" Seeing as Cian had been locked in his gargoyle form for nearly a century, he couldn't say a damn word about the price he'd paid for Tristan taunting a sorceress.

Cale pushed away from the railing. "I've got something to take care of tonight, so if I'm not back before dawn, we'll meet at the house tomorrow night to figure out how we use it to break the curse."

If not for Rhiannon's fury following Arthur's death, they could have damn well discussed it in the morning. The goddess hadn't cared that her son was prophesized to awaken and finish the war begun centuries ago. She'd blamed the gargoyle clans for his defeat at Camlann and believed it fitting they should spend their daylight hours trapped in their stone form as punishment.

With centuries to get used to her punishment, he should have been less bitter about the whole thing. Maybe if the lost daggers weren't the only way to return Excalibur to Arthur and have the curse lifted against his people. A seemingly colossal undertaking when it had taken him over a hundred years to locate just one of them.

Tristan nodded as his brother walked away. Exhaustion pulled at him, the long hours of searching for the dagger finally catching up to him. He finished off his beer and managed to occupy himself with watching the band for a while.

More than sleep, he needed one of the females below if he stood any chance of forgetting the human tonight. One redheaded enchantress in particular had glanced in his direction half a dozen times in the last hour.

Sparing a brief look at the bar, he noticed the dragon had wisely moved on and Kennedy busied herself with tidying up. He swore the woman didn't know how to stand still. Countless times he'd imagined helping her burn off the excess amount of energy she radiated.

Seeming to sense his gaze, Kennedy glanced up. The flashing lights and thick shadows should have prevented her from picking him out so easily, yet he felt the moment she locked on to him.

The cat growled softly then louder, tearing to get loose as Tristan eased back into the darkness and out of sight.

Kennedy didn't know the inner workings of her Chevy Impala any more than she knew quantum physics or how to speak Chinese. And that was a problem for three reasons.

One—the secondhand car she'd scraped every cent to buy refused to start. Two—the flickering street lamp overhead made the quiet stretch of road downright eerie with its pulsing light and crackling hum. Three—and undoubtedly the most troubling of all—she couldn't shake the feeling someone was watching her.

She peered at the maze of hoses and wires under the hood, struggling not to give into the paranoia that slithered across the back of her neck. Even with the late hour, she wouldn't have considered the area treacherous. Acknowledging that did nothing to stem the creeped-out sensation that crawled under her skin. If anyone had followed her from the bar, they were doing a damn good job of staying out of sight.

For the millionth time, Kennedy cursed her roommate. If not for having to cover all the bills after her *ex*-roommate had bailed on her, she would have been able to afford a vehicle with a purring engine, not a death rattle. Unfortunately her choices had been limited, as her depleted bank account could attest to, proving yet again the only person she could count on was herself.

Herself *and* roadside assistance.

Kennedy reached in through her open window for her cell phone. Staring at the engine block wasn't getting her anywhere. Give her unruly drunks, temperamental waitresses and bouncers with more brawn than brain and she could work wonders. Stranded at three in the morning, however, made those skills feel as useful as tying a cherry stem into a knot using just her tongue.

She glanced at the display screen of her cell phone and groaned. No signal. *Perfect.* Giving the area another quick scan, she walked a few feet away from her car, hoping to figure out why her phone wasn't getting any reception. She was right downtown, for Christ's sake.

A black BMW convertible cruised past her, its brake lights brightening the surrounding gloom as the car came to a stop a few meters in front of her. Kennedy's heart sped up before she got a hold of herself. The familiar vehicle reversed, and while she should have been relieved to no longer be alone, her insides stretched taut.

"Car trouble?" Tristan asked, turning the volume down on the music pumping out from the speakers.

She glanced over her shoulder at the raised hood of her car. "Nah. I just like playing grease monkey in the middle of the night for kicks."

Tristan grumbled something under his breath and turned off his car before throwing open his door. A few confident strides carried him to her crap car, its faded blue paint looking even less attractive when parked so close to Tristan's shiny BMW.

"Do you know much about cars?" she asked when he started poking around under the hood. She tried to bite back as much of her skepticism as she could, which wasn't much. It was either be skeptical or stare at his phenomenal ass, and the former seemed like a smarter move.

He spared her a sharp glance, but said nothing. She hovered over his shoulder, watching him check caps and fluid levels. She was opening her mouth to point out that she had known enough to check the obvious, when he straightened abruptly and pivoted on his heel, knocking into her.

Kennedy clutched the front of him to steady herself, her grip on his T-shirt seeming to drag him even closer. Too close. Heat radiated from him and his rich masculine scent overwhelmed her senses. She studied the strong column of his neck—she didn't dare meet his gaze—thinking she'd like to press her mouth to the small scar where his neck met his shoulder.

His muscles tightened beneath her hand and a soft sound, almost a growl, rumbled in his chest. Then he moved past her, sliding behind the wheel of her car as though she hadn't been a heartbeat from crossing the line. And running her tongue up his throat to meet his mouth definitely would have qualified.

As if she hadn't already pushed her luck with him tonight.

Kennedy closed her eyes, leaned her forehead against the edge of the propped-up hood. If this kept up, she was seriously going to have to consider looking for a new job.

Drawing one more steadying, get-over-him-already breath, she edged around to the driver's side. No matter how many times Tristan cranked the ignition, the engine didn't turn over. An expression that bordered on desperation furrowed his brows.

He didn't look at her when he climbed out, slamming the door behind him.

"If I'm keeping you from something or someone..." She trailed off, thinking of the slinky redhead she'd noticed him with earlier.

"You're not." His annoyed tone suggested otherwise.

"Look, if your cell is working I can just call a tow truck and you can be on your way."

He turned around quickly, scanning the area for something. "Yours isn't working?"

She shook her head. "No signal."

He pulled his phone out of his pocket, tearing his gaze from across the street long enough to check the screen. He tilted the phone up as though it would suddenly capture whatever waves the damn things transmitted on.

"No reception either, huh?"

Shaking his head, he shoved the phone back in his pocket. He propped one hand on the edge of the hood, his expression wary.

Kennedy turned to follow his gaze, a chill darting up her spine as she searched the dark street behind her.

"I'll give you a lift home."

She wouldn't have objected if he hadn't sounded as though he'd rather lie down in the middle of the street and wait for the next car to run him over. "You know—"she reached into her car and grabbed her purse, "—I think I'll just walk back to work and catch a ride with one of the girls."

"Everyone's gone already."

She frowned. "Even Cale?" She swore the man slept at the bar most nights.

Tristan scowled. "My brother had plans. I'll take you." He didn't wait for her to agree before opening the BMW's passenger door.

Knowing she'd be stupid to refuse a second time, especially when the sensation of being watched continued to linger, she locked her car and joined him. The lowered roof gave her an uncompromised view of the convertible's expensive interior. Still, she hesitated to slip into the black leather seat that looked soft enough to melt beneath her.

She turned her head in Tristan's direction, disturbed to find him standing closer than she'd realized. Close enough that his thigh brushed hers, forcing her to tip her head back to meet his eyes. She might not have a water hose pointed at him now, but the fierce gaze he pinned her with made her wish she did.

He planted an arm on the car behind her, blocking her in. In case she changed her mind?

He leaned forward, and her pulse jumped as his rough jaw whispered across her cheek. She closed her eyes, a wave of delicious warmth uncoiling deep in her belly.

"Don't forget to buckle up."

Tristan was already rounding the front of the car when she realized he'd moved away from her. She sank into the seat and closed the door, resisting the urge to fan her face. Between the lingering humidity that promised a sheet-tangled sleep and her internal temperature skyrocketing, she had to be flushed from head to toe.

Hand on the door, Tristan froze.

"What's wrong?"

He whipped around. The sound of a wild animal—a pissed off animal—rumbled on the air.

It wasn't...coming from Tristan? Kennedy straightened to get a better look around.

Without warning, Tristan vaulted over the door and dropped into his seat. He shoved the key into the ignition and the car roared to life just as something sailed past the front of Kennedy's face.

"Down," Tristan yelled, pushing her lower in the seat. "Fuck."

She raised her head enough to see something red sticking in his neck. No sooner did he pluck it out than another dart struck his shoulder. The snarl of fury that burst past his lips made her heart pound faster.

His head lolled forward and he forced it back, his hand clumsily searching for the gearshift.

"Drive," he mumbled. "Kennedy...drive..."

His words slurred together before his head fell to the side, his eyes closed.

Shit!

Another dart lodged into the trim around the windshield. Without a clue where they were coming from, she scrambled into Tristan's lap, her feet tangling with his in search of the gas pedal. She didn't take even a second to glance around before shoving the gearshift into drive and punching the gas.

The BMW shot forward and her fingers tightened on the wheel that dug into her bare thighs. She drove right through the stop sign ahead, and then the next one. She half hoped a cop car might notice and offer some kind of help from whoever had just attacked them.

Her gaze snapped to the rearview mirror in search of pursuing headlights. But instead of seeing the dark stretch of road behind them dotted with the occasional street lamp, her face stared back at her.

Her face but for the black, bleeding eyes.

Kennedy let loose the scream she'd been clinging to for the last two minutes and looked over her shoulder. The backseat was empty. Another terrifying glance at the rearview mirror revealed nothing but passing landmarks that blurred past.

What the hell?

Grateful for almost no traffic, she ramped up their speed, taking turns at random to throw off anyone who might be following. The tops of her thighs felt rubbed raw from each crank of the steering wheel, but she didn't stop driving. Not until she hit the other side of town and found herself facing the docks between the industrial park and acres of land slated for condo development.

She shoved the car into park, but didn't turn it off. Neither could she pry her eyes off the rearview mirror.

Shock. There was no other explanation for what she'd seen. The feeling of being watched, coupled with the attack and Tristan losing consciousness had drop-loaded too much adrenaline into her system.

When a few more minutes passed and no one pulled up behind them, she relaxed back against Tristan. Feeling around the wheel, she released the catch and tipped it up, giving herself a little more breathing room. Once her heart stopped threatening to break right through her ribs, she turned to check on Tristan.

The slow rise and fall of his chest confirmed he was still breathing.

Kennedy cupped his face. "Tristan?"

No response.

She tapped his cheek. "Come on, wake up." Nothing. She dropped her head to his shoulder. "Please, please wake up."

A flash of red between the seats caught her attention. She plucked the small feather-tipped dart from the leather, careful not to stick herself with it.

What was in it, some kind of tranquillizer? And why the hell had someone shot *darts* at them to begin with? A drive-by, carjacking or mugging she could understand—even if she'd been parked in a fairly safe part of downtown—but darts?

Kennedy tried again to rouse him, then reached for her purse. Half the contents had been spilled across the floor of the car during her drag race through town. She gave up on feeling around for her cell phone when she remembered Tristan's. Turning so she sat across his lap, her feet in the passenger seat, she dug into his pocket. Her fingers had just brushed the phone's edge when a soft sound left Tristan's lips.

She nearly whimpered in relief. "Tristan? Tristan, wake up!"

His lashes didn't so much as flutter. Hoping she hadn't imagined the small response, she waited another few seconds, willing him to open his eyes, then continued to try and free his cell phone.

"Oh, come on." She squirmed forward, twisting a bit to get a better grip inside his jeans pocket.

An arm clamped around her. "Don't. Move."

Part warning, part plea, the growled command stopped her in her tracks.

Chapter Two

Sweet Avalon.

The cat in him stretched its claws in pure pleasure, wanting more of the soft female slowly driving him out of his mind. Indulging the beast, Tristan pressed his face against her throat. Silky tendrils of her hair slid along his cheek.

Kennedy.

He breathed deep, inhaling her enticing scent until his blood ran hot. She resisted the hand pressed against her back, the one coaxing her closer, but he only smiled against her skin. The more she resisted, the more both man and cat craved a brush of her fingers, a taste of her lush mouth.

She wanted him. That she planted a palm in the middle of his chest did nothing to change that fact. Not when his senses drowned in the tease of her increasing arousal. Needing to feel more of her, he slipped a hand beneath her shirt and spanned his fingers across her lower back.

Her sharp intake of breath echoed in his ears, and he knew she felt it too. The same tangle of need that caught him hard in the gut every time they were in the same room.

"Closer," he demanded, opening his mouth on the curve of her neck. She arched beneath his lips, slowly sagging against him, her body melting into his. He wanted to roar in primal satisfaction.

Tristan tunneled his fingers through her hair, cupping her nape as he ran his tongue from the soft hollow of her throat to the corner of her mouth. Gods, he'd known she'd taste this good, feel this good. And he wanted more. More bared skin. More quick catches of her breath. More of her wrapped around him.

She murmured something but the words ran together in his head. The hazy fog he couldn't shake drenched her voice in lulling dips and waves that drove the cat wild. With one hand buried in her hair, his other swept up the inside of her leg. He bit at her bottom lip, catching the lusty sigh that rolled off her tongue the moment he molded his palm along the inside of her thigh.

Kennedy squirmed in his lap, and he hissed out a breath at the sweet friction against his cock.

"Tristan." Her voice sounded far away, but no less turned-on than he was.

He inched higher, groaned louder when she squirmed again. He knew without slipping beneath the hem of her shorts that she was growing hotter, wetter. Nipping a path along her jaw, he skimmed his fingers higher to her shirt, tugging at the fabric until he could work a hand beneath to cup her breast.

Her nipple jutted against her lacy bra. Fumbling with the clasp, he jerked the material down and grazed the puckered flesh. He needed to see her breasts, to run his tongue between them, over them. He ached to watch her face as he licked the dark pink tips before sucking her into his mouth.

"Tristan, listen—"

He trapped her nipple between his thumb and finger, tugging gently. Her whimper of pleasure only made him harder. Lifting his hips, Tristan tugged her down to grind against his shaft. With the sweet curve of her ass nestled so snug to him, it was all he could do not to thrust against her like a savage animal.

The cat didn't think there was a damn thing wrong with that.

"Touch me." The gravelly plea didn't sound like him, but that didn't stop him from snagging her hand and bringing it between them.

The first tentative brush of her palm was nothing more than a tease. He laced his fingers through hers, tightening her hold on his cock. They both moaned as she stroked him through his pants.

"We have to stop," she whispered, her protest quickly lost beneath his tongue.

He angled her head back, sinking fast and hard into a hungry kiss. He'd been thinking about it for months. Every time he noticed her smile or glower he'd thought about covering her mouth with his, pushing his tongue inside until she gave it up to him. Gave him everything.

And everything was exactly what he wanted right now. The hot, naked, burying himself inside her kind of everything. The finding ways to make her scream in pleasure kind of everything.

"Harder." He gripped her fingers tighter, guiding them up and down his shaft, then turned his attention back to the sweet spot between her legs.

The brush of his thumb inside the hem of her shorts made her tremble, so he did it again and again, moving a little higher each time. The lacy edge of her panties was the only thing preventing him from tracing the damp folds of her sex.

"Stop."

The demand managed to penetrate the silky fog clinging to Tristan's mind. He reluctantly forced his eyes open, knowing the dream was going to slip away from him. With one more lazy sweep of his mouth across hers, one more slick stroke of his tongue, he drew back, prepared to find himself alone.

A maze of fuzzy colors blurred across his vision. He struggled to focus.

"Tristan?"

Kennedy's voice no longer sounded far away. Second by second he processed the dry ache in his throat, the faint pain that throbbed in the back of his skull—the female curled up in his lap.

Not a dream.

He glanced down. His hand really was halfway up her shorts, the heat of her skin warming him straight through to the bone. Lifting his gaze, he took in her raised shirt. A glimpse of one full breast peeked out from beneath the bunched material. Her chest rose and fell in rhythm with the shaky breaths that whispered across his cheek. A rosy flush clung to her neck and throat, and her damp lips...

Tristan forced his attention all the way to her eyes. Definitely not a dream.

Shit.

Don't freak out.

Kennedy repeated the same three words to herself for the

dozenth time since Tristan had finally opened his eyes. Staying calm after the last twenty minutes was about as likely as a bachelor party turning down a free strip show.

Tristan's possessive hold on her thigh was the only thing keeping her halfway grounded—at least until he looked at her. *Really* looked at her. Her earlier relief evaporated as his brows drew together in confusion. Not that she blamed him. She wasn't entirely sure how she'd gone from reluctantly accepting a ride to letting him feel her up.

She'd been so damn grateful he wasn't out cold that her brain took a while to catch up with her senses. The ones headed for full-blown short circuit since the moment he'd tugged her closer. Forget what his mouth had done to her, the lazy trace of his tongue, the scrape of his teeth…

"You're okay." They were both okay. Mostly.

"Am I?" He glanced down, drawing his hand away from her.

Without the added distraction of his hands trailing over her skin—not to mention the slightly panicked expression on Tristan's face—she scrambled back into the passenger seat.

"What happened?"

Kennedy righted her clothing, not meeting his gaze when she felt him watching her. She plucked the dart from between the seats and held it up. "Someone was either really bored tonight or a zookeeper couldn't wait until tomorrow morning to go postal."

"Zookeeper?"

"Can't really think of who else carries around tranquillizer darts." And that was a serious stretch of the imagination. So why didn't he look half as confused as she felt? "Are you in any trouble?" Cale hadn't said much about Tristan's month-long vacation.

"Me? You were the one stranded on the side of the road."

"I'm not the one they shot, unless they have really bad aim." She studied the dart he took from her. "Could this just have been someone's idea of a sick joke? Otherwise, wouldn't you have been unconscious longer?"

Tristan set the dart in the console beneath the mounted GPS. He stared out at the harbor. "You drove us here?"

"Like a bat out of hell." The memory of black, bleeding eyes staring back at her in the mirror made her shiver.

"What?"

She shook her head. "Still a little freaked out is all." And struggling not to look over her shoulder to make sure they really were alone in the car.

"I'm not sure what happened," he began.

"It's fine," she interrupted. "You weren't yourself...and I..." Hadn't cared why he'd kissed her. Hadn't cared about anything but enjoying the way he opened his mouth over hers, slowly drinking her in.

God, did taking so long to slow things down count as taking advantage of him?

Tristan arched a brow. "I started to say that I'm not sure what happened back at your car, but I'm pretty sure it wasn't a mentally unstable zookeeper."

Her gaze slid to his. "Oh. Right." Clearly she was the only one wondering how she'd let her hormones override her commonsense. At least he could blame his actions on whatever had been in the dart.

A sexy grin curved his lips.

"Why are you smiling?"

"I've just never seen Kennedy Beaumont flustered before."

"Stick around. I'm just hitting my stride," she mumbled, raking her hands through her hair.

A chill danced down her spine, and she whipped around.

Empty backseat. Deserted development lots stretched back into the darkness. No poltergeist Kennedy waiting to pounce.

If she'd been back at the bar she would have poured herself a double shot of whiskey right about now. The alcohol would have gone a long way to soothe her frayed nerves and, if she was lucky, erase the taste of Tristan that lingered on her lips.

He started the car, adjusting the wheel before he put his hand on the gearshift.

"We need to call the police." Since attempting to use his phone had landed her in a hot situation moments ago, she bent to feel around at her feet for hers.

A tight grip on her wrist jerked her upright. The worried look on Tristan's face made her stomach roll. "What?" She followed his gaze to the black mark on top of her hand.

"Where the hell..." Kennedy rubbed at the ink stain that reminded her of a spider web. The mark didn't fade no matter how hard she rubbed it. “I don’t know where this came from.”

“Did you let someone draw this on you?”

“Yeah. In between the wet T-shirt contest and my pole dance.” She snorted. “You saw how busy we were. I think I’d remember someone playing Picasso on my hand.”

He didn’t comment, and his silence made it harder not to be seriously creeped out by the flawless design she couldn’t explain. She tried rubbing it off on her shorts, but he pulled her hand up to his face for closer inspection.

“What did you see tonight?”

“Not much. One minute you were jumping into the car and the next you were out cold. I didn’t see anyone, but then I didn’t exactly sit there and bask in my surroundings.” She’d no doubt broken a few speed records getting out of there.

Releasing her hand, Tristan leaned forward, and she could have sworn he...smelled her. “You’re afraid.”

“Can’t say the experience was typical for me.”

He shook his head. “I mean now. You’re afraid now.”

“Let’s see you hallucinate and wind up with a weird mark on your body and not panic a little.”

“Hallucinate?”

Kennedy closed her eyes. “My imagination just ran away with me when I played Indy 500.” Or so she’d thought. She glanced at her hand, damn sure she wasn’t imagining the black mark.

“Tell me what you saw.”

The deadly serious tone had her focusing all of her attention on Tristan for the first time since she’d scrambled off his lap. The same tension from earlier radiated from him, and she half expected another dart to come sailing through the darkness and embed itself in his neck.

“Could we put the top up now?” They might be miles away from the quiet street where she’d parked her car, but the longer they sat there, the more vulnerable and exposed she felt.

“Kennedy,” he prompted after the roof rose with the press of a button, sealing them in.

She let out a breath. “I saw myself, but not. I looked in the mirror, but I had black eyes. *Bleeding* black eyes.” She shuddered. “Definitely not the CoverGirl look I was going for with my mascara tonight.”

"Do you have to be a smartass all the time?"

"It's sarcasm or rock quietly in the corner. Forgive me for picking the option that doesn't involve a strait jacket."

"Where were you when you saw it?"

It, not *yourself*. The distinction felt important somehow, and Kennedy searched his face wondering why he sounded so reasonable. Shouldn't he be looking at her like she was one signature short of being admitted for a full psychiatric work-up?

"A couple miles from my car. It was there one moment and gone the next." And still freaky as hell to recall. She curbed the impulse to look in the back seat again. Barely.

Tristan shifted the car into drive, leaving the harbor behind.

"Are we going to the police?" Not that they could offer much in the way of descriptions of the assailant.

"No. Cale's."

"Your brother's? Don't you think we need to report what happened? The guy who shot you could have hurt someone else by now."

"What makes you think it's a guy?"

She shrugged. "Pendragon's does attract a wild crowd. I suppose you could have pissed off the wrong woman tonight." Enough of them had spent the evening checking him out.

He scowled at her. "I think the mark on your hand proves that this isn't about me."

She watched the speedometer rise as he cruised through the next green light. "That's working under the assumption that it's connected to my crippled car and our mystery dart shooter."

"Don't forget your hallucination."

Like that was possible. "There's no way all those things are connected." Not unless someone had slipped something a hell of a lot stronger than a roofie into her water tonight and she was actually passed out somewhere dreaming all this up.

"Anything is possible."

Kennedy stared at him. "I think I liked it better when you ignored me." At least her life was a whole lot less surreal then.

"I don't ignore you."

"Yeah, you're Mr. Sociable whenever you get within ten feet of the bar," she quipped.

He shot her an impatient look. "I just got back into town."

"Please. You chatted up every waitress in the place tonight. Bouncers too." And if she didn't change the subject, he'd know exactly how closely she'd followed his every move. She didn't want to think about how that made her look, let alone coupled with how she hadn't been in a rush to stop his roaming hands earlier.

"So how will going to Cale's help?" she asked when they fell into a strained silence.

He didn't answer her.

Turning in her seat to face him, she cocked her head. "What was it that you said about not ignoring me?"

The throbbing in the back of Tristan's head intensified—until she shifted in her seat and her sweet scent enveloped him.

Ignore her? Not likely. Not when he couldn't draw a breath without taking her in. Had he really been so long without a female that every whisper of movement on the seat next to him could so thoroughly snare his attention? He was pretty sure she could fall asleep and he'd find it as equally fascinating as watching her nibble on her bottom lip. The same plump lip he'd sucked into his mouth earlier.

Cale was going to kick his ass. By now his scent was all over Kennedy and no "roadside assistance" explanation was going to justify that. Certainly not when he could barely get his lust, let alone his hard-on, under control.

Avoiding her questions wasn't completely intentional. It took far too much concentration to keep his hands off her, and even more to figure out why she'd been marked by a wraith.

Like the gargoyle clans, the former Knights of the Round Table had also been punished for Arthur's fall. Forced to drink blood to survive, wraiths were bound to fulfill the terms of any pact made with Rhiannon for their services. The elusive mercenaries were usually contracted to take out immortals. Tristan had never heard of them targeting a human before. They rarely posed a serious enough threat.

So who wanted Kennedy dead?

He chanced a quick glance in her direction. She stared out the passenger window, idly rubbing at the symbol on her hand. He knew the bartender rarely backed down from a confrontation, a trait he'd been convinced would come back to bite her in the ass when Cale had hired her. So who the hell had she pissed off without him or Cale hearing about it? Or had they both been too preoccupied with tracking down the dagger?

It didn't make any sense. It would take a serious offense for an immortal to use a wraith instead of handling it themselves. Unless they didn't want to be linked to her death.

His chest constricted, and he shoved thoughts of the wraith's success out of his mind. Cale would know how to handle it. He'd hired her, making Kennedy and her problem Cale's responsibility.

The cat growled in protest.

"I still don't see why we're not going to the police first." Kennedy studied him, confusion lingering in her pretty brown eyes.

He jerked the wheel to the right, swerving at the last second to avoid a pothole he would have noticed if he hadn't been staring at her again. "We're closer to Cale's."

A few minutes later he stopped in front of the gate that kept unwanted visitors—mainly humans—off the property. He frowned at the security console. The number sequence that would open the gate jumbled together in his mind, and the harder he tried to recall the code, the harder his head pounded.

"Problem?"

Not compared to the spider web on her hand, but he didn't tell her that. Instead, he shook his head and hit the intercom button. Whatever the wraith had used in the darts was still screwing with his head. The mercenary couldn't have been expecting Tristan would show up to give Kennedy a ride or the darts would have been loaded with something a lot more potent.

Cursing his sister, who should have answered, he stabbed the intercom again. Another minute ticked off, and he gave up, digging out his cell phone this time. When Briana still didn't answer, he shoved the phone back in his pocket. Reversing back onto the street, he parked the car and climbed out. Kennedy followed suit, glancing around.

"It's safe."

She cast him a dubious glance, trailing after him as he walked the front perimeter of the stone wall bordering the property. "This *is* Cale's place, right?"

"Last time I checked." He spotted the tree towering above the wall on the corner of the lot. "Stay right here."

Her spine snapped straight. "Where are you going?"

"I'll just be a few seconds. You're safe. Promise." Until the wraith tracked her here, but that was one more certainty he didn't plan on sharing. "I'll be right back."

Ducking around the corner, he sprang up—high enough Kennedy would have asked questions—and grabbed the top of the stone wall, pulling himself over. From there he jumped easily into the tree and then back to the front of the wall overlooking the street.

"Give me your hand."

Kennedy peered up at him. "How did you get up there?"

"Footholds on the other side."

She stared at his outstretched hand. "I'm sure I can climb it too."

"This is faster. Unless you're scared of heights," he taunted, grinning when she planted one foot on the wall and pushed off, catching his hand.

A burst of warmth exploded up his arm, the sensation tunneling straight to his groin. He tightened his grip and hauled her up the wall.

She grabbed ahold of him when she reached the top to steady herself. "Work out much?"

His grin widened as he savored the feel of her body tucked close to his. Her hand drifted down his arm, but the narrow wall didn't leave her much room to back away.

"Do you do everything the hard way?"

"This coming from the woman who relies on water hoses to settle disputes at a crowded bar."

A reluctant smile drew his attention straight to her mouth. He spanned his fingers across her lower back, preventing her from edging away from him. He'd let her go in just a minute, first indulging the cat's need to touch her. The man, however, wanted a whole lot more. Hours more. Days.

Kennedy shivered. "You're not still mad about that, are you?"

He shook his head. "But I can't promise I won't retaliate the next time." Because the need to lower his head and run his mouth along the slender curve of her neck threatened to overwhelm him, he nodded to the thick branch extending from the tree. "Ladies first."

Easing out of reach, she stepped gingerly onto the branch,

clinging to the overhead limbs for balance. When she reached the trunk, she moved to another branch and waited for him to climb down first.

The cat wanted to climb higher in the tree and wait for the wraith to make another appearance, but he needed to get her inside first. His feet hit the ground and he reached up to help her down.

"Crap," she hissed, skidding down the tree.

He should have caught her easily and kept them both upright. Maybe it was the drugs slowing his reflexes, or maybe he wanted to feel her sprawled across his chest when the impact knocked them both to the ground.

"Are you okay?" Her eyes widened and she tried sliding off him.

He anchored one arm across her back, keeping her still. "Not really." He probably wouldn't be okay for a long time. The closer she got, the more he wanted her there, proving his attraction to Kennedy ran much deeper than he'd imagined.

"You're bleeding." She caught her bottom lip between her teeth, wincing in sympathy.

"Just a scratch." He barely registered the scrape on his cheek from connecting with the tree bark during the fall. Barely registered anything but all the places she was nestled against him. The only thing better than having her draped across him, would be her draped across him *naked*.

She stared in the direction of the main house, exposing the tempting curve of her throat.

Tristan didn't think about it, he lifted his head and closed his mouth over her skin.

Kennedy moaned, and he ran his lips higher, sliding one hand into her hair and coaxing her down. Her thigh slipped between his legs, rubbing his arousal. The friction unleashed a groan in his chest, and he grazed her with his teeth before sucking her harder between his lips.

Why did she feel so good, taste so good? Attempting to wrap his mind around it didn't matter to the animal basking in the feel of her fingers threading the ends of his hair, dragging him closer.

In the distance a lone howl, then a series of barks echoed through the night, and he tried to remember why that was important.

Fuck. The dogs.

"Oh, shit." Kennedy scrambled off him, and he rolled to his feet as a pack of Dobermans tore across the grass toward them.

Chapter Three

"Run!" Tristan laced his fingers through hers, pulling her after him.

"Can't you call them off?"

"No."

If the dogs were actually real, he would have made the effort. The Dobermans, however, were nothing more than an elaborate glamour Briana bargained with a Fae for. Tristan knew they weren't real, but there was no way to convince Kennedy of that with the pack bearing down on them. As long as she believed they could hurt her, damage could be done.

Shifting was a last resort as far as he was concerned. She had enough questions without witnessing him shift into a large black cat, and he didn't need her running from him too.

"They're too close."

Only a few dozen meters to the house. "Don't look—" The rest of the order lodged in his throat when the ground rushed up to meet him. The fall dragged Kennedy down with him, giving the dogs time to rapidly close the distance.

He rolled, pinning her beneath him. "Don't move."

Her chest contracted with every sharp breath she sucked in. "Somehow I don't think running helped things."

Tristan glared at the snarling animals circling them. He shot a quick glance at the house, hoping Briana had returned with dawn approaching and heard her favorite new toys getting on his last nerve.

Kennedy stared up at him with wide eyes, then turned her head to follow the lead dog as it stalked closer. The fingers she fisted in his shirt twisted tighter. "I always liked dogs."

When the lead Doberman got too close, the need to shift rippled beneath Tristan's skin. The cat prowled the edges of his mind, ready to break free. He kept his gaze locked on the threat, growling in warning.

Kennedy went motionless beneath him, but he didn't take his eyes off the dog. Where the fuck was Briana?

"Tristan." Her fingers dug into his skin.

"It's okay."

"What's wrong with your voice?"

He didn't look at her, didn't want her to pay any closer attention to his eyes. At least if the Doberman had been real it would have noticed Tristan's eyes now reflected the light from the house, would have caught the scent of a predator and backed the fuck off.

The muscles under the dog's fur bunched in preparation for attack. Tristan's claws burst from his fingers, and he ducked his head, shielding Kennedy.

Silence.

The padding of impatient feet no longer treaded the ground. The menacing snarls evaporated on the night air.

He lifted his head, relieved to find the dogs had vanished.

"Where did they go?" Some of the tension drained from Kennedy's body, but she didn't let go of him.

Tristan was saved from answering by the sound of approaching footsteps. A moment later, Briana rounded the hedge leading back to the garage.

"Aren't you a little old for wrestling like a cub?"

Scowling at his baby sister, Tristan pushed to his feet and helped Kennedy up.

Briana's gaze flickered to the woman next to him, surprise blinking across her face. "Hey, Kennedy." Her attention darted back to Tristan. "Where's your car?"

"I couldn't remember the secret password," he snapped, motioning for Kennedy to precede him to the house.

"What happened to your shirt?"

He followed Briana's gaze to the jagged rip on the back of Kennedy's shirt. One more tug would probably tear the fabric in two.

Kennedy looked over her shoulder to check the damage. "My night keeps getting better and better."

"A little rough, weren't you?" Briana snickered.

Tristan narrowed his eyes. "It wasn't me." He glanced at Kennedy for confirmation, second-guessing himself the moment the words left his mouth. It wouldn't have been that big of a stretch if things had gotten out of hand in the car. He'd damn well wanted her enough to tear through layers of clothing to reach bare skin.

"I think it snagged on a branch when I fell out of the tree."

"I see you still know how to show a girl a good time," Briana mocked, opening the door and heading inside.

"Did you call off the dogs?" Kennedy asked.

"Yeah." Briana shot him a questioning look.

"A little bloodthirsty, aren't they? Or have you guys had a problem with break-ins?"

Briana shrugged, nodding to the room on the left. "You look like you could sit down and I need to borrow my brother for a second."

Kennedy hesitated.

"I'll just be a minute and then I'll find you something else to change into." For reasons he didn't want to think about, Tristan gave her hand a reassuring squeeze before letting her go.

"Cale is going to kick your ass," Briana hissed, spinning on her heel and striding farther down the hall.

"It's complicated." And getting more complex by the hour. No wonder the dagger hadn't been that difficult to acquire. Fate was keeping tonight as her ace in the hole.

"He is *so* going to kick your ass. Sex is never complicated for you, so if that's your first line of defense, I'd seriously reconsider using that when Cale gets home."

"We didn't have sex."

Briana scoffed.

"We've got a bigger problem than what happened when I was a little...high," he settled on, though he knew the drugs had merely paved the way for what he'd been thinking about doing to Kennedy for months.

"High? Don't tell me you were diddling with an enchantress?" Briana didn't bother to veil her distaste for the Lady of the Lake's wanton offspring.

He shook his head. "Kennedy was marked by a wraith."

For the hundredth time, Kennedy stared at the mystery mark on her hand. The drive to Cale's had given her plenty of time to mentally run through her night and pin down when someone might have had an opportunity to...what? Rub a temporary tattoo on her skin without her being aware of it or noticing it hours ago?

Marks didn't magically appear on a person's body, and yet she had no explanation for the creepy spider-web design. At the very least she would have noticed it when she'd fiddled with the wires and hoses under the hood of her car. Then Tristan had shown up, but he hadn't touched her hand.

And everything had really gone to hell after that.

She leaned back against the plush beige sofa and closed her eyes. Her heart no longer threatened to punch straight through her chest, but she couldn't stop her stomach from twisting her insides into knots.

Nothing made sense. Not her piece-of-crap car dead on the side of the road, the darts, the hallucination, the dogs vanishing without a sound. And then there was Tristan. Cool and remote when offering her a ride. Hot and intense when she'd been in his lap and headed for the best orgasm of her life.

She wasn't even going to wonder why his voice had sounded more animal than human or think about the feral glow she'd glimpsed in his eyes outside before he'd covered her body with his. If she did, she might lose the tenuous grip she had on her mind.

Holding up her hand, her gaze traced the web's intricate pattern. Tristan knew something. More than once he'd avoided answering her in the car. While she'd like to think he chose not to comment because he didn't want to outright question her mental stability, her gut said otherwise. Life had taught her to scrutinize the telling silence more than any excuse and explanation, and Tristan hadn't said much at all.

The only thing more surreal than the events of the last hour was the possibility Tristan had information that might begin to explain any of it. She would give him another minute with his sister and then he really needed to start talking. Starting with his reason for coming here instead of going to the police.

"How are you doing?"

Kennedy forced her eyes open, vaguely annoyed to see that familiar, distant expression on his face. He didn't move from the doorway, which she should have been grateful for considering how much his presence distracted her on a completely physical level.

She had never been one to be led around by her libido, but twice tonight she'd let herself be distracted by him. First in the car and then lying on the front lawn for Christ's sake. Even now she tried not to think about the tease of his mouth on her throat.

A knowing grin ghosted across his lips, and she remembered he'd asked her something.

"Like I've worked back-to-back double shifts during Ava-fest." Pendragon's week-long anniversary party was nothing short of exhausting and nearly as wild as tonight had been.

"Cale will hopefully be home shortly."

"And he'll make it all better, will he?"

Straightening, Tristan crossed the room. He settled on the arm of an overstuffed chair. She couldn't help but notice it was also the furthest piece of furniture from her, short of the dainty bench that probably wouldn't have held his crossed legs, much less the rest of him.

"Cale's the problem solver of the family."

"And you're the troublemaker."

A glint of wickedness brightened his eyes. "How do you figure?"

"Seems like I've been in trouble since you walked into the bar tonight."

He averted his face, and she cringed.

"That didn't come out right." She sighed. "Just tell me this kind of stuff isn't the norm for you."

"I can admit that coming to with an attractive woman curled up in my lap doesn't happen nearly enough."

"I was trying to get your cell phone out of your pocket." She frowned, realizing he hadn't actually answered her question. The evasion felt important, but her mind was too overwhelmed. The more she tried to align the pieces, the more her thoughts ran together.

He frowned. "What's wrong?" He moved to the sofa, the cushion dipping under his added weight.

She studied him from beneath heavy lids. The concern in his voice didn't match his stiff shoulders or the way he seemed careful not to get too close. He fisted one hand in his lap, his gaze sweeping over her.

"I shouldn't be so tired, should I?" Shouldn't she be pacing the room, pressing him for answers to the questions that hovered on the edge of her mind?

"You've had a busy night." His attention slipped to the mark on her hand.

"What does it mean?"

"More trouble," he answered, smiling crookedly.

Kennedy suspected the playful grin was supposed to soften the serious response. Too bad those gorgeous blue eyes of his didn't sell her on the whole there's-nothing-to-worry-about package.

No doubt sensing more questions, Tristan stood, offering his hand. "Let's get you cleaned up and maybe we can figure this out."

We? Did that mean he wasn't planning on ditching her the second Cale showed up? He'd certainly left her with that impression moments ago. She glanced down. "It's the grass-stained knees, huh?"

Another slow smile, one that succeeded at catching her in the stomach. His hand closed around hers, gently pulling her up. She brushed against him, and he went completely still.

She tipped her face up. "You okay?" Because she wasn't. Not when they were this close. For a moment her exhaustion and disbelief faded, replaced by a slow burn that tunneled through her middle.

His grip on her hand tightened, and he closed his eyes.

Her gaze dropped to his mouth, the memory of his lips sliding across hers drenching her mind until she leaned up and brushed his jaw. The coarse layer of stubble rasped her cheek and a needy whimper stuck in her throat.

Feeling the weight of his stare, she tilted her head back, unprepared for the dangerous glimmer shining in his eyes. She scrambled back a step, as surprised at the warning imprinted on his face as she was by the wave of lust that caught her hard in the belly.

"Tristan?" Had some secondary side effect of the drugs kicked in? Or now that the drugs were clearing out of his system had he remembered how much he disliked her?

"This way." His granite tone left no room for argument or questions as he led her away.

The maze of halls and rooms blurred past as she watched him from the corner of her eye. He clenched his jaw, his expression strained as he strode through the mansion, his usual confident stroll abandoned in favor of a clipped pace she worked hard to keep up with.

He moved through an open door, closing it soundly behind them. Releasing her hand, Tristan passed through the main room of a small suite. Though the main room boasted all the necessary furniture—sofa, chair, desk, flat-screen television—it lacked the personal touches that would make the room feel really lived in.

When he didn't reappear, she trailed into the next room. A dresser, bedside table and king-sized bed filled most of the space. Light spilled from yet another doorway and from the sound of water running, she assumed it led to a bathroom.

He poked his head out, motioning her inside. The tight quarters made her instantly aware of how close he stood, and she tried to pay attention to the clean clothes and towels he pointed out. Her knees shook a little, but she could no longer be sure if it was triggered by some kind of delayed shock or his proximity. The longer she spent in his presence, the faster her blood pushed through her veins.

"I'll give you some privacy."

"Wait." She grabbed his hand, and he hissed out a breath. Ignoring the protest that rose to his lips, she pushed him toward the tub. "Sit."

Wary, he lowered to the porcelain edge, watching her as she ran warm water, then wet a face cloth folded neatly next to the taps. She wrung out the cloth and turned to face him.

Still as a statue, he leaned away from her. "What are you doing?"

Without answering she dabbed at the dried blood on his face.

"You don't need..." The rest of his objection was lost to a deep sigh. His shoulders relaxed and he leaned into her palm, his eyes drifting shut as she tipped his face up to clean the scrape.

"I'm not hurting you, am I?" She gently probed at the worst

of dried blood.

"Not like you think."

Her gaze slid down to meet his. Closing his fingers around her hand, he took the cloth from her. She didn't look away as he set it on the vanity behind her, didn't breathe as he drew her fingers down his cheek to his jaw.

A hundred questions rose in her mind but quickly felt distant and unimportant compared to the desire licking through her body.

Tristan gripped her waist, tugging her closer. Close enough to nuzzle her stomach, his warm breath seeping straight through her thin T-shirt. For a long moment, neither of them moved. She threaded her fingers through the ends of his hair, afraid to ask what he was doing.

Whatever it was, she wanted more. She'd been wanting more for months and the short distraction in the car had only flamed her hunger for him.

Slowly, he pushed her shirt up and pressed his lips to her sensitized flesh. Kennedy shuddered, her breath catching in her throat as he trailed lower. The hot sweep of his tongue circled her navel and he murmured something she didn't understand. Then his fingers tugged at the snap on her shorts.

The sound of her zipper giving way made the soft ache between her thighs pulse fiercely. This time she understood him when he whispered her name, his voice rough, seductive. Her shorts slid down an inch, and he opened his mouth on her skin. The wet heat sent a shockwave of need tearing through her.

Tristan repeated the decadent exploration, laving each inch of her he exposed until her shorts were pooled around her feet. Left in her T-shirt and lacy thong underwear, she clung to his shoulders, suddenly feeling more vulnerable than she had all night.

"Very nice." He traced the edge of her thong, his finger rubbing up the middle of her cleft.

She bit down to soften her moan of pleasure, already thinking about his fingers sliding along her damp sex. The urge to squeeze her legs together and catch his hand between them made the back of her knees tremble.

He raised his head, his blue eyes glittering possessively as they locked on hers. He didn't ask for her permission as he hooked his fingers on either side of her underwear and tugged them off.

"I have to know," he growled, teasing his thumb through her short curls.

Only a whisper of a touch and she rocked up on her heels. "Know what?" Breathless, she stared down at him.

"How good you taste." His thumb slid up her damp seam, parting her for his mouth. "Already wet for me," he mused, satisfaction flashing across his face. "Have I made you wet before, Kennedy?"

"Yes." Even if it hadn't been true, she would have lied to make sure he didn't stop the lazy caress of his fingers. Every torturous brush closer to her clit sizzled along her nerve endings.

"Good." Two fingers pushed at her snug opening, and she cried out when he buried them inside her.

A moment later she felt his hot breath tease across her sex, and then he pressed his mouth against her. She wasn't sure who groaned the loudest. The slow, wicked strokes of his tongue made it impossible to concentrate on anything but the curls of release that uncoiled deep in her womb.

Raking her fingers over his shoulders, she arched into his greedy mouth. "Harder," she pleaded, unable to stop herself from rocking against him.

His lips closed around her clit, his tongue swirling around the aching knot.

"Yes, more." God, she needed more. Her pulse raced and a steady warmth streaked across her skin, drawing her nipples into hard points. She lifted one hand to her stomach, sliding beneath her shirt until she grazed the underside of her breast.

"Let me see," he demanded.

Caught on the edge of release, she found no reason to deny him, and tugged impatiently at both her shirt and bra. She sighed as the restrictive fabric gave way, moaned when she drew her thumb across the tight peak.

A growl of appreciation burst from Tristan's throat. He pumped his fingers into her drenched sex harder, matching the ruthless rhythm with his mouth. The quick teasing licks lengthened, the sweet suction deepened.

Kennedy buried her fingers in his hair, holding him to her as she came. Wave after searing wave rippled through her, dragging her under. She wasn't aware her legs had given up on keeping her upright until she slid to the floor.

Tristan's arms locked around her, trapping her against him. He pushed her hair back from her face, his finger delicately tracing her jawline. The look of raw need imprinted on his face made it impossible to slow her thundering heart. He lowered his head, and Kennedy curled her fingers around his shirt in heady anticipation.

His stubbled cheek grazed her skin as he slid down to meet her mouth. He hesitated, his lips drifting across hers. The feather-light contact made her whole body clench, and when she thought she couldn't take any more of his teasing, his tongue pushed between her lips, sweeping fast and deep.

Steadier, she kneeled between his parted legs, meeting the hungry thrust of his tongue with her own. Kissing him in the car had been slow and hot. This time his mouth scorched her, conquered her. She tasted herself in his kiss, and it ignited a fresh wave of lust that settled between her thighs.

"Need you," he gritted out, a noticeable tension tightening his limbs.

Fisting her hair in his hand, he moved down her neck, nipping a little harder with his teeth. He followed each scrape with a lap of his tongue, curving around her shoulder and lower...

She whimpered when he abruptly stopped. Then his hands gripped her shoulders and he jerked her around.

"Where did you get this?" His thumb circled the tattoo at the base of her spine, the accusation in his voice icing her bloodstream.

"From a tattoo parlor," she offered, glancing over her shoulder at him.

"When? Why?"

She frowned at the clipped questions. Having seen the kind of women who often snagged his attention, she couldn't imagine he found the tattoo distasteful. "My twenty-first birthday. Had a little too much to drink and discovered the evidence of my wild night the next morning."

His gaze dropped to her tattoo one more time, and then he stood. He drilled his hands through his hair. With his back turned to her, she snagged her shorts and panties from the floor and hastily stepped into them. She'd adjusted her bra and shirt when he finally glanced at her, his expression unreadable.

"I'm going to see if Cale is back yet. Feel free to have a shower if you're up for it. Then we'll talk."

He vanished through the door before she could object. She followed him back into the main room, but found it empty. The hall too. The man clearly excelled at making a quick exit.

Given their history, or lack thereof, she shouldn't have been surprised by his abrupt departure. Still, she understood why his vanishing act stung a little, but what she couldn't wrap her head around was why she suddenly felt more alone than she had in a very long time.

Not the least bit eager to analyze that on top of everything else, she turned on the shower and stripped down. Once beneath the hot spray, she closed her eyes, almost grateful to be alone. She needed some time to unravel her thoughts about the rest of the night without his proximity screwing with her hormones. When they shared the same space she struggled to concentrate, and when he actually put his hands on her...

Before she got herself worked up again—and after that kind of orgasm it wouldn't take much—she pushed Tristan out of her head. After rinsing shampoo from her hair, she found herself studying the mark on her hand. The longer she stared at the black curves and angles, the more exhaustion pulled at her.

Keeping the shower brief, and still no closer to figuring out how she ended up here instead of talking Tristan into taking her to the police, she toweled off quickly. She dragged on the pair of borrowed drawstring shorts and oversized T-shirt. Immediately, Tristan's scent filled her head and her nipples hardened as the fabric settled against her breasts.

Kennedy shook her head, clinging to her determination to get some real answers. She wouldn't allow Tristan or anyone to sweep her concerns under the proverbial rug. She wouldn't let herself settle for anything but the entire truth, a promise she'd made to herself after her mother's death.

Insanely attracted to Tristan or not, she'd get some answers. And he'd need a lot more than his sister or a pack of vicious dogs to save his ass if he lied to her about any of it.

Satisfied that she had at least one thing worked out in her head, Kennedy scanned the top of the vanity for a comb. Finding nothing, she checked the medicine cabinet. No comb there either.

She closed the cabinet, her hand freezing on the corner of the mirror. Heart in her throat, she lifted her gaze to her reflection.

Snaking shadows framed her face, making her skin deathly pale. Hideous black tears streamed down her cheeks, her dark eyes closer to empty pits. A scream rocketed up from her lungs only to die on her lips as the shadows behind her congealed into one form.

Holy fuck!

She bolted for the door, not bothering to look over her shoulder.

She knew it was following her.

Tristan dragged his claws down the wall, breathing in through his mouth to keep Kennedy's addictive scent from overloading his senses any more than it already had. Closing his eyes wasn't helping, not when he couldn't stop picturing her arching against him—eyes closed, lips parted, her hands drawing her shirt up and showing off her incredible breasts.

He dropped his forehead to the wall. Thinking about her breasts wasn't helping him quiet the animal demanding that he return to her. The cat raked at the edges of his mind as he raked at the walls, fighting the urge to give in. To make her scream for him as he thoroughly fucked her until neither of them could move.

The taste of her lingered on his tongue, driving him out of mind with lust. Every time she'd moaned, raked him with her nails or pushed her slick sex against his mouth, his cock had throbbed harder.

Sweet Avalon, he needed to get a grip. She was off-limits, an employee—*human*. The latter should have been enough to cool his insides. It had in the past. Indulging in a one-night stand with a human to scratch an itch was one thing, but no human had ever come so close to unchaining him completely.

What was it about her that pulled him in so many directions? One minute he ached to see her smile, to talk to her the way so many Pendragon's regulars did, laughing and flirting. And the next he could think of nothing but ripping her clothes off and sinking deep between her thighs, filling her, making her *his*.

The cat growled in feverish agreement, confusing him further. Tristan enjoyed sex as much as any male and never had a problem keeping things simple in that department. But the animal in him had never before displayed such a preference for anyone. The cat's need for closeness and touch had always been easily satisfied.

But with Kennedy...

He paced the length of the hall, ordering himself to think this through. There was more at stake here than him losing his mind. More unknown variables he needed to figure out. Like the tattoo on her back, or more importantly why she'd chosen that particular tattoo.

Was it just a coincidence that she'd branded the sexy curve of her lower back with a Fae glyph? Or had a Fae seduced her and left his mark behind as some kind of inside joke? Tristan's insides turned to stone at the thought of anyone branding her that way...

His head snapped up, the scent of an enemy invading his senses.

The wraith.

He sprinted toward his suite, jerking his shirt over his head. Colors blurred across his vision, muscles lengthened and bones realigned as the cat broke loose. The familiar comfort of the shift barely registered beneath the furious need to protect Kennedy and rip out his enemy's throat.

A moment later he heard her scream.

Chapter Four

Why was there never a bouncer around when you really needed one?

Kennedy judged the distance between her and the shadow closing in. One bouncer wouldn't get the job done anyway. She'd need a whole freakin' team, and that frantic realization definitely nudged the boundary between sane and losing her damn mind.

Another scream stretched up her throat as she darted around another corner, quickly silenced when she slammed into a sidewall that jutted out into the hall. Knocked backward on impact, she scrambled away from the all-too-real hallucination mere feet away. Her back came up against the wall, her damp palms sliding across the polished floor in vain. She couldn't get enough traction to regain her footing.

Not real. Not real.

An inky black hand materialized within the shadow. Five distinct claws lengthened to deadly razor-sharp points and reached for her. A burst of adrenaline exploded through her bloodstream, and she shot across the floor, escaping the shadow's lunge. Real or not, she felt the current of air rush across her face as she narrowly missed a swipe of the thing's claws.

"Tristan!"

For the first time, his name made it past her lips. She planted her hands and shoved her weight forward, poised like a runner primed for the hundred meter dash—a runner frozen in her tracks.

Oh Jesus.

Suddenly the shadow behind her didn't seem that big of a

threat at all. Eyes wide, she couldn't move, didn't dare. In front of her another dark blur shot around the corner. Its monstrous paws pounded across the floor, its large black head lowered, mouth agape, revealing one too many sharp teeth. The menacing growl that rode the air stopped her heart in her chest.

Unlike the shadow, the large black cat didn't seem like a hallucination at all. She could all but feel the puffs of air that flared the animal's nostrils, could smell the wild, earthy scent as it stalked closer.

Its gaze darted to her face, the animal's iridescent blue eyes sweeping over her before fixing on the darkness behind her. Not even the certainty that the shadow hovered over her shoulder, its gnarled claws prepared to slash at her, could make her look away from the cat.

She might have laughed then, a hysterical no-fucking-way laugh that probably echoed the halls of every loony bin in the country—if she could have drawn enough oxygen from her lungs. Instead, she remained paralyzed and out of options.

Moving would draw the cat's attention, and while she had no clue if or how the shadow would hurt her, she could far too easily imagine the cat's teeth tearing into her skin.

"Nice kitty." She cringed as the words left her lips. The last thing the animal looked was *nice*. Vicious predator. Deadly meat-eater. Those were a much better fit. And if she didn't get a grip, didn't lock down the panic slithering up her spine, she might as well dangle a damn string in front of the animal and prepare to lose an arm.

And that was probably a best-case scenario.

Pain sliced through her hand, and she cried out, cradling it against her chest. As she frantically rubbed at the invisible ice pike drilling through the webbed marking, the cat's growl deepened and she held her breath at the whisper of movement behind her.

The cat sprang forward.

Kennedy hit the floor, unsure which of the two had knocked her sideways. The cat, she thought, remembering the brush of smooth fur across her arm before she'd been knocked over. Another burst of pain shot up her arm but was quickly forgotten as the snarls and growls managed to drown out the sound of her pulse thundering in her ears.

If Alice had smoked crack before falling down the rabbit

hole, she would have undoubtedly witnessed something exactly like the confrontation unfolding no more than five feet from Kennedy. Right about now, though, she'd gladly take the Mad Hatter and Cheshire cat over the pair circling each other.

She knew she should move, run while the two faced off, but her limbs refused to cooperate. Maybe she clung to the hope she was imagining everything and moving meant believing it. Or maybe she knew she was better off doing nothing to draw attention to herself. Or maybe...

Moving almost too fast for her to see, the pair collided, all dark shadows and vicious slashes of claws. The phantom's eerie silence chilled her to the bone, second only to the hissing and growling coming from the cat.

Move, Kennedy.

This time the internal command took hold, and she scrambled up on all fours. Then she made the mistake of looking over her shoulder. The shadow's claws caught the side of the cat and a trail of crimson dripped from its paw. The sight of the blood pooling on the floor didn't faze her nearly as much as the murderous growl that echoed through the hall.

Darting to the right, the animal planted itself firmly between Kennedy and the phantom. Neither moved as the seconds stretched into minutes. Kennedy inched backward, freezing in place when the phantom retreated, melting into the surrounding shadows as quickly as it had appeared.

She didn't tear her gaze away from the dark hall until she sensed movement from the corner of her eye.

The cat had soundlessly closed the distance between them. On instinct, she jerked back against the wall. There wasn't a doubt in her mind she wouldn't get far before the animal took her down.

One foot. Two. Three.

Another inch and she'd feel the brush of the cat's whiskers against her cheek.

Oh God.

Smooth fur brushed her cheek, and her eyes shot open. She hadn't realized she'd even closed them until she found herself staring into the cat's blue eyes. Again, the animal nudged her with his large head. She waited for another growl or a flash of its teeth. Sitting back on its haunches, the cat stared at her. Unprepared for any more surprises, Kennedy shook her head.

"Are you another hallucination?" she asked, more to be sure she could still speak. She had to be dreaming, right? Why else would it be there, let alone rolling to its side and settling one massive paw over her hand instead of chewing it off.

No one kept an animal like this as a pet, did they?

The lazy drum of the cat's tail thumped on the floor, and her heart began to slow.

"This is crazy."

Closing its eyes, the cat pressed his cool nose to her arm. Kennedy tensed, waited. When the cat made no move to use her fingers for an appetizer, she wiggled her hand out from beneath the heavy paw.

The cat cracked open one eye, the intense color almost shocking against the shiny black coat. Holding her breath, she tentatively ran her thumb across the top of its paw. The cat exhaled, the sound reminding her of a sigh. Feeling braver, she ran her palm a little higher, her gaze darting to its eyes.

A soft rumble echoed in the hallway.

She scanned the hall before bringing her attention back to the large animal sprawled next to her. Was it...purring?

Like a deflated balloon, she slumped back against the wall. Now what? She dragged her hands through her hair.

Almost as though he read her mind, the cat climbed to its feet. With another nudge, Kennedy forced her rubbery knees to hold her weight. She took her time standing, hindered by her lingering fear and the certainty she was much too close to overdosing on adrenaline, if such a thing were possible.

She sidestepped away from the cat, wanting to go find Tristan. She could handle a lot, but was clueless when it came to wild animals that weren't safely tucked in large cages.

The animal moved to block the hall.

Great.

She tried edging around to the other side. The cat countered her move, then began padding closer. Backing up, she found herself being herded toward Tristan's room. She spared half a thought for slamming the door, keeping the cat in the hall, but it moved too quick.

Once her knees hit the edge of the sofa, the animal sat and watched her. Kennedy scanned the room, searching for what she didn't know. A way past her furry savior? A way to let Tristan know she needed him?

"You have no idea how much I wish I was more of a cat person right about now," she said.

The cat cocked its head.

"Only had a Husky growing up," she rambled on. "Called him Buck, like from *Call of the Wild*."

A sound that reminded her of a snort puffed past the cat's nostrils.

"No, I don't suppose you'd be a fan of dogs, huh? You should have been around earlier. Could have used you to chase off some Dobermans."

The cat flicked its tail as though it were annoyed, then turned and padded out of the room.

Kennedy stared at the empty doorway.

Holy shit.

"You're bleeding."

Tristan ignored his sister, keeping his forehead pressed to the wall. The smooth surface helped to cool his feverish skin. He drew in another steady breath, followed by another, and another.

He didn't know why he bothered, the caged animal prowled restlessly inside, demanding to return to Kennedy. He'd shifted back to think, a near impossibility in his cat form when his instinct to protect the human trumped everything else.

Everything but the lust streaming through him in choking waves.

Gods, he needed her. Needed her hands in his hair, her mouth crushed beneath his, her body pinned under him. His stomach clenched, his muscles stretched taut, caught on the fierce edge of desire so hot it burned through his veins.

"Tristan." His sister's voice turned impatient. "I said you're bleeding."

"I know." The sting from the gash barely registered compared to the overwhelming urge to take the remaining steps to his suite and return to Kennedy.

And then what? Try to explain? Tell her it had really been him moments ago? Kiss her?

Yes. Kiss her. Trace every naked curve with his tongue, learn every sweet spot that would make her shudder for him.

Fierce arousal battered away at his resolve to keep his distance, undermined his determination not to overwhelm Kennedy. And if he barreled through the door and dragged her into his arms—into his bed—overwhelming her would be one hell of an understatement.

Whether she recognized it or not, she'd responded to him on another level. She felt the intense physical connection between them, hungered for his touch the way he did hers. Not even the incident in the car or with the dogs had stopped her from inviting his touch, from craving it.

Not taking advantage of that fact, not dismissing her need for answers in favor of satisfying the primal instinct to take her was the only thing keeping him in the hall.

But for how long?

He felt every move she made on the opposite side of the door hum under his skin. The whisper of her hair, the rush of breath past her lips, the rustle of clothes he ached to peel away. His heightened awareness of her made any logical attempt at an explanation a fading possibility.

"Is it from the wraith?"

He glared at his sister, wishing she'd go away so he could concentrate on Kennedy.

"The wraith cut you, Tristan."

He glanced at the already healing injury, struggling to figure out why it should matter when the woman in his room was all he needed. Her intoxicating scent wrapped around him, pulling him back to her.

"Focus, Tristan. The wraith," Briana prompted.

Yes, the wraith. His claws burst from the ends of his fingers. He needed to find the mercenary first, then he could return to Kennedy.

He shoved away from the wall and strode down the hall.

"Wait a minute," Briana hissed.

"Can't," he shot over his shoulder, preparing to shift back.

"The wraith. It's Lucan."

He stopped, but didn't turn around. The soft reminder tempered the cat's thirst for the wraith's spilled blood. Lucan was an ally. Reminding himself of that helped Tristan get a better grip on his control. "I know."

"So you also know he's bound by his contract whether he wants to kill Kennedy or not."

"That's all that kept me from ripping his throat out." Barely.

"Then he's waiting on the west perimeter."

That caught his attention. "You're monitoring him?"

"From the moment he stepped foot on the property."

"So why didn't you put in an appearance a few minutes ago?" He forced the question out, determined to focus on the situation at hand.

She shrugged, her expression almost distracted. "You had it under control. And I didn't want to freak Kennedy out any more than she already was."

"How did you know he was here?" He searched his sister's face, wondering why he got the impression she wasn't telling him something.

"Shouldn't you be asking yourself why he's hanging around?"

"He has a job to finish?"

"Or?" she pressed, sounding irritated that he wasn't catching on.

"I'm really not in the mood for twenty questions, Briana."

She planted herself in his path. "Or he figured out something you still haven't." She nodded to the cut that had already stopped bleeding. "Any other time you would have gone Stonehenge by now."

He frowned at the cut, focusing. The venom in a wraith's claws, resulting from the vast amount of blood they drank, could weaken other immortals when exposed. The venom, like the sun, triggered the shift to stone-cold gargoyle instantly. As indestructible as he was in his stone form, it would have left him completely helpless. Would have left Kennedy vulnerable.

The cat snarled at the thought of being unable to protect her.

Only those who had found their mates could control the shift to stone that might otherwise leave their loved ones…

Oh hell.

He stared at the cut as though the slice from Lucan's claws would somehow confirm the bewildering possibility.

"You've finally connected the dots I see."

He swallowed past the dry knot lodged in his throat. "It's not possible. I would have recognized it sooner."

"Obviously not."

"Kennedy's my mate?" Only his mate's presence could give him control over Rhiannon's curse.

"So it would seem."

"But she's human." He shook his head, searching for another explanation. "She can't be my mate." The denial outraged the cat.

"Why else would Lucan have backed off?"

"You're the one who pointed out that he's bound by his contract to kill her."

Brianna's expression softened. "That doesn't make him a complete monster. He's in control right now, and he'll fight it as long as he can."

The underlying compassion in his sister's voice didn't escape Tristan's notice.

"If he left without eliminating his target, it's obvious he wants to talk to you."

"Knowing I'll kill him."

She arched a brow. "And why would you kill him over a human?"

"To protect what's mine." The snarled response was automatic. Instinctive.

The satisfied look on his sister's face had him closing his eyes. Sweet Avalon, could Kennedy really be his mate? He'd been drawn to her, intrigued by her from the beginning. No other female had snared his attention so completely. If it was true, shouldn't he have figured it out before now?

"Nothing else explains why you're still standing here. Or why you need her so badly," she added.

He stopped, realizing he'd turned around to return to Kennedy. "How do you know what I need?" he asked, irritated that he couldn't keep his thoughts from straying to the human. Even talk of the wraith and protecting her didn't stem the need to see her, talk to her. Touch her.

"It's...ah...a little obvious."

He gave her a blank look.

His sister cleared her throat and nodded to his groin.

"Jesus, Briana." He jerked around, hiding his erection like an embarrassed teen caught jerking off. One quick snap finished the button he'd left undone after yanking them back on earlier.

He dragged his hands through his hair. "I met her months ago and still spent every damn day as a statue."

"Meeting your mate doesn't automatically prevent the shift at sunrise. It only gives us control over it. Your need to protect your mate gave you control over it when Lucan cut you."

He shook his head against her logic even though the doubts were slowly receding.

"Have you actually tried fighting it at dawn?"

Why would he? For over a millennium the change had been an unavoidable part of his existence.

Gods, could Kennedy truly be his mate?

The cat roared in affirmation.

Eager to return to her—whatever the reason—he strode for the front door.

"Tristan." Briana touched his arm as his hand closed over the knob. "The sun will be up in a few minutes." Meaning she'd be heading to the roof. "Lucan is..." She trailed off. "Just be careful, okay?"

Something in her tone made him think she'd wanted to say something else but held back.

He nodded and slipped out into the night. Because he could travel faster on four legs, he stripped off his pants and shifted. Around him the night came into sharper focus, but it was the wraith's scent that hit him first, filling his nostrils.

Growling, he retreated a few steps, then clamping down on the need to find Kennedy, he sprinted toward the western perimeter. His steps slowed as he padded up a short incline that looked down at the mansion.

Lucan stood with his back to him, his earlier phantom form abandoned for his human one. "I had no idea," the mercenary said without turning around. "Not until I tracked her here did I realize how fully you were involved in the situation, and even then I never expected her to be your mate. I was only instructed on how to deal with Cale."

His brother? Tristan waited for the wraith to explain, preferring to stay in cat form should the wraith attack. He wanted to give his friend the benefit of the doubt, but he'd witnessed the bloodlust that consumed Lucan when a contract compelled him to kill. Tristan knew better than most how vicious the former knight could be when he gave in.

Lucan finally turned to face him. Already Tristan noticed the signs of strain on Lucan's face from denying himself the kill. It was only a matter of time before the tremors that made his friend clench and unclench his fist worsened.

"I've been ordered to negotiate for the dagger. If it's not turned over in forty-eight hours, I'm bound to fulfill the terms of the contract."

Tristan snarled.

Lucan gave him a weary look. "I'm sorry my friend. I'll be close if you want to talk." He paused. "Two days, Tristan. That's all I can give you." Lucan's shape grew dark at the edges, then he was no more than a shadow fading into the night.

Two days. Two days to turn over the dagger or Lucan would hunt down Kennedy. Two days to figure out how in the hell he could sacrifice his brother's freedom.

But if she truly was his mate, how could he possibly sacrifice her?

Kennedy stared at the closed door, unable to talk herself into opening it and searching for Tristan. She clutched at a faded leather belt, tightening her grip until her knuckles whitened. As far as weapons went she might as well have been armed with an arsenal of cotton balls, but holding onto something felt better than cowering in the closet. Too bad doing exactly that wouldn't seriously sabotage the image she hadn't lost her ever lovin' mind.

Movement on the other side of the door made her pulse pick up speed, and her gaze locked on the turning handle. Unless the oversized pussycat also had an opposable thumb, it wouldn't be opening the door. Breaking through it, sure, but slowly twisting the knob around until she felt every near-soundless click...

"Hey."

Tristan. Relief swept through her, relaxing her spine. Marginally. "Shut. The. Door."

"Kennedy—"

She shook her head. "Before Puss in Boots comes back, preferably."

He arched a brow, but did as she asked. His gaze dropped to the belt in her hand and the chair she'd dragged in front of her.

"Don't tell me you were a lion tamer in a former life?"

"Are you laughing at me?"

He struggled not to smile. "No."

"You take off and leave me to deal with something from the Phantom Zone and a wild animal jacked up on super catnip, and now you're laughing at me?" Death wish, meet Tristan.

His half grin faded. "You're not hurt, are you?" In the space of a heartbeat his gaze turned critical. "I didn't think it touched you." Closing the distance, he frowned intently as though he might see any injuries through the borrowed clothing.

She stared at him, gripping the belt tighter when he tried tugging it loose. "It. You said 'it'."

Tristan tugged again. "Are personal pronouns against some bartending code I'm unaware of?" He changed tactics, smoothing his fingers across her wrist.

The soft caress succeeded in slowing her runaway heart, and she found herself relinquishing her weapon.

"I didn't imagine it, did I? That thing. The cat. They're both real." She didn't want them to be. If there was something wrong in her mind, she could fix that. A shrink, some meds, something. Accepting Casper and his furry nemesis actually existed would be a whole lot harder. "I've stepped into the Twilight Zone, haven't I?"

"He's harmless."

Somehow knowing Tristan referred to the cat, she shook her head. "A week-old kitten is harmless. That beast could have used my bones for toothpicks."

"He prefers his meat cooked most of the time, if that makes you feel better."

"Oh, much." She snorted, then closed her hand, only to remember Tristan had taken the belt and tossed it on the nearby table. "Please tell me what the hell is going on. Because the more I try convincing myself none of this can actually be happening, the more real it becomes."

He didn't say anything.

"Please." She touched his hand, barely curbing the urge to launch herself straight into his arms. Not since her mother's death had she felt so helpless, so unsure of what the hell to do.

His fingers curled tightly around hers, too tightly. Her gaze darted up to meet his. For a moment she thought he meant to kiss her, triggering a flare of warmth in her belly that defied reason. Uncertain, afraid, bewildered—sure. But aroused?

Caught off-guard, she stumbled back a step. Tristan spun away from her, driving the tension up between them with his silence.

"I need to know what's happening."

"Give me a minute," he snapped.

Frustration swelled inside her. "You've already had a whole lot longer than that to start explaining."

He said nothing.

She took the few steps separating them and planted herself directly in front of him. "Damn it, Tristan. Talk to me."

"I can't." The words sounded forced, almost growled.

"Why the hell not?"

"Because talking is the last thing I want to do right now."

It took her a minute to see past the rigid shoulders, clenched jaw and the tense lines bracketing his mouth. Another moment to search his eyes for the cause of his sudden anger.

And just a heartbeat to fully realize he wasn't pissed off at all.

"Tristan?" Wary, she backed up. "What's wrong?"

He laughed, the sound laced with frustration. "That same thing that's been wrong for months." He moved toward her and she retreated further.

A devilish smile, one that instantly reminded her of a cat cornering a canary, curved his lips. "What's wrong is watching you, catching your scent and craving your touch. Night after night. Always wanting what I couldn't have. Never giving in."

"Until tonight," she said softly. He had certainly given in when she'd all but wrapped herself around him in the car. Forget what his mouth had given her in the bathroom earlier.

He cocked his head, his gaze sliding down her front, lingering on her chest before dipping lower to the borrowed baggy shorts. The heated look on his face made her feel as though she were wearing a string bikini bottom instead, emphasis on *string.*

"Yeah," he agreed. "Until tonight." Another confident step in her direction.

Another retreat, one that brought her up against a small table. "That doesn't explain—"

He silenced her with a shake of his head. "This is going one of two ways, and neither of them involve any explanations."

The annoyance she wanted to feel, that she should have felt, deserted her, leaving her confused and just a little bit nervous. "Because talking is the last thing you want to do?"

He nodded, erasing the last of the space between them.

"So what is it that you want to do, because I'm really not up for another hour—"

His thumb brushed her bottom lip, silencing her before he splayed his fingers along her jaw. The same eyes she'd been fantasizing about for months bored into hers. She knew what came next, and her belly tightened in anticipation even as she braced herself for it. As she hungered for it.

Everything from the brush of his thumb at her throat to the way he moved in, his chest crowding her, his leg nudging her thighs apart, said soft and slow. But when he opened his mouth over hers, his lips hot and greedy, his tongue pushing in to sweep across hers, the kiss turned fast and hard and downright explosive.

She rose up on her toes, snatching a breath before he captured her mouth again. He tangled his hands in her hair, angling her head back a little more. Despite the fierce kiss that promised she'd beg for more before he was through, he gently cupped her nape.

The scorching trail he followed down her neck would have turned her into a puddle at his feet if not for his other hand grazing her breast. Tension, hot and sharp and so damn good, echoed in her core, keeping her feet firmly planted.

It wasn't the first time he'd kissed her—and she hoped like hell it wouldn't be the last—but this felt more...real. Not a sleepy seduction or a coaxing tease, just raw and unrestrained and breaking her apart inside.

Looping her arms around his neck, Kennedy hung on, rubbing herself against his thigh. Tristan's appreciative groan slid into a thick growl when she sucked his bottom lip between hers. He pressed against her, jostling the table behind her.

Something shattered on the floor. Probably something expensive.

"—of guessing what you're thinking," she finished when the crash succeeded in thankfully slowing things down. She needed a second to process everything.

"Do you really need to guess what I'm thinking about?"

She swallowed, her eyes sliding shut as he ran his mouth down her throat, nipped her shoulder.

"Stop." She planted a hand against his chest, ignoring the soft ache between her thighs. "I can't do this now. I need to know what's going on."

At first she thought he planned on giving her some space, then he lifted her, setting her on top of the small table. He flattened one hand on the wall near her head. The other slipped beneath the hem of her shirt, his fingers trailing across her skin.

Nothing about the predatory look on Tristan's face matched the lazy caress, as though he were holding back. She shivered, resisted closing her eyes and sinking into another kiss that would surely fry the last of her rational brain cells.

She refused to let that happen. Not again. Twice tonight she'd let her hormones override her common sense. It couldn't—wouldn't—happen again. "We need to slow down."

A frustrated groan rumbled past his lips, lips lazily brushing the corner of her jaw. "We need to stop talking." His teeth grazed her throat.

She thought about pushing him away, but anticipating the brush-off, Tristan snared her wrist and brought it to his mouth.

"Please, Kennedy."

"This doesn't make sense. Before tonight, you didn't even like me." Clinging to that fact helped to slow the flames that licked through her veins wherever his lips touched her skin.

He tucked her hair behind her ear, giving him uncompromised access to her neck. "I liked you too much."

"Then why ignore me for months?" Why drive her crazy wanting him when he felt the same way?

"To stop this from happening."

She parted her lips to ask him what this was. He bit her bottom lip, dragging it between his before sliding his mouth over hers completely. She moaned, felt herself melt a little into his arms. Strong, muscular arms, lifting her up, wrapping her around him, and carrying her toward the other room—the bedroom.

"Wait." Kennedy wiggled free of his hold, putting some distance between them. She couldn't keep a clear head when he touched her. Even out of arm's reach she felt the pull of him. Every cell in her body craved him like an addictive drug, yet she clung to the faint voice warning her to tread carefully. "We can't do this."

"Yes. We can." He might as well have said, "Yes, we will." The subtle tilt of his head, as though he were already imagining them doing a whole lot more with a lot less clothing on worried her.

Worried her because every second that passed left her achingly aware of him. Her skin still buzzed from the last brush of his fingers. Her lips still damp from his mouth.

Why was it so damn hard to concentrate? "Tell me why you brought me here. What came after me? Where were you and where in the hell did that animal come from?"

"Is that everything?" He moved toward her, his steps casual, his expression determined.

She shook her head. "Why can't I stop this?" She pressed her hand to her belly, which clenched with every purposeful step in her direction.

He stopped in front of her, his gaze burrowing right into her heart. "Because right now this is more important than anything else."

"It shouldn't be." Nothing should matter but getting this figured out, and at the same time the deepest parts of her knew he was somehow right. And that made even less sense.

He lifted a hand to touch her face, and her breath caught then locked in her lungs when he changed his mind. "This goes one of two ways. Either I walk out the door and try getting a hold of myself. Or—" his gaze darkened, his voice low and rough, "—I start peeling your clothes off."

Chapter Five

Arousal streamed through her. "Why does that sound like some kind of ultimatum?"

"Choose."

The demand unleashed a wave of molten butterflies in her stomach. Instead of moving toward him, she skirted back toward the leather sofa, anticipating his pursuit.

He didn't disappoint her.

"Okay, now it feels like you're stalking me."

He grinned, never letting her get too far from him. "Then tell me to leave, Kennedy."

"And be alone in the house with that big-ass cat? Doesn't sound like a bright move to me."

"I don't think he would mind keeping an eye on you."

"It's not his eyes I'm worried about." Too bad the image of all those teeth and razor sharp claws didn't stay with her long enough to cool the fever burning her up inside. She was starting to think nothing could, and even worse, that she didn't really want it to.

"Then tell me to stay."

"Of course I want you to stay. I just need—"

"Answers? Later."

"Now," she insisted, dodging back toward the doorway only to stop short of opening it. She didn't know what scared her the most. Facing the panther or jaguar or whatever the hell it was, or staying and giving in to Tristan.

He stepped up behind her. "Am I making you nervous?"

"No."

"Angry?"

"I want to be."

"Aroused." It wasn't a question.

Kennedy shook her head, unable to voice the denial.

His soft laugh called her a liar. "Then tell me to go. Now. Before I lose the last of my control."

She turned her head and her cheek brushed his jaw. "You're not going to hurt me."

"I want to do a lot of things, but hurting you definitely isn't one of them."

Closing her eyes, she said, "I need a minute." But not nearly as much as she needed him to touch her right that very second.

"You've already made up your mind," he challenged.

Had she? Kennedy started to shake her head, wondering if she'd ever been so confused and impossibly turned on.

"Okay then." He moved around her.

"This is insane, Tristan."

He gripped the door handle.

Everything inside her cried out to stop him and it had nothing to do with being afraid of being alone. There was a lot more to be scared of in here, with him.

Tristan opened the door.

Don't leave.

He stepped through.

She parted her lips.

"You're killing me here, you know that?" The almost playful comment was lost beneath the desperate edge in his voice, like hot steel dragged across granite.

"Stay." One word was all she could manage when she feared letting him stay more than letting him walk away. She knew attraction, she knew all about getting caught up in something hot and unpredictable, but none of that felt anywhere close to riptide threatening to drag her under now.

Tristan didn't move and she waited, half expecting him to ask her if she was sure.

He didn't. In two short strides he stood in front of her, his hands sliding into her hair, his mouth opening over hers. And the moment he slipped his tongue into her mouth, sweeping slow and deep, she came dangerously close to climaxing.

From a kiss.

She gripped his shirt, clinging to him as her knees trembled and all the hot places inside her jumped a hundred degrees.

His hands slid down her back, then easily beneath the borrowed shorts. “No panties.”

“After my shower...” she trailed off, the feel of his palms on her bare ass negating any need for explanations.

“Your next one won’t be alone.”

His grated response set fire to her belly, and then he urged her backward, toward his bedroom. Keeping track of their progress became impossible when the more he kissed her, the more she wanted to feel his mouth everywhere.

Moments later, the back of her legs bumped the edge of the bed, and she looped her arms around him to keep from falling back.

Tristan laughed. “I’ve got you.”

“That’s what I’m worried about.” She didn’t wait for him to come back to her mouth, going up on her toes to steal another kiss instead.

The arm that snapped around her back, dragging her hard against his chest, made her grin. If she could get to him half as bad as he got to her...

As if sensing her thoughts, he shook his head. One quick glance at his face and she knew whatever patience he had left, whatever had been stopping him from peeling her clothes off, had run out.

He caught the bottom of her T-shirt and tugged it over her head. When the material bunched around her wrists, he closed his fingers around them, holding them above her head.

“So beautiful,” he murmured, running his thumb down her throat, between her breasts...

Her eyes drifted shut.

He abruptly released her wrists. “Who did that to you?”

She frowned at the harsh demand, then remembering the jagged pink scar on her left side, turned away from him. Habit had her searching for the top she’d allowed him to strip off without thinking. A first for her. It had taken weeks for her to show the scar to the few men she’d let into her bed in the past.

“Tell me who did that to you.”

She folded her arms across her chest, hiding the scar as

best she could. "Easy, Billy the Kid. There's no one to meet at sunset for a showdown. I was in a car accident when I was twelve."

His expression softened. "Were you badly hurt?"

"I was in the hospital for a few weeks." Damn it, where had her shirt gone?

He moved closer and she angled her right side away from him.

"You don't need to hide yourself from me."

"I'm not." She might have stood half a shot at sounding convincing if she'd met his eyes when she said it.

"It doesn't matter to me."

Spotting her shirt, she bent down to scoop it up. "Uh-huh." Not only had she heard that before, she'd caught the sneaky, appalled glances of more than one man when he noticed the scar. And then there were the flawless women she regularly spotted Tristan with, the kind who probably didn't even have a smudge in their nail polish let alone a permanent scar five inches long.

Kennedy wanted to think it was a good sign that after the night she'd had, she could still be self-conscious enough to feel like she wouldn't measure up to them. At least that was normal. Stupid, but normal.

"Wait." Tristan reached for her, catching hold of her wrists and trapping them behind her back with only one of his hands.

She really didn't want to be turned on by how strong he was, how easily he cut off a retreat, and at the same time managing to eliminate any space between them. Their bodies touched from chest to knees, his T-shirt rasping over her bare skin with every ragged breath he drew, his hard thigh between hers and pushing against her sex.

"It *doesn't* matter." As if to prove his point, he ran his gaze down her body, and when his attention focused entirely on her breasts, her heart pounded at the heat that flashed in his eyes.

He didn't give her a chance to voice another objection. Cupping her breast, he dragged his thumb back and forth across her nipple, the friction from her bra magnifying the heady sensation. He trapped the puckered tip, tugging gently.

The answering echo of pleasure in her core demanded attention, and she rubbed against his thigh, biting her lip to silence her moan.

"Don't." His mouth covered hers in a long, hungry slide. "I want to hear it, want to hear how much you like it."

"Oh, I like it." Too much. Way too much.

Releasing his grip on her arms long enough to pull his shirt off, he wasted no time in returning to her mouth. He anchored one arm around her back, keeping her close. Her breasts were crushed against his chest, the smooth wall of muscle warming her straight through.

She tensed when his fingers grazed her scar, and as though he realized the source of her tension, he let his hand drop to her waist and thrust his tongue between her lips, coaxing her up on her toes for another bone-melting kiss.

And then another, and another.

His arousal brushed her abdomen and they both groaned. The rough denim triggered a wave of heat that tunneled straight through her middle. Needing to feel him, she drew her palm down his chest and past the button on his jeans.

She heard his breath hitch, knew he waited.

"Do it," he growled.

Kennedy closed her hand over his arousal, sliding upwards just as he rocked his hips, grinding against her palm.

Without warning, he spun her around, jerking her back against his chest. The rough gesture should have worried her. Instead she reveled in it, reveled in the seeming power she had over him, making him come a little more undone with every passing second.

Tristan sank to the edge of the bed, pulling her into his lap. His cock fit hard against her ass. There wasn't much time to think about how she wanted to arch her hips and sink back on him without any clothes getting in the way. He pushed her bra strap down, replacing the thin material with his mouth.

Bringing one arm up, she locked it around his neck, indulging in the scuff of his stubble along her shoulder. And then her bra fell away from her heavy breasts, the sudden tease of air hardening the tips even further. She watched him lazily pluck at her nipple, squirming until not even squeezing her legs together eased the ache between her thighs.

"You want to come, don't you?" He rested his palm against her sex, circling, drawing the hem of her shorts higher and higher.

"Yes." God, yes. The first threads of release churned in her belly, snaking lower...lower. "Tristan," she begged.

A soft laugh against her ear. He slipped a finger under the edge of her shorts, and she cried out when the pads of his fingers teased her opening. Slick and soft, he worked higher, parting her folds.

Kennedy lifted her hips, silently guiding him.

She didn't need to. His fingers expertly stroked her cleft, and when she bounced just a little in his lap, seeking the release that whispered across her nerve endings, he clamped an arm across her waist.

Unable to wait, she arched up to meet his hand, his slippery strokes circling her clit. Pleasure streamed through her, drawing her muscles tighter. She didn't hold back, moaning deep in her throat as she came, rocking to the slowing rhythm of his fingers.

Boneless, she relaxed against him.

"Wow," she murmured.

Tristan didn't respond, didn't even move.

She tipped her head back, surprised by the strain edging his mouth and around his closed eyes. "What's wrong?"

"I need a minute." For the second time tonight his voice bordered on feral.

"You wanted this, wanted me. Don't put the brakes on now."

"I don't want to scare you."

Scare her? "Look at me," she pleaded, and when he didn't, she laced her fingers through his, guiding them along her sex. "Don't stop, Tristan."

His eyes snapped open, the startling blue depths brighter, wilder.

"Your eyes," she whispered releasing his hand. But instead of moving away from him, the fear imprinted on his face stopped her. She turned around in his lap, her movements slow and tentative. "How?"

Not contacts, she realized, gently tipping his face up as though it were just a trick of the light. Her pulse kicked into next gear. Definitely not contacts, almost not even human.

"What are you?"

"Yours." He gripped her waist, his hands sliding higher to splay across her bare back. "Just yours."

Tristan thought his heart would hammer straight through his chest. He stared at Kennedy, caught between waiting for her to decide what to do, and burying himself deep inside her. He needed his jeans off, needed to feel her slide along his hard length so bad he couldn't sit still.

Studying him intently, she inched closer. He couldn't help it, he shifted on the bed, brushing against her and fighting the urge not to jerk his pants around his ankles and sink further between her thighs.

Kennedy tensed, and he knew she deserved some answers, but it was increasingly impossible to concentrate on anything but how good she felt in his arms. If he started to explain anything—and he highly doubted he could—they would have to stop, and he was damn sure he couldn't do that.

She was his mate and he couldn't let her go without making her his. It was as simple and as incredibly complicated as that.

He dared to run his fingers along the waistband of her shorts, dipping his fingers inside. She didn't object, so he kept going, sliding them down over her ass until he could reach the damp crease from behind.

Wet, so hot and wet, it was a wonder he only slipped a finger inside her. She gripped his neck, but she didn't stop him. Pumping softly, he pushed two fingers into her snug opening, groaning when her slick inner walls clenched around him.

Her whimper of pleasure spurred him on.

Bolder, he thrust harder, filling her more completely. When she sank her hands in his hair, pulling him closer, he knew he'd overcome a huge hurdle. The cat roared in satisfaction, and Tristan knew there would be no stopping, no slowing down. Not until he claimed her in every way.

He rolled, ripping off her shorts and pinning her beneath him. He spared a moment to indulge in the feel of her body arching up to meet his, then he slid down, dragging his tongue across her skin. Every few inches he paused, sucking her between his lips.

Kennedy moaned, and he grinned, pleased she responded to his touch. Moving back up, he nuzzled her neck, tasting the curve of her shoulder, nipping at her. He wanted inside her so damn bad his insides shook. He needed another minute to get under control before he even touched his zipper. Having watched the pink tips of her breasts get hard, her lips part with her shuddering breaths, her thighs slide open, he knew he was close to exploding.

"Tristan." Unafraid, she used her hold on his hair to coax him back to her mouth.

This time he couldn't keep the kiss slow or soft. He thrust his tongue between her lips, taking a long, deep taste. She rocked her hips, grazing his cock, and he pushed her harder into the mattress.

Catching a hold of her hands, he trapped them against the bed and bent to close his lips over her nipple. She tugged at his hold, but he didn't ease up, focused instead on sucking her into his mouth.

Her back arched, her breath hissing out as her fingers dug into his. He sucked harder, finally releasing her wrists as he traced the curve of her breast on his way to her other nipple.

A flick of his tongue, a graze of his teeth and Kennedy moaned, her hands trailing down his back, then around his hips to the front of his pants. Her palm brushed the length of his cock, and he groaned against her breast.

As much as he wanted to drag this out for her, he couldn't wait a moment longer. He stood and stripped off his jeans, freeing himself. Her hot gaze slid down his body, fixing on his cock. She sat up, drawing his attention to her breasts and then the damp center of her he wanted most to lose himself in.

She closed her hand around him, and his jaw snapped shut. His eyes slid closed and he sucked in a harsh breath. Counted to five. None of it helped. None of it could slow down the clawing need to claim her.

Tristan leaned over her, grinning when she inched further up the mattress away from him, as if she sensed the predator in him craved the pursuit. He snagged her ankle, dragging her toward him. Her legs parted further, letting him see everything from her pale inner thighs to the soft curls and glistening sex.

He easily covered her body with his, and the sensation of skin against hot skin triggered a wave of lust that grabbed him hard in the gut. Kennedy ran her fingers along his jaw, her expression hungry, and at the same time almost anxious.

His eyes, he realized.

"You're—" he stopped himself from saying *mine* at the last

second, "—safe with me. Always."

She nodded, lifting her hips and nestling herself snuggly against him.

His eyes damn near rolled back in his head. He slanted his mouth across hers, wanting to take his time, wanting to reassure her that she hadn't made a mistake giving in, but couldn't stop himself from taking her mouth the same way he ached to take the rest of her—hard, fast and deep.

He gripped her hips and thrust inside her. Their raw moans of pleasure rode the air, and when he could force his eyes open, he found her staring up at him. Her eyes glittered with the same relentless need that had him in a choke hold.

"Wait," she murmured wrapping her legs around him.

He forced himself to relax his grip, a near impossibility when the walls of her sex tightened around his cock.

"Just..." She lifted her bottom, deepened the angle, let him slide a little deeper.

Sweet Avalon.

And then he reared back and plunged in...deeper. A fierce growl ripped from his chest, and then he pumped his hips, fucking her harder. Tension licked along his limbs, drawing him tighter...tighter.

Kennedy cried out beneath him, her sex clenching. He grit his teeth, riding the waves of her release until she softened beneath him. Still, she protested when he slid from her, then eagerly rolled to her belly when she realized he wanted her from behind.

A moment was all he allowed himself to stare at her, to memorize the image of her up on her knees, her hair trailing down her back, her gorgeous bottom turned up, her sex wet and ready. So few women realized how incredibly sexy they looked this way, and his mate made every other female in existence pale in comparison.

He grabbed her hips, fitting himself against her opening.

"Tristan," she pleaded.

He buried his cock deep inside her. She moaned loud and deep, her fingers clutching at the blankets as he rocked back and filled her again, and again and again. Release stormed through his body, and pumping his hips, he bent down, sealing his lips over the curve of her neck and her shoulder.

And as his fierce orgasm rattled him to his very soul, he bit her.

Kennedy cringed at the icy ache in her hand and shoved it under her pillow. It didn't help. She took her time waking up, wondering what she'd banged her hand on. After prying open her gritty eyes, she lifted her hand up for inspection.

One heart-pounding glance at the spider-web tattoo and everything came crashing back. Work, her useless car, the cat, Tristan.

This was Tristan's room. His bed.

She looked under the blanket, confirming she was spectacularly naked. Naked and alone. Clearly something hadn't gone right even though she remembered every second of the sex. Hot, amazingly incredible sex. Even thinking about it reawakened every cell in her body. Her nipples hardened, and for a few seconds, she wanted nothing more than to find Tristan and do something about her very aroused state.

Thankfully she glanced at the mark on her hand and the sensation was short lived. She needed to know what the hell was going on, starting with how he'd managed to make her forget her need for answers earlier.

If she possessed half his skill at avoidance, never mind how easily he'd distracted her from the truth—with sex no less—she could turn in her bartending apron for a healthy political career.

Kennedy sat up, ignoring the aches in muscles she hadn't used in quite sometime. She tracked down her clothes, stepping into her shorts before dragging the borrowed T-shirt over her head.

A sting on her shoulder made her wince. Gently, she probed at her shoulder, felt a scratch of some kind. She glanced at the bathroom, then remembering what had happened in there the last time she was alone, decided she'd take a look at the minor scrape later.

At the door she hesitated, thinking about the oversized feline that was hopefully locked up somewhere. Given Tristan's determination to avoid answering her questions, she wasn't about to sit around and wait for him. Though she couldn't lay all the blame at his door. As much as she wanted to be angry that he'd managed to call most of the shots, she knew she'd let him.

She couldn't remember ever letting the need for sex consume her like that, but it sure as hell wouldn't get in the way now. She hoped. Worried that calling out would bring super kitty her way, she quietly wandered the halls. The moment she stepped foot in the empty kitchen, her stomach growled. Food, she decided, would have to wait a little longer.

Kennedy turned to leave, stopped by a flicker of movement from the corner of her eye. Crossing the checkered tile floor, she opened the French doors, blinking at the bright sunlight that warmed her face.

Beyond the large patio, Tristan stood with his back to her. Wearing just his jeans, he stood barefoot in the dewy grass, his eyes closed, face turned up to the sun. He didn't turn at the sound of the door closing behind her, or even when she padded across the chilled stone patio and stepped up beside him.

The sheer blissful smile on his face surprised her.

"Tristan?"

He grinned and nodded at the sky without opening his eyes.

She squinted at the puffy clouds. "What is it?"

"The sun."

Ooookay. "And?"

"It's the first time I've felt it on my face in centuries."

Chapter Six

Tristan watched her brows draw together, unprepared for how much such a simple gesture could awaken the cat that wanted to spend hours curled around her, feeling her touch.

She shook her head. "I don't think I heard you right."

Letting out a breath, he shoved his hands in his pockets. Her wary expression and straight spine weren't exactly inviting a brush of his fingers across her cheek, let alone a long, slow kiss. Burying his hands in his pockets was the only way he could think of to avoid stroking her plump bottom lip.

Another breath. "I haven't seen the sun since the fifth century."

"And by century you mean..."

He inwardly braced himself. "Hundred year spans."

She glanced at her hand and his stomach turned over at the reminder of her death sentence. "I don't suppose you're just off your meds?"

Leave it to Kennedy to try brushing it off as a joke. He shook his head.

She sank to the ground so quickly he could only flinch when she landed on her butt.

He crouched next to her, mesmerized by the way the sunlight glinted off her hair. He touched the ends of the blond strands shot through with shades of bronze and gold. How had he never noticed that about her hair before?

Tristan tipped her face up so it was not lost in shadows. He'd lived in the dark long enough. For months he could have felt the sun warm his back as it did now, and if he'd listened to the cat, to the instincts that drew him to Kennedy from the start, he would have been able to.

Her eyes slid shut. "I want to be dreaming."

"And last night?" He studied her brows, her lashes, her lips.

She looked away from him. "Are you talking about the pre-feline part of the evening or after that?"

He smiled. "You're not still scared of him, are you?"

"Right about now there isn't much I'm not scared of."

"But not me?" He'd been rougher with her than he'd wanted in bed, unable to completely control the cat's need to dominate.

"You? No. But the things you make me feel scare me to death."

He cupped her face, trying not to hope she felt half as much of a bond as he did. "What things?"

"Things I'm having a hard time controlling."

Having no idea what humans experienced when bonding to immortal mates, he struggled to find the right words to say. "Maybe you need to loosen the reins then."

She eased away from him. "You can't keep doing that."

"What?"

"Making me want to kiss you."

He grinned. "I'm not making you do anything."

She snorted. "You're supposedly fifteen centuries old. I'm pretty sure that must come with a few perks."

"Like coercing you into getting naked?" If he didn't catch the heat that flared in her eyes he might have been offended.

She shoved to her feet. "I don't know." He trailed after her, but she spun around to face him. "Stay there."

"Aren't you worried I can hocus-pocus you into stripping from a distance?"

"You find this funny?" She sounded even less impressed than she looked.

"Just the part where you think I can snap my fingers and have you naked and in my bed. Though it would be a neat trick." And gave him all sorts of images in his head.

She gave him a doubtful look.

"Trust me, if I could do that we wouldn't be standing here right now."

"What are you?"

"Besides turned on?"

She scowled at him.

"You need answers and I need to be close to you, so let's go inside."

"Bed is a bad idea."

He noticed she didn't say no. "I was thinking more along the lines of breakfast, but I'm fine with returning to my room."

"Breakfast is good," she said hastily, preceding him inside.

Tristan took his time, watching her first-class ass until she grabbed a stool. She'd no sooner plunked down before pushing back to her feet and pacing nervously. He crossed his arms and leaned back against the counter closest to her.

She shot him a wary look, but continued to eat up the stretch of floor between him and the island in the middle. Every few steps she turned and changed direction, and each time he caught her scent, his gut tightened.

Finally, she stopped directly in front of him. It only took her a moment to realize her mistake. He didn't give her a second to retreat, backing her up against the island. Planting a hand on either side of her, he leaned in. Her hair tickled his cheek as he ran his jaw along hers, then down her neck.

"Back off."

Quiet but undoubtedly sincere, and just a little bit dangerous, the order succeeded in getting his attention. There was no way he could keep his hands off her, but he wouldn't be able to talk to her if he didn't distract himself with something else.

He turned away long enough to gather a few things from the pantry and fridge.

"You're cooking?"

"It keeps my hands busy." He nodded to the stool directly beside the island. If he couldn't touch her, standing close to her would have to do. For now. "Ask your questions."

"How can you be so old?"

Of course she'd start with a hard one. Hard for her to hear the answer to. "I'm immortal."

She stared at him.

"I can't die," he began.

"I know what immortal means." Her gaze moved over him top to bottom, and hopefully missing how aroused he was. "You can't be human."

He grabbed her hand, held it over his heart. "I am right

now."

"And the rest of the time?"

Gods, when had just talking ever turned him on so much? Paying attention to her very valid questions couldn't have been harder when the urge to kiss her nearly overwhelmed him.

Forced to give in or release her hand, he went with the latter.

"How is it even possible?" Kennedy continued. "How can you be so old and have never felt the sun? I guess I can cross vampire off my list." She paused, and her eyes narrowed as she recalled what he'd done. "You bit me."

"I got a little carried away." Uncomfortable with his guilt over that, he cracked a few eggs so he didn't have to look at her.

"Is that some kind of immortal fetish?"

"Not exactly."

She pushed her hands through her hair. "Okay. Let's start with last night." She held up her hand. "How did I get this?"

"You've been marked by a wraith." At her arched brow he added, "They'd be the ones closer to vampires."

"Is that what came after me in the bathroom too?"

The cat prowled in the back of his mind, disliking mention of the wraith. "Yeah."

"It wants me dead right?" She didn't wait for him to acknowledge that. "Why?"

"Because I have something it wants." He hadn't expected many to learn he had the dagger so soon, let alone have time to make arrangements to take it from him. He must not have been the only one to learn the sorceress possessed a dagger, simply the first one to reach it.

"So why didn't it mark you then?"

"Going after you was more effective."

Her frown matched his earlier confusion. "I don't understand. We've barely spoken."

"The wraith originally planned on making a deal with Cale."

"None of this is making sense. Cale is just my boss." She stopped. "He's immortal too, isn't he?"

Tristan nodded.

"So what did you take?" The accusation in her tone rubbed him the wrong way.

"I'm not a thief." Not exactly anyway. "It's a mystical

dagger."

"Mystical. Of course it couldn't be something simple, like priceless."

"It's that too." And judging by the look on her face, hearing that hadn't helped.

"So it does something?"

He set the bowl of eggs aside. "It's part of a set. Once united the daggers will lead to a sword."

"Someone wants me dead over a sword? Gee, whatever happened to the good old-fashioned greed, passion or revenge motives?"

"They're after Excalibur."

She laughed. "As in Knights of the Round Table and King Arthur? That Excalibur?"

"That would be the one."

Kennedy's laughter faded, and she searched his face for a sign he was conning her. The sincere expression on his face didn't reassure her at all. Either he was telling the truth, or he'd convinced himself he was. Neither possibility seemed all that favorable.

"You're looking for Excalibur? And when you find it?" Maybe if she could figure out why they wanted the sword, she'd know how to get herself out of this mess. Although *mess* didn't seem to come close to describing the last ten hours.

"We'll guard it."

"Until?"

Tristan hesitated. "Until Arthur reawakens to claim it."

"*The* King Arthur. So you're what, friends with the guy?" Wasn't the brain built to shut done when there was too much information to process? And if discovering that immortals, wraiths and mythical monarchies actually existed wasn't too much to handle, she'd dance topless on the bar during her next shift.

Assuming she lived that long.

He held out his hand. "Come."

She reluctantly placed her hands in his. Last night he'd pulled her through the halls so quickly there hadn't been time to notice much of her surroundings. Now she simply had too much going on in her head to register anything but a blur of polished tile floors and painting-covered walls.

At least until they passed through a series of rooms and reached a large heavy wooden door that looked like something out of a Brothers Grimm fairytale. Half expecting to find a stone staircase descending into a dungeon on the other side, she glanced around the empty room, empty but for the floor-to-ceiling mirror on the far wall.

She took her time following him to the mirror. There was nothing in the room to give off a heavy vibe, but the sense of *something* in the room with them slowed her steps. Both her hand and lower back tingled the closer she drew to the mirror.

"If this is something—"

Tristan cut her off, speaking in a language she didn't recognize.

"—kinky..." she finished, watching the mirror's surface shimmer, their reflection awash in a silvery rainbow that faded, leaving an image of a sundrenched meadow. "That can't be real."

He took her head and when she realized what he meant to do, she resisted.

"Trust me," he pleaded, those fathomless blue eyes of his sucking her in.

"With the exception of some bad choices in boyfriends, I haven't trusted anyone since I was twelve."

His lip curled at the mention of *boyfriends*, then he frowned. "Since the car accident," he guessed.

Surprised by his perceptiveness, she focused on the mirror. There were way too many questions to allow herself to be coerced—distracted—into talking about the past.

"I would never let anything hurt you."

Part of her believed him. The other part was simply too stunned by how much she already trusted him to give in entirely. Still, the soft caress of his thumb along the inside of her wrist soothed her apprehension, and she let him guide her closer to the mirror.

She brushed her fingers across the surface, still expecting to find it hard and cool. Instead, her fingers pushed through the shimmery membrane. A breeze whispered across her hand, the meadow's bright sun warming her instantly.

"How is this possible? And if you say hocus-pocus I'll hit

you, I swear."

Tristan smiled.

"What is that place?"

"Avalon."

She let her hand drop and the world skidded a little sideways for a moment.

He wrapped an arm around her waist as though he expected her to hit the ground again. "I know it's a lot to take in."

"Assuming I believe it." Being drugged seemed like such an easier explanation for everything.

"You're right."

"I am?" Somehow she'd expected him to be annoyed she doubted it, doubted him. But how could she not? Even Alice really only had a talking cat and the Mad Hatter to deal with.

"Seeing is believing, right?" His tone made her heart pound so fast it nearly burst through her chest.

He took a step back, unsnapped his jeans.

"What are you doing?"

"Giving you answers."

Even though it was what she wanted, what she'd demanded, she reached out to touch him, to stop him.

A shimmer of silver, like with the mirror, waved in front of her. The tattoo on her hand tingled like it was moving across her skin.

She drew her hand back, frowned at the unchanged brand. Weird. No, she'd surpassed weird a few thousand light years ago.

A soft thump, followed by a familiar purr snapped her gaze up.

Tristan had…vanished, run, hid—all of them would have worked for her, but she knew none of them would have been right. God help her, she knew, even though she didn't want to.

Tristan and the black cat were one and the same.

"I need a drink." Two hours later and Kennedy's urge to get blindingly wasted hadn't passed.

"Try eating something," Tristan encouraged.

"I really have no urge to see what regurgitated omelet looks like, thanks."

He pushed a stack of pancakes in her direction instead.

She didn't glance at the plate. "Pass."

He forked one onto an empty plate, poured syrup over it and cut off a chunk. "Come on, one bite."

Her stomach growled despite the dubious glance she spared for the fork he held up. "I'm a little old to be fed."

"That's not what this is." At her doubtful look, he shrugged. "Come on, I make kickass pancakes. Seriously."

She took a bite to humor him, waiting for the dripping piece to settle like lead in her stomach. Instead the heavenly taste lingered on her tongue long after she swallowed. "Wow." Not even her mother's family recipe had tasted this good.

He grinned, started to cut off another piece, but she snagged the fork instead.

"I'll feed myself."

"Spoilsport."

Kennedy leaned away from him. After shifting back to his human form—naked—Tristan had tugged his jeans back on. She'd figured out an hour ago that he knew just how much the sight of his bare chest played havoc with her senses.

Focusing on her plate was the only way she could ignore how he deliberately invaded her personal space, finding one excuse after another to touch her. It had started off innocent enough. Asking her to pass him something when he returned to answering her questions and cooking, stealing every chance he could to brush her hand or lean into her while reaching past her.

By her guess, one more innocent touch would permanently rewire her insides.

Finished with her pancake, she pushed the plate aside. Tristan countered the move by nudging the plate of omelets—undoubtedly cold omelets—in her direction.

"No thanks."

"Who's going to eat all this?"

She glanced at the breakfast feast laid out across the table in bowls and dishes. "I'm not the one who felt compelled to cook way too much food." Enough for a football team probably.

"The only thing I'm compelled to do is touch you."

"And risk losing a paw."

A threat he obviously no longer took seriously since he stepped in front of her. His reluctant agreement to give her some space to process everything—which would probably take days, weeks really—looked to be running out.

And heaven help her that she didn't care half as much as she should.

Even when she'd fired question after question at him, she'd remained intimately aware of every move he made. The long, hot glances she ignored, the way he tilted his head when he got close enough to smell her hair, the rough edge that took hold of his voice each time she denied his touch.

A freaking cat. A very big, very lethal cat.

Alice had nothing on her.

Exhausted and overwhelmed, Kennedy couldn't fight the yawn that snuck up on her.

Tristan tucked her hair behind her ear. "You're tired."

"Would have guzzled a few Red Bulls if I'd known how last night was going to turn out."

He tugged her to her feet. "You need to sleep."

She slanted him a suspicious look. "Is that code for sex?"

"Later."

Kennedy snorted, but he merely shrugged and led her out of the kitchen. By the time she reached his room, she'd yawned three more times and could barely keep her eyes open. That didn't stop her stomach from tightening the moment she noticed the bed, its sheets still rumpled from earlier.

Shutting the door, he looked over his shoulder at her. A long, sexually charged look.

Oh my. "I've really had one hell of an afternoon..."

His hand went to the fly of his jeans.

"...and think sleep would be best." Somehow she managed not to choke on her words, suddenly preoccupied with watching him tug down his zipper.

Tristan cocked his head, dragging his gaze from her feet, up to her eyes. "You're a lot of things, Kennedy, but a convincing liar isn't one of them. You would welcome my touch and we both know it."

"If that's true, what's stopping you?" As far as challenges went, it fell miserably short.

His hand encircled her wrist and she nearly whimpered at

the contact. He coaxed her into the bathroom.

She glanced in the mirror and tried not to cringe. "Bad hair days are a turn off for big cats, huh?"

"Not even close." He nuzzled her neck, and her eyes drifted shut. "You're exhausted, and to be honest, so am I."

Trailing back toward the bed, she skidded to a stop when he stepped out of his jeans.

Her every nerve ending stood at attention as he tossed his pants onto a chair, not displaying a hint of modesty as he stood before her beautifully naked—and aroused. She couldn't help but let her gaze roam down his powerful chest, then lower…lower.

Tristan grinned at her blatant perusal.

She cleared her throat. "You sleep naked."

He laughed. "Yes, but this is to keep you safe."

"From who, the clothing fairy?"

His laugh deepened, and that was all the warning he offered before the air between them shimmered and she found herself staring at the cat.

The instinctive urge to run lasted only a second, maybe two. She'd forgotten how big he was like this, bigger than any animal she'd seen in a zoo or on television. Now she almost wished she'd paid attention to those documentaries. Maybe then she'd feel like she could handle being herded toward the bed by a man-eating predator.

Did Tristan eat meat in cat form? Had she anticipated him shifting on her like this, she would have made a point to ask that rather important question when she'd been interrogating him earlier.

The cat batted her hand with his head, and her pulse jumped. Hesitant, she opened her palm and he rubbed himself beneath her hand, arching his back. He circled her and a flick of his tail caught her across the butt.

"Cute."

He jumped up on the bed, pawed at the blanket until satisfied with the arrangement, then sank down. Crossing his paws, he lowered his head, but didn't close his eyes until she stretched out next to him—very, very slowly.

Without warning, he dropped his big head on her stomach, effectively pinning her in place. As if that wasn't strange enough, he nudged her arm until she got the point, purring when she ran her fingers along his sleek coat.

"Have I mentioned how completely surreal all this is?"

He cracked open an eye, puffed out through his nostrils.

"You're right," she said, guessing at what he was thinking. "If you could talk like this, I would have really freaked out."

Kennedy turned her face into the warm spray of water, then leaned forward, letting the water sluice down her spine. Unlike in her own cramped apartment shower, she wasn't in a hurry to rush through the motions. The longer she lingered behind the frosted glass panes, the more she could put off facing the very real, very black and furry reality curled up in the middle of Tristan's bed.

She squeezed some shower gel into her palm, and the familiar soapy scent—Tristan's—made every cell in her body stand up and take notice. She closed her eyes, breathing in the soap, and regretted it the second another whiff of the stuff made her nipples harden.

The near-constant state of arousal really had to let up. Yet even as the pro orgasm but pro self-control part of her brain came to that conclusion, she trailed her hand down her stomach, wishing it was Tristan's. Wishing it was Tristan's palms cupping her breasts, his thumbs swirling through the soap to circle her nipples.

Kennedy darted a look over her shoulder, toward the closed bathroom door. Her hand slid lower, gliding across her skin. She closed her eyes, sinking deeper into a fantasy she'd entertained dozens of times before. Only now she knew the animal that lived inside him, and damned if knowing he walked that fine line between the logic of a man and the savage instincts of a predator didn't take her fantasy to a whole new level.

One so deep she didn't notice she wasn't alone in the bathroom until the door clicked. Knowing who it was didn't stop her heart from quickening.

Naked, Tristan opened the shower door, lingering in the doorway. A heated smile curved his lips, his gaze sliding up her body. "Morning."

Completely exposed, Kennedy turned away on instinct.

Fantasizing about him sharing the space and experiencing it were apparently two different things. She glanced over her shoulder, tracking his progress across the wet tile floor. Not until he stood within arm's reach did she look away from his face.

He stepped closer to the spray and water beaded on his chest, dripping down...down. The trail snaked over his defined abdomen before reaching his aroused cock. Kennedy let out a breath, clenching her thighs around the heavy ache deep in her core.

"Need some help?" He took the shower gel from her and set it aside, reaching for a bottle of shampoo instead. After squeezing a generous amount into his palm, he nodded for her to turn around.

She took her time, just a little bit preoccupied with the brush of his arousal against her bottom. The moment he started working the shampoo into her hair, her spine turned to rubber, and the longer he massaged her hair into a heavy lather, the harder his shaft bumped against her.

"Turn around and close your eyes."

When she complied, he tipped her head back, rinsing the shampoo out. Without opening her eyes, she knew right down to the centimeter how close he was to her mouth. As if he'd read her mind, he brushed his lips across hers.

Somehow, she managed to contain her frustration when he pulled back.

"I think you missed a few spots earlier." Tristan returned to the shower gel, soaping up his hands and running them down her arms.

"Good thing you showed up when you did then."

His hands slid around to her belly, roaming higher.

"I thought cats didn't like water."

"I happen to be a big fan of a little water play." To emphasize his point he bent and sucked her nipple into his mouth.

She moaned, slipping her hands into his hair and holding him against her. He curled his tongue around her, flicking the tip before pulling her hard between his lips.

"Again," she begged.

He laughed and dropped to his knees, pushing her out

from beneath the full onslaught of the spray. She flattened her palm against the wall when he lifted her leg, carefully setting it on the ledge running the perimeter of the shower.

"Much better," he murmured, having improved his view of her damp sex.

Kennedy shivered at being on complete display, unprepared for the sheer pleasure that came from the very slow, very hot kiss Tristan pressed to her sex. Riveted, she watched his tongue slide up her cleft, moaning low and deep as he laved the slick knot nestled between her folds.

She clutched at the slick tiles, needing leverage to keep from sliding to the floor in front of him. As though he understood her problem, he slipped his hands up, cupping her ass. Pressing his mouth to her inner thigh, his tongue hot against her cooling skin, he took his time returning to her sex.

He ignored the not-so-subtle roll of her hips and the half-hearted pleas that came out rough and just a little bit desperate. She couldn't help it, the agonizing pace of his lips sliding across her body, the alternating chafe of his stubble with the smooth, slick sweeps of his tongue were steadily driving her out of her mind.

Tristan sealed his mouth over her, laving her clit with soft, quick strokes. Crying out, she arched up, her muscles tight. He gripped her bottom harder, his fingers digging into her and keeping her trapped against his mouth.

As if she'd try to escape the decadent torture pushing her toward release. Knowing he hand a good hold of her, she dared to let go to the wall and slid her hands into his damp hair. She rose higher on her toes with every lazy flick of his tongue, eased down again with every slow suck until she writhed shamelessly against his mouth.

The more she bounced her hips to his mindless pace, the more ruthless he became, licking and sucking, pushing his face against her.

"Oh God," she whispered, reaching for the climax coiling deep in her sex, moaning loudly when it crashed over her, stealing her breath.

Slowly the rest of her surroundings came back into focus. The water still beat the tile floor relentlessly, steam clouded the air, making what just happened more like a dream than real.

Tristan softened his grip on her ass, but didn't let her ease away from him. Not that there was anywhere to go with the wall at her back and him at her feet, keeping her exactly where he wanted her. She met his gaze, her cheeks flushed, her lips parting around the breaths she sucked in.

Without looking away, he dipped his head, tasting the very center of her.

She trembled, but kept staring down at him. "I need a minute. I can't..." she shook her head, "...again."

Oh yes she could.

Anticipating the attempt to squirm free, he pressed her even harder against the wall, keeping his lips soft. Knowing how sensitive she was only made him that much determined to make it good for her. Again and again. If this was all she believed was between them for now, he'd make damn sure she never doubted how incredible it was.

Tracing her folds with his tongue, he took his time memorizing the taste of her. She whimpered softly and the sound grabbed him hard in the gut and groin. Her hands left him, stretching over her head as if to pull herself away from the feather-light tease of his tongue, only to drop back to her sides on a shaky moan.

He loved watching her sink farther into pleasure, her breasts rising and falling with her quickening breaths, loved feeling the press of her thigh against his cheek, holding him to her. And most of all he loved knowing he could do this to her, could stroke and lick and suck her to the point she threatened to slide into his arms.

"Tristan," she hissed, grinding against his mouth.

Faster now, he ran his tongue up her cleft, stopping at her clit. The slick knot felt plump beneath his lips, and he greedily closed his mouth over her.

She threaded her fingers through the ends of his hair, tugging just hard enough to make staying on his knees a testament to his control. His cock hung heavy and aching between his legs, and he wanted inside his mate.

Soon. He pushed two fingers against her opening, pumping them into her wet sex. She rocked her hips forward, and he laved at her damp flesh, pushing a little harder and a little harder. Her body bowed against him, her release filling his senses until he could have pleasantly drowned in it.

Pushing to his feet just slow enough to avoid them both slipping and ending up in a tangled heap, he pressed her against the wall. His shaft hit her belly, and he groaned, sliding his arms around her.

She pushed up on her toes and her sweet sex teased along the head of his cock. Catching her thigh, he lifted it to his hip, opening her wider and sinking between her folds.

They both moaned, and he found her mouth, thrusting his tongue between her lips to tangle with hers. The hot walls of her sex clenched around him, and he surged forward, sliding deeper. But it wasn't enough. He gripped her waist, lifting her until both legs locked around his waist.

They hit the wall hard, and he almost lost his grip. Already so close, he didn't care. She flexed her hips, rocking against him, and he used what little leverage he had to thrust into her.

Her head fell to the side and he buried his face against her neck, driving himself in and out of her sex and falling apart faster than he could have imagined. It shouldn't have been possible to need her so much so quickly, to want to give her everything, to share his bed, his life, his heart.

"Oh...oh." She dug her heels into his ass, grinding harder. "Tristan, please."

Working his hips, he pumped deeper, groaning when her climax hit and her sex spasmed around him. His own release ripped through him, leaving him rocking inside her even after his orgasm faded and his muscles relaxed.

The sky was nearly dark outside when Tristan finished drying off and reached for his pants. He could hear Kennedy in the bathroom, easily pictured her slipping another one of his shirts over her head. As much as he liked the idea of her wearing his clothes, he liked the idea of taking them off her later even more.

He pulled his pants up just as she emerged from the bathroom. She stopped in the doorway and the flash of carnal interest in her eyes made him achingly hard. Now he realized why newly mated gargoyles were rarely seen. If he had his way he'd take Kennedy back to his lair on Avalon right this second and spend weeks keeping her all to himself, learning about her, teaching her about his clan, showing her his favorite spots, discovering every way to wring pleasure from her body for hours on end.

Except she was human. Humans couldn't cross the mirror without stopping their fragile hearts. Not even the Avalon-born humans, who had escaped Morgana's enslavement after Arthur's fall, could cross over.

Kennedy strolled toward him. "What's with the scowl? I thought cats were fairly nocturnal."

He yanked on a clean T-shirt, ignoring the tension that clutched his heart. "Which is why I want to get this over with."

"Get what over with?"

He took her hand and led her into the hall. "We don't have much time."

By the time they climbed the stairs and reached the roof, the last stretch of sunlight faded from the western skyline.

"Wow." Kennedy stared at the two stone gargoyles in front of them. "They look like you."

The pair were identical to anyone who didn't know his siblings in their cat form, anyone who didn't recognize the sly prowess imprinted on Briana's form. Few could hunt and corner their prey as fast as Briana.

Normally Cian's playful side came through in his gargoyle state, his endless amusement most noticeable in the curl of a paw or the tilt of his head. For the last century he'd looked riled, ready to strike and forever prevented from it.

Next to him, Kennedy froze, the sound of stone cracking making her frown. She ventured closer as fine lines of bright white streaked across Briana. Anticipating the explosion of light, Tristan stepped closer to his mate.

Kennedy brought her hands up to protect herself from the chunks of stone that broke away, and he watched her expression morph from surprised to curious when the pieces disintegrated before reaching her. That didn't stop her from tensing up when Briana padded through the settling dust and stared up at Kennedy with glittering feline eyes.

"My sister," Tristan said.

"When you mentioned gargoyle, you really meant it, huh?"

Briana circled Kennedy once, pacifying the cat's instincts to rule out any threat, then disappeared down the stairs.

He started to follow her inside, stopped when Kennedy

hadn't moved to do the same.

"Is that Cale?"

Tristan shook his head. "That's my other brother, Cian."

"Does he like playing statue or something?"

A vise clamped down on his chest. "A sorceress did that to him. He can't break free." He headed for the stairs, relieved when she followed.

"Some kind of spell?" she guessed, and when he nodded asked, "How long has he been like that?"

"Over a century."

"And there's no way to free him?"

They reached the hall, and he headed for Briana's room. "We're working on it."

Fully dressed, Briana stepped into the hall before they reached her door. "I guess you told her everything, huh?" Her gaze zeroed in on the mark on Kennedy's neck, and she arched a brow, silently asking if everything included the truth about their bond.

He gave a subtle shake of his head, but Kennedy caught the cryptic look passed between them. "What?"

"I've got something that will help." Briana nodded to the puncture marks on his mate's neck.

Kennedy probed at the healing bite mark. "It doesn't hurt anymore, actually."

Briana nodded down the hall. "Can I talk to you for a second?"

With a suspicious look, Kennedy jerked her thumb in the opposite direction. "I need coffee, so come and find me when you're done."

"You didn't tell her?" Briana hissed the moment Kennedy was out of earshot.

Guilt gave his stomach a good, hard nudge. He ignored it. "I think learning what we are is a big enough shock for one day, don't you?"

Briana scoffed. "Seeing as you're not a woman, I think you might be seriously underestimating how big a deal being claimed can be."

Not wanting Kennedy to get too far away, he started for the kitchen, choosing not to acknowledge Briana's are-you-out-of-your-mind glare.

"How did you explain that to her anyway. Just a love bite?"

"Things got out of control." And then some. "I hadn't exactly planned on it."

"Remind me to step out of the line of fire when you break it to her like that."

Curious and just a little bit worried, he had to ask. "Think she'll be mad?"

Briana's expression said it all—he was a dead man. "Forgetting for a moment that she's human, what woman wouldn't be *thrilled* to know she's been bonded to an immortal for the rest of her life without her consent?"

Tristan winced. "It won't be pretty, huh?"

"Assuming she lives long enough to hear it."

The cat growled first, then the man.

"I'm sorry. It's just..." She blew out a breath. "She's been marked. Short of finding out who engaged the wraith to take her out, there's nothing much to be done except give Lucan the dagger."

He whirled around. "And leave Cian trapped like that?"

"At the cost of your mate?"

Closing his eyes, Tristan curbed the impulse to lash out at his sister for the impossible position he was in. "I know."

Briana stopped just outside the kitchen. "Where's Cale?"

"He never came back last night."

"That's not like him."

"Keeping tabs on him?"

His sister rolled her eyes. "He always tells me when he won't be home by dawn."

"Why don't you try tracking him down."

She nodded. "What about you?"

He'd spent most of the time Kennedy had slept working out a game plan. "I'm going to find out who's using Lucan to get the dagger. Dolan was watching her closely last night."

"Dolan?" Having overheard them, Kennedy stepped into the hall. "You think he could have something to do with this?"

"After the way that Fae was watching you? Yeah."

"Fae? Another immortal race?"

Surprised they hadn't touched on the subject of the Fae during that afternoon's question and answer period, he nodded. "The oldest in Avalon."

Kennedy's doubtful expression caught him off guard. "Dolan has never been anything but nice to me."

"How nice?"

She rolled her eyes. "Not like that. He usually watches my back. I think his scar tends to intimidate people."

Scar?

"How long has he been hanging around?" Briana asked.

Kennedy shrugged. "A few weeks I think."

Briana crossed her arms. "He could have been learning her routine to make it easier for the wraith."

"What if you can't find out who wants me dead?" Nothing in Kennedy's voice betrayed her worry, but she edged closer to Tristan, accepting the hand he wrapped around hers.

"Tell her."

"Briana," he warned.

His sister ignored him. "The only way to save you is to turn over the dagger that will free Cian, or Tristan will have to fight Lucan."

"Lucan?" Kennedy visibly struggled to keep up.

"The wraith," he answered.

"You know him?"

"He's a friend," Briana said.

Tristan snorted.

Kennedy shook her head. "You can't give him the dagger."

"Tristan won't win a fight."

He glanced at Briana. "Your faith in me is staggering. I'm not going to die," he added, turning his attention to Kennedy. "One of those perks to being immortal."

"I'm pretty sure you mentioned something about beheading earlier. Immortal or not that sounds pretty permanent, wouldn't you say?" She glanced at Briana for confirmation.

His sister nodded, and he glared at her.

"We'll find the contractor," he promised.

"Are you sure Dolan is involved?"

Tristan searched Kennedy's face, wondering at her skepticism. "Are you sure he isn't?"

"I don't know." She pushed her hair back from her forehead. "How are you going to find him?"

"We'll make him come to us."

Her brow furrowed. "How?"

"We offer him a bargain."

Kennedy stared at the stone cat inches from her feet. She hadn't moved for twenty minutes, running the events of the last two nights through her head and coming back to the same conclusion every time.

She couldn't let Tristan die for her.

One person had sacrificed their life for hers already, and that had been enough. Tristan only had twelve hours left to track down whoever was using her as a pawn, and the odds of him finding that immortal weren't looking too good. He hadn't given up hope Dolan was involved, but wanted to wait to summon the Fae until he'd regained his strength, something only achieved by playing gargoyle for a while.

She'd told him she'd be fine for a little while. Turned out, saying it wasn't nearly as hard as believing it. Not even Briana's assurance that Lucan would keep his word to give Tristan time kept Kennedy from scanning the corners of the room in search of shadows that shouldn't be there. Tristan had insisted that he'd know if she needed him, though she still wasn't clear on how if he was solid as a rock, and he hadn't offered much in the way of explanation.

Ignoring her promise to wait for him, she sat up. She couldn't put it off any longer, not when her life and Cian's were at stake. Tristan had only known her for a few months compared to the centuries spent with his brother, yet he was willing to risk his life for her for reasons he continued to keep to himself.

And she knew there was something he wasn't saying. More than once she'd caught the knowing glances between him and Briana. The fact that he continued to hold out on her made it easier to follow through on her plan. She excelled at taking care of herself, and despite how much she wanted to trust Tristan to fix everything, the thought of him dying trying to protect her...

The sudden pressure on her chest threatened to cut her in half. She closed her eyes, gripping the edge of the bed until the crippling sensation eased and she could stand. That she had to force herself out of the room, away from him, proved just how attached to him she'd gotten in such a short time.

Too attached. She was falling for him. Fast and hard and without a clue how to slow it down.

She paused at the front door, her hand clenched around the handle. Having been introduced to Tristan's world so recently, she didn't harbor any illusions that she actually knew what she was doing. Odds were her instincts had been way off, but she couldn't sit back and do nothing.

She'd done that once, let her fear paralyze her and lost the only thing that had mattered to her. She wouldn't lose Tristan too.

Taking a breath, Kennedy wrenched the door open and stepped outside. Goose bumps raced across her skin despite the warm afternoon air. Each step out of the shade felt one step closer to salvation and one step closer to death.

She closed her fist around the charm she'd taken from Tristan's room. "Dolan of the Fae, I wish to make a bargain."

Chapter Seven

"And why would I want to make a bargain with you?"

Kennedy whipped around at the amused inquiry and found Dolan leaning against the front door, arms crossed. He looked the same as he had the other night, right down to his faded jeans and plain white T-shirt. Given the little she'd learned about the Fae from Tristan, she'd half expected something about him to look different this time.

She squared her shoulders. She'd never been intimidated by Dolan before, and she'd be damned if she started now. "I thought the Fae enjoyed bargaining."

"And what else has the cat told you?"

"Not much," she admitted, most of which she'd rather forget at the moment. Like how easily Fae could bewitch humans, leaving them at their mercy.

Dolan shoved away from the door. "So why are you coming to me for help?"

She frowned. "You're not surprised I know about you."

"It was inevitable." He started to say something else, but stopped, his gaze locking on her hand. Something akin to concern flashed across his face. "When did you get that?"

"Two nights ago."

An inexplicable rage darkened the Fae's face, turning the scar a deeper pink. "He let you be marked? I knew I should have gutted the bloody gargoyle the second I noticed him watching you."

Kennedy cocked her head, puzzled by Dolan's reaction. "If you're referring to Tristan, he plans to fight the wraith."

"I never figured the cat was annoying *and* stupid." He

paced away from her, swiveling back to face her. "What is the wraith after?" When she hesitated, he added, "You're the one who called me for help, *deifiúr.*"

Going with her gut, Kennedy met his gaze straight on. "A mystical dagger."

His sighed, proving she hadn't needed to elaborate any more than that. "And of course the selfish bastard won't just hand it over."

"His brother—"

Dolan waved a hand, cutting her off. "So you would make a bargain with me for his brother's benefit?"

She shook her head. "I can't let Tristan die for me."

"Why not?"

Not caring to examine her feelings for Tristan at the moment, let alone share them with anyone else, she arched a brow. "Do I need to complete a medical questionnaire too, or can we get on with it already?"

A hint of a smile touched Dolan's lips, quickly overshadowed by a disapproving scowl when he noticed the bite mark on her neck. If she hadn't suspected it meant something significant before, she certainly did now.

"Will you help me or not?" Kennedy prompted.

"And if I refuse?"

"I'm screwed."

Dolan shook his head, and her heart sank. She turned away, heading for the front door.

"There are rules, you know. The bargain is void the second you tell anyone the terms."

Despite Tristan's warnings about bargaining with the Fae, she nodded for Dolan to continue.

"In exchange for helping him with the wraith, you will come with me at the time of my choosing."

A sliver of unease shot through her veins. "Go with you where?"

He crossed his arms, but didn't answer her.

"For how long?"

His expression turned calculating. "A week."

"And then I go back to my regular life?" Assuming she didn't end up bewitched and catering to Dolan's every whim. A risk she'd take if it meant Tristan wouldn't end up killing himself to keep her safe. She couldn't live with two deaths on her conscience for that reason.

"Regular is a bit boring, don't you think?"

It was her turn to scowl.

Dolan rolled his eyes. "I hope he's worth it."

"He is."

The moment the cold stone broke away from his body, Tristan knew Kennedy wasn't in the room. It took only a few moments to pick up on her scent, and he padded down the hall in the direction of the kitchen.

Oblivious to the large cat stalking her, she bent over to dig a pan out from a bottom cupboard. Not wanting to freak her out, he quickly shifted and stepped up behind her. The floor creaked under his foot, and Kennedy whirled around, a wooden spoon clutched in her hand.

Tristan caught her wrist a moment before she would have nailed him in the chest with it.

Her shoulders relaxed, a relieved smile curving her lips. "Good reflexes."

He grinned. "Come back to bed with me and I'll show you how good they really are."

"Back to that, are we?" Her breath hitched on the last syllable, her eyes sliding shut as he opened his mouth on the inside of her wrist.

"Can't help it." He nipped the tender skin, then gently sucked it between his lips.

Kennedy gave a soft whimper and tugged her hand free, then turned around. "I'm hungry for something else at the moment."

The cat growled, eager to play her game. Her words said one thing, but her scent said something very different. Something hot and tangled...

He eyed the mess of scrambled eggs in the frying pan, cringing when she poked the massacred food with the wooden spoon. He didn't think it was possible for anyone to screw up scrambled eggs, but the slightly charred lumps proved him wrong. "Maybe you should put that down before one of us gets hurt."

"Is that some kind of dig about my cooking?"

He brushed her hair aside. "Let's just say you make a better bartender."

"I'll have you know that my cooking hasn't killed anyone."

Yet. Smart enough to keep that thought to himself, he tugged the spoon out of her hand. "Let me help ensure it stays that way." He snapped off the burner and shoved the frying pan to the back of the stove. Before she could protest, he turned her around and set her up on the island.

"You're naked." Arousal hummed beneath the innocent observation.

"So glad you finally noticed."

She slipped a hand between them and cupped his balls. "Hard not to." Running her palm up his cock, Kennedy kissed his neck. "So how did you…sleep?"

Tristan shook his head.

"No more talking, right?"

"You're catching on." Wrapping his hand around her ponytail, he playfully tugged her head back and slanted his mouth across hers.

Moaning softly, she relaxed against him, and he slid his tongue between her lips. The first wet taste of her drop-loaded a rush of pure, carnal lust into his system, and he groaned against her mouth.

Her fingers tightened around his cock, and he eased his legs a little wider to give his mate complete access.

"What happened to going to your room?" she teased.

"Can you do that and walk at the same time?" He didn't wait for her to answer, guessing at her response. "I didn't think so."

Her rich laugh whispered across his cheek, and he turned his mouth to catch hers for a drugging kiss. Smooth, hot and—

Another scent lay buried beneath her arousal, almost masked somehow.

He leaned back, scrutinizing her face. "Is there anything you want to tell me?"

The flicker of guilt in her eyes said it all. She'd been talking to the Fae.

Clamping down on his anger, he stepped back, crossing his arms. "What was Dolan doing here?"

Kennedy shook her head, remaining silent.

She wouldn't—couldn't—have summoned him. The longer he stared at her, however, waiting for her to say something, the worse the ache in his stomach became. Damn it.

Intending to demand an explanation, he paused, the hair on the back of his neck rising.

The wraith.

He headed for the door. "Stay inside."

"Wait."

"The wraith is here," he said without turning around. "Go back to my room and wait for me. Please?" he added when he realized his voice sounded more animal than man.

"Okay."

On the way out, he snagged a pair of pants from the closet. Lucan had promised to give him forty-eight hours. Knowing his friend hadn't given in and gone after Kennedy while he'd been regaining his strength was the only thing preventing him from going for the wraith's throat.

He found Lucan in the same spot as before. The undeniable scent of blood filled Tristan's nostrils. The wraith had fed recently. Tristan spared a quick thought for the unlucky human who would have been killed by the infection from the bite, assuming the wraith hadn't bled the poor bastard dry.

"Not as threatened tonight?" Despite that he'd fed recently, the wraith wasn't looking too hot. Dark circles hung under the mercenary's eyes, his face pale, his pulse more erratic. Already the signs of denying himself a kill were taking their toll.

"My sister seems to think I can trust you."

Lucan smiled weakly. "You wouldn't have needed her to vouch for me once upon a time."

"That was before you targeted my mate."

The wraith sighed. "I didn't come to rehash our last conversation." He glanced toward the house. "She met with the Fae."

"I guess you haven't strayed too far from the property then." At Lucan's unapologetic look, he clenched his jaw. "When did they meet?"

"Just a few hours ago. She bargained with him."

Fuck. "What were the terms?" he asked, already suspecting the answer.

"I think he realized I was close and prevented me from overhearing anything."

"Worried?"

"When a Fae is involved? Always."

"You didn't need to tell me."

Lucan shrugged. "She's your mate. How can you best protect her if she's conspiring against you?"

Conspiring? Annoyance flared in Tristan's chest. "If Kennedy talked to Dolan then it was to find out he wasn't involved."

"And you know the human so very well?"

"Well enough," he growled.

"So it's not possible she's working with the Fae to get the dagger from you?"

Tristan crossed his arms. "If Dolan engaged you, you'd be rolling on the ground in pain for revealing him."

"Perhaps my contractor simply beat them both to it."

The memory of the Fae glyph on Kennedy's back surfaced. Tristan dismissed it almost immediately. "If they're working together she wouldn't have needed to bargain with him."

"Complications arise." Lucan glanced down at the house. "Does she know she's your mate?"

"No."

"Are you certain? Maybe she figured it out and didn't care for the match to be permanent."

The cat roared in denial. "Who engaged you?"

Lucan stared at him.

Tristan shrugged. "You seemed awfully chatty, figured it couldn't hurt to just ask."

"If you're looking to tip the scales, you'll have to find that information somewhere else." His eyes darkened to black pools, revealing how close to the edge the mercenary already was. "You a few hours left, maybe not even that." He turned away, paused. "I am sorry, Tristan."

"You sound convinced you'll defeat me if it comes to that."

"If only I couldn't."

Tristan didn't wait to watch the mercenary leave, suspecting he wouldn't venture too far from Kennedy.

Briana waited for him at the edge of the driveway, her attention locked on the trees in the distance. "Cale still isn't back. He's not answering his phone and no one at Pendragon's has seen him since the other night."

"The sun just set."

"He should have been back last night. Something is wrong."

Tristan wished he could disagree. His brother wouldn't have disappeared without a word, not when they had the dagger and were one step closer to freeing Cian. "We'll find him."

"Before or after your suicide mission?"

"I'll be fine." He opened the front door and stepped inside.

Briana grabbed his arm, bringing him to a halt. "No, you won't. Did you know there isn't even one instance of a wraith being killed? Not one, Tristan."

"I can't give him the dagger and I won't let him kill Kennedy."

"We'll get it back again."

"I can't just leave Cian like that." Not when it should have been Tristan trapped in his gargoyle form for taunting the sorceress.

"And when you're killed, I'll have lost two of my brothers."

Kennedy came around the corner.

Briana glanced at her. "He won't survive this. Lucan is a trained killer. That's what he does."

Reading his sister's intentions, he snarled. "Don't."

"No. You won't listen to me. Maybe you'll listen to your mate."

"Briana!"

Kennedy frowned. "Mate?"

Briana nodded. "That's right. You're his mate. That bond doesn't survive death."

"I can't... I didn't..." Disbelief flickered across Kennedy's face.

"Somewhere along the way fate and Mother Nature got together and figured out who your perfect match is, biologically, emotionally, physically." Briana nodded to Tristan. "He's it."

Gaze critical, Kennedy turned to him. "Is that true?"

"He wouldn't have claimed you otherwise," Briana answered for him.

"Claimed me?" She followed Briana's gaze to the healing bite mark on her neck. "As in property?"

"It's not like that." Tristan glared at his sister. "I'll explain everything but first I need to know what Dolan was doing here."

Briana whistled. "The Fae? Didn't see that one coming."

"You made a deal with him, didn't you?" Tristan pressed.

Kennedy said nothing, her expression bordering on defiant.

"You need to tell me. Dolan can't be trusted."

She gestured to the bite mark. "And you can?"

"Yes." The doubt in her eyes twisted his insides. Although frustrated, he couldn't expect her to blindly trust him. It would have been helpful—unrealistic—but damn helpful.

"Because you're my mate?"

Yes. However, he was smart enough to realize that sharing that probably wouldn't win him any points here. "Because no one else will protect you like I will."

"Because no one else will die for me, you mean? I can't live with another death on my conscience." She spun on her heel and strode away from them.

Briana stopped him from pursuing Kennedy. "Give her a few minutes before going all Neanderthal on her."

"Thanks to you," he snapped.

She threw out her arms in disgust. "Someone needs to get through to you."

"It wasn't your place."

"And it's not your place to determine this family's future."

"But it's Cale's? Sorry, but he is not my keeper."

Her eyes flared at the comment, and she turned away.

Damn it. "Wait a second. Look, it may not come to a fight. Lucan said something about tipping the scales."

"And?"

"Maybe it's nothing, but I think he was trying to tell me something. There was a dragon talking to Kennedy the other night. He was tall and lanky, had dark hair and wore the mark of the McKibben clan. I need to know who he is."

"Since when did the dragons care about Excalibur?"

"Maybe Morgana is starting to make them nervous." Tristan couldn't imagine the dragons getting involved after this long unless the power-hungry sorceress was eyeing their territory.

She let out a breath, nodded. "Give me an hour and I'll get you a name."

"You should have said something," Kennedy said through the closed bathroom door. Already the walls felt like they were closing in, but short of another face-off with her phantom assassin, she didn't trust herself not to reach for something worse than a water hose where Tristan was concerned.

"I wanted to give you some time to get used to being with me first."

A fresh wave of disbelief and anger swept through her. "You say that like I don't have a choice."

No response.

"Oh, that's right," she added. "You took that choice away from me. It's a wonder you didn't just club me over the head and drag me home to your cave." She considered her surroundings. "Although you pretty much did, huh?"

"Kennedy," he began.

She planted her palms against the door. "If this is where you tell me you're sorry or that you're going to fix it, you'd be better off batting around a ball of yarn right now."

"I'm not fixing anything. I'm sorry you found out that way, but it doesn't change anything."

She wrenched the door open, unprepared to find Tristan leaning against the wall next to the bathroom door. Ignoring the instinct to back away from him—very, very slowly—she took another step forward, planting her feet directly in front of him. Although terrified that her life was spinning beyond her control for the second time, she refused to back down.

"You might come from a different world than I do, but that doesn't mean you control me."

The stubborn look on his face softened. "I just want to keep you safe."

"From the wraith, maybe. But who's going to protect me from you?" At his confused expression, she added. "You both branded me. Why is your mark any different?"

He cocked his head, his gaze turning perceptive. "What's bothering you more? That we're mated, or that someone told you before you realized how deep the connection between us runs?" He palmed her cheek, his proximity sending off warning bells in her head even as her whole body clenched. "You know there's something between us."

"Lust," she provided.

His devilish grin should have annoyed her. Maybe it would have if he wasn't sweeping his thumb back and forth across her jaw like that.

"It's more than that." His tone dared her to deny it.

"Like whatever it was that made you bite me?"

"Claim you," he corrected.

"And what if I don't want to be claimed? What if I don't want to belong to you or anyone else?"

He arched a brow. "Just *if*? I must be growing on you."

She jabbed her finger into his chest. "Don't you dare make light of this."

"I take my mate very seriously." His attempt to look solemn didn't even get off the ground, not when a cocky grin tugged at the corner of his mouth.

Kennedy scowled, proving how unimpressed she was. And if it also masked just what that grin did to her, all the better. "How long have you known?"

"A couple of days."

"And it's just okay with you? That I'm the one biology and fate somehow determined was meant for you?"

His hand slid down her neck, his thumb doing that seductive sweeping thing to her throat. "If it means that I get to spend every day figuring out how to make you laugh and smile, and every night learning how to drive you absolutely wild in bed, then that's more than okay with me."

"This is crazy."

"Crazy is denying it because you didn't anticipate it." He pressed his lips to her cheek. "Crazy is pretending you don't feel what I do to you."

Her breath hitched. "Good sex does not guarantee a lasting relationship."

"Good?" He slid lower, heading straight for her mouth. "I was thinking more like phenomenal. Earth-shattering even." His lips grazed hers.

Kennedy didn't dare let herself draw a breath. "You're doing it again."

"I don't know what you're talking about." She heard the smile in his voice.

"You're trying to distract me." And it might not have been such a bad thing if she wasn't a tad preoccupied with the whole *mate* development.

Desperately needing space, she eased back a step, then two more.

Tristan didn't even try to hide his satisfaction.

"Stop it," she warned, then at his innocent look added, "Stop looking like you enjoy pursuing me."

He shrugged unapologetically. "The hunt is half the fun."

"I am not your prey."

"Then stop trying to figure out a way to get past me."

She eyed the bedroom door again. "You can't just keep me in here."

"I could always restrain you." His hot gaze roamed over her. "For your own good, naturally."

"I want you to leave." Preferably before she gave serious thought to giving in to the feverish buzz humming under her skin. There was too much at stake to sweep it all under the proverbial rug to be dealt with later.

He came closer. "Say that again, only try sounding like you mean it this time."

She bolted, huffing out a breath when he caught her around the waist and pushed her against the door. How in the hell had he gotten it closed so damn fast?

"Look at me, Kennedy."

Not until he repeated the throaty demand a second time did she realize she'd squeezed her eyes shut. "No."

"Please."

She shook her head, biting down on her lip to silence the thoughts that would sabotage every survival instinct she possessed.

"Come on, Kennedy." He nipped at her jaw. "Look at me."

The past and present collided and she shoved past him. "Do you know how I got this scar?" She jerked her shirt up, intentionally exposing her marred skin. "A drunk driver ran our car off the road and into the river. I was barely conscious and my mom couldn't get my seat belt undone right away.

"The car was taking on freezing cold water and the impact of hitting the drunk driver and guard rail had smashed up the door frames. In the process of freeing me and getting us clear of the car, my mother severed her femoral artery. She died a few minutes after dragging me to shore."

He pulled her into his arms. "Kennedy—"

She averted her face. "Don't kiss me," she pleaded. "Don't make me want you more than I already do. Don't make me fall for you. Not when..." The words stuck in her throat. She lifted her hand to his face. "Don't die on me too."

"After I've just found my mate? Not a chance."

"God, I don't even know what to do with that."

"Just give it some time. Give *us* some time."

Time to get even more attached? Not a good idea. Something on her face must have said exactly that because Tristan gripped her arms.

"Nothing is going to happen to me. You need to trust me. I'll be fine."

There wasn't time to voice her doubts. He trapped her face in his hands and captured her mouth in a drugging kiss, one that wrenched her heart into a dizzying backspin. She covered his hands with hers, leaning into him. One by one her reservations and fears retreated, stripping her down to the bone.

For one heart-crushing moment she thought about putting an end to the kiss, an end to the ever-deepening feelings she had for him before she ended up hurt and alone all over again.

But she couldn't do it, couldn't stop herself from twining her arms around him and holding on, and it had nothing to do with biology or fate or being claimed. She'd been so overwhelmed by everything she'd learned in the last few days she'd failed to notice how alive being with him made her feel.

"Don't shut me out," Tristan pleaded, pressing his face against her neck. "Be mad, be scared, but don't be alone in it."

She started to shake her head, trying to find the words that could begin to express just how much she didn't want to be alone.

"Do I have to beg?" He dropped to his knees, the playful glint in his eyes undermining his solemn expression. He wrapped his arms around her waist and nuzzled her stomach. "Be with me," he murmured against her.

"Unless you're afraid," he taunted when she couldn't speak past the lump in her throat.

A smile tugged at the corner of her mouth. "I'm not afraid."

"Prove it." He followed the arrogant challenge up by tugging at the hem of her shirt.

She brushed his hand away, anticipating his next move. As eager as her body was to feel his rough palms sliding over her skin, he couldn't be the one always calling the shots.

She nodded at the bed. "Sit."

He hesitated, and when she ran her finger along the hem of her shirt, drawing it higher, he moved to the edge of the mattress. Since she hadn't expected him to go along with her so quickly, she paused, questioning her next move.

"Don't stop."

She pressed her finger to his lips. "No more talking."

Heat flared in his eyes, the wild blue depths more feline than human. Kennedy grasped the edge of her shirt and drew it up, exposing her midsection, then dragging it higher. When she caught herself turning instinctively to the right to keep her scar out of his immediate line of sight, she stopped.

Forgetting yesterday and refusing to worry about tomorrow, she needed to share all of herself with him, even if it was only for tonight. Holding his gaze, she stripped off her shirt.

A sound somewhere between a groan and a growl rumbled in Tristan's chest. She smiled, taking off everything but her bra and panties. His fingers curled into the blanket, as though he knew he couldn't yet touch her.

Kennedy took the last step remaining between them. She slipped her bra strap off one shoulder, then the other, drawing out every second until she unclipped the back and let it fall to the floor. Her nipples hardened under Tristan's scorching gaze.

He shifted on the edge of the bed, but waited, a predator knowing that eventually his moment to strike would come. Words escaped her as she tugged off his shirt, running her fingers down the smooth layers of muscle stacked atop muscle.

Tristan caught her hand, pressing a soft kiss to her palm before letting her go. He didn't wait for her to tell him to lie back, stretching out on his own a moment before she could get the words out. Propping one hand behind his head, he managed to look like he'd orchestrated the show, only his clenched jaw and hungry dark eyes betraying his increasing restlessness.

Catching the edge of her panties, she slipped them over her hips and slowly down her legs. Naked to the core, she took another breath, wondering where her courage had suddenly fled. She stood up to rowdy drunks and stone-cold assholes on a nightly basis, and yet one look at Tristan waiting for her made her tremble inside and out.

His lips parted, and she half expected him to order her to get on the bed already.

Instead he drank in the sight of her for what felt like hours, then, “I need you.”

Not *I want you.* Not *I’ll keep you safe.* Just *I need you*, and never before had three little words ever touched her or unleashed such sheer longing that her knees almost gave out.

Crawling across the bed, she didn’t waste any more time. She didn’t object when he fumbled to help her get his pants off. That he didn’t rush her when she pushed him back and straddled his hips, brushing the full length of his cock, spoke volumes about his restraint.

She leaned down, sliding her mouth over his. “Touch me,” she whispered against his lips.

“I don’t know that I trust myself to just yet.” The rough confession sizzled through her bloodstream like fire streaking toward gasoline.

Stealing another kiss, letting the savage intensity lick through her system, she then leaned back and took every inch of his shaft deep inside her.

Chapter Eight

Sweet Avalon. Tristan sucked in a breath, grappling for the control she'd effectively shredded, first with her tantalizing strip show and then with a kiss that slayed him on the spot.

She rocked her hips, and he pushed up, sinking deeper. He fisted his hand under his head to keep from grabbing her and rolling her beneath him. Every sweet bounce of her ass, the soft grind when she took him fully inside her, the rapid rise and fall of her breasts—so damn close to his mouth and much too far away—threatened to undo him here and now.

She rode him slow and easy, her quick breaths growing faster and closer together. Damn but she was gorgeous. Everything about her—the fiery spark in her eyes, the unabashed arch of her spine, the sexy, confident smile—spoke of her strength, even the scar she didn't try to hide from him this time.

He ran his hand up her thigh, squeezing his eyes shut to prevent them from rolling straight back in his head when she quickened her pace. Digging his heels into the mattress, he rocked up, wanting it harder.

She shook her head, and at first he thought she meant to draw the torture out, to take him to the edge one soft, carnal bounce at a time. Not a bad way to go really, but then she dropped her head back and all he could think about was pulling her down to catch one of her nipples between his lips.

Sliding his hands higher, he cupped her breasts, thumbing her jutting nipples. Kennedy moaned, and he took a chance, coaxing her down. She hovered over him and he leaned up, closing his mouth over one hard tip. He caught her hips, holding her down where he fit so deep inside her.

He didn't know how long they just held on that way, the sweet walls of her sex clenching around his cock as he sucked her nipples between his lips, laving the swollen tips with his tongue.

Whimpering, Kennedy pushed him back down, riding him harder, almost ready to come. His jaw clamped down, his own release streaming closer and closer. Tension wound his spine tighter, and he slipped his hand up the inside of her thigh. He brushed his thumb over her clit and she cried out, pumping wildly.

Tristan couldn't tear his gaze away from her, not when she brought her arms up, catching the mass of blond waves and drawing it away from her face. The raw seductive heat in her eyes would have pushed him right over the edge if she hadn't arched up and cried out, her orgasm setting him off. He bucked his hips beneath her, driving himself hard and deep until his own release crashed over him.

And when Kennedy collapsed against his chest, breathless, a soft smile on her lips, he wondered for the first time exactly who had claimed who.

Tristan turned his head to look at Kennedy stretched out beside him. As much as he wanted to spend the rest of the night just like this, he knew he couldn't put the discussion off any longer. "Tell me about your bargain with Dolan."

She closed her eyes briefly. "I can't. You know that."

"You don't know him."

"And you do?" she challenged.

Frustration ate at him. "I know his race. The Fae never agree to anything unless it's to their benefit. That's how they work."

Kennedy rolled away from him, and his stomach turned to lead.

"Tell me."

"I can't."

"You mean you won't."

She sat up, jerking the sheet off the bed and trapping it against her front when she whipped around to face him. "I haven't had a damn say in any of this since it started. Not being marked, or brought here or *claimed.*"

Judging by her tone, what just happened between them hadn't brought her much closer to accepting their bond.

"But this," she continued. "My deal with Dolan...I'm in control of that."

"That's exactly what he wants you to believe, but whatever you asked for, whatever he demanded for the trade, he'll twist it around."

When she remained silent and turned away from him, Tristan snagged her wrist, jerking her back down to eye level. "Damn it, tell me."

"Or what? You'll claim me again, only this time stripping me of my free will as well? You expect me to trust you, just like that, when you don't trust me."

"When it comes to the Fae, I trust no one."

She pulled her hand free, but remained seated on the edge of the bed.

"You wear their mark. Your tattoo, it's a Fae glyph."

Surprise blinked across her face. "It's coincidence."

"Is it?"

"Whatever you're thinking—stop. I knew nothing of your world until a couple of days ago."

"Yet you managed to summon Dolan pretty easily."

Her eyes narrowed. "So because I was smart enough to pay attention when you and Briana were talking about it, my motives are suddenly suspect?"

"That's not what I meant." He shoved his hand through his hair, struggling to figure out how the conversation had taken such a turn.

Kennedy stood ten feet away, arms crossed, waiting. For what he didn't know. An apology? A solution? A way out of being his mate?

Thankfully a knock on the door saved him from saying the wrong thing and making the situation undoubtedly worse.

"Tristan? I have the name you're looking for."

"I'll be right there." He yanked on his clothes. "We'll finish our conversation when I get back."

"Can't wait," she quipped. She didn't so much as glance in his direction as she gathered up her clothes and vanished into the bathroom.

"It's a lot to take in, isn't it?"

Kennedy turned from the window, abandoning her study of the drops of rain splattering on the glass. A flash of lightning followed a boom of thunder loud enough to rattle the panes.

Briana turned away from her computer. "Whatever Dolan agreed to, it won't be to fight Lucan. The Fae don't interfere with Rhiannon."

"Afraid of her, are they?"

"Trust me, you would be too if you came face to face with her."

Kennedy started to shrug, then silently questioned the wisdom of inviting that kind of trouble. She knew little of the goddess, but wouldn't put it past fate to throw a few more wrenches into the mix.

"He's not so bad you know. Tristan," Briana added as if there were any doubt who she meant.

"We barely know each other."

"And you think knowing each other is what keep marriages together?"

Massaging her temples to ease the headache she'd had since Tristan left hours ago, Kennedy sank down on the sofa. "Are we even talking about marriage here? Mated. What does that mean? Should I expect him to woo me by leaving dead birds on my doorstep?"

Briana laughed. "You know the part in traditional wedding vows about till death do you part? Being mated is a lot like that. I'm sorry I blurted it all out at you like that."

"Are you really?"

"Not sorry that you knowing might give Tristan a reason to reconsider. But I'm sorry I sort of shoved it down your throat that way."

"Did you recognize your mate right away?"

Briana didn't say anything.

"Tristan and I met months ago. If we really have some kind of bond, how come he didn't realize it before now?"

"You're not worried about being his mate, are you? You're worried that he made a mistake."

Pushing to her feet, Kennedy paced back toward the

window. "I'm human. You're all immortal. Doesn't that seem like someone screwed up somewhere?"

"I can see how it would be easier to believe that," Briana said gently.

"Nothing about any of this is easy." She rubbed at the spider-web tattoo, shivering for the dozenth time in the last half-hour.

"He's not wrong."

"How do you know?"

"We just do. Even when our mate is someone we never expected, even when we try to pretend it can't be or know we can't be together, we know."

Kennedy couldn't imagine what was worse. Discovering that kind of connection to someone else—an immortal someone—or acknowledging that bond and knowing you couldn't have a future together.

"Tristan?"

The alarm in Briana's voice had Kennedy whipping around.

The sight of Tristan leaning in the doorway, his shirt ripped, blood staining the front of him, pushed her heart into her throat. "You're hurt."

"Just a scratch."

He might have been able to keep the pain from his voice, but the way he favored his right leg as he crossed to the sofa and sat wasn't so convincing.

Carefully, Kennedy eased down next to him. He cupped her nape and drew her closer, rubbing his cheek against hers.

"Who did this to you?"

"See, I *am* growing on you."

"The dragon got away, didn't he?" Briana asked.

Kennedy didn't need to look at Tristan to know the answer. His grip on her tightened, his other arm coming up to pull her against his chest. Relieved he'd returned in one piece, she didn't say a word when he growled something about his mate against her hair.

"What happened?" Briana sat opposite them.

"I shredded one of his wings pretty bad, but the bastard still somehow managed to fly away."

"Over the city? Rhiannon's huntresses won't be happy to hear that."

"Huntresses?" A sharp pain in Kennedy's hand caused the last syllable to stick in her throat.

Tristan frowned, but didn't notice the way she rubbed the tattoo. "They keep the rest of us from betraying our existence to humans. If he's not already on their radar, he will be now."

"And soon wishing he had let you put him out of his misery." Briana shuddered.

"So this guy was the one you thought hired the wraith?"

"Him or another of his clan and he was tasked to deal with Lucan."

Kennedy closed her eyes. "So that's it then."

"No." Briana stood. "We give Lucan the dagger."

"You need it for Cian," Kennedy argued.

"We found it once, we'll find it again." Tristan's sister strode out of the room.

Tristan grabbed Kennedy's hand, leading her along as he followed his sister. "Briana, wait. This isn't your call to make."

Briana scoffed. "Says who? I haven't listened to you since we were kids, and Cale... Cale is not my keeper either. He knows what it's like to lose a mate and would never expect you to sacrifice yours for anyone."

"Cale lost his mate?" Kennedy followed them down a winding staircase off the mirrored room.

Tristan nodded, his attention returning to his sister. "What about Cian?"

"He wouldn't want you to die freeing him." At the bottom of the stairs, Briana opened a door that led into a state of the art room that looked like some highly classified military lab straight out of spy movie.

"It's a glamour," Tristan explained when Kennedy stared in awe around the room. "An illusion courtesy of a Fae who owed Briana a favor."

"Is that why it looks so—" she cocked her head, "—fuzzy?"

Tristan and Briana exchanged puzzled glances before she punched in a code on a keypad.

"Briana," Tristan began.

"It's gone."

"What?"

His sister stepped to the side, revealing an empty safe. "The dagger is gone."

Tristan shook his head. "I put it there myself."

Ignoring the icy itch beneath the spider-web tattoo, Kennedy asked, "Who else besides you two had access?"

"Only Cale," Briana answered.

A sudden stab of pain in her hand made Kennedy cry out. *Son of a bitch.* She clasped her hand to her chest as the burning sting traveled across her wrist.

Tristan gently brought her hand up to eye-level.

Before her eyes, the tattoo began to disintegrate, the black ink melting into her skin. "What's happening?"

"It's a toxin." Fury darkened his words. "It's meant to weaken the target, make the kill easier."

Gritting her teeth against the fire that clawed up her arm, Kennedy shook her head. "Why didn't it happen before? Why now?"

"Because our time is up."

Tristan jerked his head at Briana. "Upstairs."

She glanced past Kennedy's head. "It's too late. Lucan's already here."

Pulling Kennedy behind him, he faced the room's only exit. Seconds ticked off in his head as the sensation of being stalked slithered up his spine.

"Show yourself."

The shadows beyond the door converged, the seething blackness stretching across the floor and into the room.

"The dagger's gone, Lucan. It's not even here to give you." Tristan tightened his grip on Kennedy. Her breathing grew increasingly ragged as she leaned a little harder against him. In another couple of minutes, maybe less, her knees would give out.

The mercenary hovered just inside the door.

Briana edged forward. "Tristan's telling the truth."

Although faceless, the wraith's attention undoubtedly shifted to his sister.

Not wanting Briana caught in the crossfire, he pushed Kennedy closer to her and stepped between them and the wraith. "We need more time, Lucan. Tell your contractor the dagger is gone."

"It's too late, Tristan." Anguish filled Briana's voice. "He's too far gone. You won't get through to him until..."

Until Kennedy was dead. "No." He watched the wraith circle them. The cat clawed and snapped inside him, trying to tear through his skin to get out.

The wraith lunged for Kennedy, and Tristan shifted, his bones reshaping and aligning. His vision sharpened, the instinct to kill the threat to his mate drowning everything else out.

"Tristan!"

He ignored Kennedy's panic, needing to stay focused on tracking his enemy. Briana had her. Or so he thought until Kennedy weaved on her feet, pitching sideways as she went down—and landing in the direct path of the wraith.

No!

Tristan sprang forward, but not before the wraith's claws materialized and slashed down. Kennedy's eyes widened and she recoiled from the strike to her midsection, curling in on herself. Blood pooled on the floor around her, the scent of it shoving him to the edge. He leapt for the wraith, catching hold of the mercenary.

Wounded, Lucan struggled to hold onto his phantom form, his black eyes void of anything but death as he fought Tristan off.

Behind him, Tristan saw Briana haul his mate back, her horrified expression turning grim. Distracted, he didn't move fast enough to avoid a rake of the wraith's claws.

Tristan stumbled, blood dripping down his limbs.

"Tristan, I think we're losing her."

Briana's words didn't penetrate until the wraith suddenly backed off, something the mercenary wouldn't do unless he sensed he'd succeeded in taking out his target.

Needing to be by his mate's side, he turned his back on the wraith, shifting to gather her into his arms. Glassy eyes stared up at him. Blood poured from the deep gashes he was afraid to look at. He knew they were bad, knew from Kennedy's cool, clammy skin, her pale face, the way her chest worked faster and harder to breathe.

"Tristan?" Confusion drew her brows together. Her gaze slid around the room before coming back to his face. "It hurts. Everything hurts."

He glanced helplessly at Briana, then back at Kennedy. "It's going to be okay." The lie snaked across his chest, made breathing impossible. He touched her face, leaving smudges of blood on her cheek.

The cat roared in denial, clawing at the edges of his mind.

Kennedy lightly gripped his wrist, her fingers slipping off him almost the second she touched him. He caught her hand and held it against his chest, willing her to hang on. There was no ambulance on the way for her, no surgery that would repair the fatal damage, no magic that could save her in time, yet he didn't let go.

He rested his forehead against hers, hating himself for what he'd let happen to Cian, for what he'd let happen to his mate. Her eyes slid closed, each of her breaths growing softer, slower. The invisible fist gripping his heart promised to leave him as lost and broken as Kennedy, and he didn't care.

"She's gone," Briana whispered, touching his shoulder.

No. He tightened his hold on Kennedy.

Briana crouched next to him. "Tristan."

An anguished sound ripped up his throat, and he turned, seeking the wraith.

"Take her," he ordered Briana, his lethal tone at odds with the way he carefully handed his dead mate to his sister.

He pushed to his feet, the ripple of his near shift humming under his skin.

"Wait."

Out of nowhere, Dolan stepped between them.

"Get out of my way," he snarled.

The bastard shook his head. "Kennedy bargained for your life."

"The Fae don't interfere with Rhiannon's mercenaries."

Dolan shrugged. "I'm not preventing Lucan from attacking you. I'm preventing you from attacking him, which would naturally force him to defend himself."

"Kennedy is dead. What she bargained for no longer fucking applies." The verbal acknowledgment of his mate's death shattered something inside him, and his claws burst through his skin.

The Fae turned, facing the wraith. "She has died a mortal's death. I believe your engagement has been completed."

Lucan hesitated as the pair exchanged some kind of silent communication, then retreated. The cat snapped and snarled, needing to feel the wraith's throat pinned beneath its jaws.

Dolan bent down next to Kennedy, ignoring the deadly growl from Briana.

Abandoning his thirst for the wraith's spilled blood, he stalked toward the Fae. "Get away from her."

Unfazed, Dolan tipped his head, considering. "Would you sacrifice your bond with Kennedy if it meant she would live?"

Hope flared in his chest even as his throat constricted. The cat snarled at the thought of living without its mate, yet the man didn't hesitate. "Yes."

The Fae searched Tristan's face, nodding slowly. He glanced back at Kennedy, watching.

Every breath Tristan drew hammered between his ears. "What are you doing?"

"Patience, gargoyle."

Still the Fae crouched unmoving over Kennedy. Seconds stretched into minutes and nothing happened. The faint glimmer of hope Tristan allowed himself slowly dimmed, replaced by the certainty that the Fae was fucking with him.

He grabbed Dolan, shoving him back. "What game are you trying to play?"

"Tristan!"

Releasing the Fae, he turned at the sound of Briana's voice, his gaze darting to the shimmery cloud surrounding Kennedy's body.

"What are you doing to her?"

"Nothing," Dolan answered.

The iridescent waves settled over his mate's skin like creamy liquid silk, seeping into her skin, brightening her color.

"If this is some kind of trick..." he warned, afraid to believe his eyes.

Dolan shook his head. "No trick. She's a changeling."

Tristan's heart stopped in his chest. "She's Fae? I thought that tradition was no longer practiced?" Long before Tristan's time Fae children were hidden and raised in the human world to ensure survival of family lines during times of war.

"There are some families who continue with it."

"And the Fae glyph on her back?"

"Sometimes we lose track of the changelings. The brand surfaces when they reach maturity and we use it to find them."

Tristan frowned. "She didn't know."

"The brand binds her magic, keeping her from harming herself or those around her until she learns what she is."

He studied Dolan. "You have a scar don't you? You hide it with glamour."

Amused, Dolan arched a brow. "Admiring my pretty face, gargoyle?"

Tristan scowled. "Kennedy said you had a scar. She saw through the glamour, didn't she?"

"It's inconsistent in changelings, but happens." That was all the explanation Dolan offered.

Impatience warred with lingering disbelief as Tristan crouched over his mate. "Why isn't she waking up?" He smoothed her hair back from her face.

"Clearly you haven't died before. You don't just bounce back from that instantly. She'll wake up when she's ready."

Almost as though she heard them, Kennedy's eyelashes fluttered. He took her hand, forcing himself not to squeeze it too tight. "Come on, Kennedy. Open your eyes."

"Give her a minute," Dolan snapped.

Tristan growled at the Fae, but never took his eyes off his mate. She groaned, struggled to open her eyes.

"Easy," he warned when she moved in his arms, surprised by her strength.

"Oh God," she murmured, cupping his face. Her eyes searched his, and she shook her head. Tears glistened in the soulful brown depths. "You died didn't you?" She locked her arms around him. "God damn you."

"I'm not dead." He eased back, trailing his fingers across her smooth skin, delighting in the feel of her warm and alive and, not surprisingly, mad at him.

Her brows creased. "Then why do you look so shiny and..." She noticed Dolan. "You promised to keep him safe. You—" She cocked her head. "You look like he does." Her attention shot to Briana. "You too. What the hell is going on?"

"It takes some time to adjust. You're in one piece and so is the cat." He held his hand out to her. "Do you remember your part of our bargain?"

She nodded slowly, but Tristan pulled her away from the Fae.

Confusion gave way to a disturbing resignation. "I have to go."

"No." He wouldn't lose her again.

"Didn't you say you would sacrifice your bond, your claim on her, if it meant she would live?"

He glared at Dolan. "You bastard." He lunged for the Fae, catching only empty air.

"I need a minute," Kennedy pleaded, pushing to her feet as the Fae appeared next to her.

"A deal is a deal," Dolan reminded her gently.

"I know, I just..." Her gaze locked on Tristan. "I couldn't let you die for me."

"Don't go," he pleaded.

A forced smile curved her lips, and she held up her hand. The wraith's mark had faded completely. "I'm not your responsibility anymore."

"It was never like that," he argued, feeling her slipping away from him even though he could almost touch her. The cat pushed at his skin, wanting out, wanting to keep her. They belonged together no matter what he had let the Fae trick him into agreeing to. To lose her now... "Stay with me." The words clawed at his heart.

"I'm sorry." A tear tracked down her cheek, but instead of reaching for him, she took Dolan's outstretched hand, and they vanished.

One month later

Kennedy didn't move when she heard the footsteps behind her. She'd run the scenario through her head a thousand times, tried to imagine how she'd feel, what she'd say. None of that factored into the sheer strength of the awareness that caught her hard in the chest.

She ran her hand across the front of the bottles lined up behind the counter. Taking a breath, she dared a glance in the mirror behind the bar, surprised to find only empty chairs and tables reflecting back at her.

Kennedy whirled around, sweeping her gaze across the

empty room.

"Looking for me?"

Her heart kicked against her ribs, and she slowly turned to find Tristan standing a foot away from her. "I forgot how quiet you are."

Rough around the edges didn't come close to describing the untamed vibe he was giving off. Judging by the state of his rumpled clothes, he'd probably slept in them. He hadn't shaved in at least a week, and his eyes were a little bloodshot.

She spied the open bottle of Jack Daniels and the solitary shot glass sitting next to it at the end of the bar.

He circled around her, his gaze assessing. "What are you doing here?"

"I heard you have an opening for a bartender." Although the layer of dust on the counter and closest tables suggested Pendragon's had been closed for a while.

"Did you?" Tristan stepped up directly behind her, his question whispered against her ear.

Her belly tightened, and she closed her eyes, unprepared for the onslaught of need that heated her blood.

"I thought you chose Dolan? Wasn't that part of your bargain?"

She swallowed. "I agreed to give him a week. He failed to mention that time passes more slowly on Avalon. Had I realized..." She turned her head, bit down on a whimper when she grazed his jaw.

"You would have what? Agreed to spend more time with him?"

"I had a lot to learn."

"And exactly what did Dolan teach you?"

She frowned at the bitterness in Tristan's voice. "You're jealous?"

He growled, and she turned to face him. She parted her lips, but the opportunity to speak was lost to the sweet slide of Tristan's mouth. His strong arms clamped around her, his hold as possessive as it was arousing.

Testing him, she resisted his grip, nipping hard at his bottom lip.

Satisfaction flashed in his eyes, and he backed her up, trapping her against the counter. Bottles clinked together and a few glasses left on the lower ledge fell over, smashing at their feet.

Neither of them looked away from each other. He threaded the ends of her hair between his fingers, his teeth grazing her jaw before he slanted his mouth over hers. She moaned this time, sinking hot and fast into the kiss.

He didn't protest when she snagged the front of his shirt and hauled him closer. Close enough she could feel the strength in his chest, the pounding of his heart under her palm, the way his breath hitched when she pushed her tongue between his lips and swept inside.

Tristan groaned, his hold on her tightening. She quickly lost track of everything unresolved between them, so caught up in the kiss rapidly slipping out of control. Each hungry slide of his lips, every silky sweep of his tongue, worked her over and inside out. If craving his touch had nearly crippled her before, now it threatened to destroy her completely.

"Touch me," she pleaded, slipping her hands under his shirt.

"And what would Dolan think about that?"

She smiled against his mouth. "If you're so hung up on him, I could call him for you."

His eyes flashed murderously, and she realized he didn't know.

"Tristan, Dolan is my brother."

He went perfectly still. "Your what?"

Kennedy grinned. "My brother. He says 'hi' by the way."

He growled, and she laughed.

"Yeah, that's what he thought you'd say."

"Why didn't he tell me?" He glanced around the room, as if eager for Dolan to put in an appearance.

She winced. "He's sorry about that, actually, making you think my survival hinged on you giving me up." She grabbed his hand when he looked ready to hunt her brother down. "Really," she added, stretching the truth a bit. Tristan didn't need to know her brother hadn't minded misleading him at all.

Sensing the truth, he scowled. "I'll bet." He cupped her face, sweeping his thumb across her cheek. "No more disappearing like that on me."

She cocked her head. "Is that an order, cat?"

He rolled his eyes. "Your brother is already influencing you, I see."

Crossing her arms, she prompted, "You didn't answer the question."

"I'm not looking for a slave, Kennedy. I don't think of my mate as any less than my equal."

"Am I? Your mate," she clarified when his brows snapped together.

Exasperation darkened his face. "What the hell has Dolan been telling you?"

"Nothing you haven't pointed out on more than one occasion." She glanced at the floor, telling herself she'd known it would all come down to this. The time spent in Avalon, the warnings from Dolan, none of it made the apprehension gnawing at her stomach any easier to deal with.

"You don't trust the Fae," she said simply. She held out her arms. "How can you handle having one for a mate?"

Relief eased his handsome face. "Fae or not, I never would have let you go if I'd thought I had a choice." He brushed his thumb across the healed mark of her claiming she still felt all the way to the bone. "I want to build a life together, if you'll have me."

She knew enough to recognize it was the closest the predator in him could come to *asking* her to stay with him. He might not have given her any warning before claiming her initially, but the worry she glimpsed in his eyes now proved he hadn't assumed he was the only one with a say about their future.

Smiling, she struggled not to throw her arms around him just yet. "And my brother? I'm just learning about what—who—I really am. I need him in my life."

Tristan huffed out a breath. "He told you to say that, didn't he?"

"No." She even managed to keep a straight face.

"Apparently becoming immortal doesn't make you any better of a liar." He gripped her hips, drawing her close. "If I have to put up with him to have you in my life, I'll deal with it."

Grudgingly, she thought, grinning.

He slipped his hand up her shirt, his fingers trailing across her skin. Her eyes slid shut, relief giving way to desire. His hand roamed higher and she tensed in delicious anticipation of him cupping her breast. He didn't.

"What's wrong?"

Puzzled, he lifted her shirt, running his finger along her scar. "You still have it?"

She nodded, watching him intently.

"You don't hide it with glamour." The approval in his voice made her heart squeeze.

She covered her hand with his, no longer just accepting that the scar was a part of her, but grateful for it. "My mother—my human mother loved me enough to die for me. I didn't want to lose the reminder of her strength."

Coaxing her up to meet his mouth, Tristan dragged her into another breath-stealing kiss.

"Where are we going?" she asked when he broke away and turned her toward the bar's exit.

"Home," he answered, then came to a stop. "We'll live wherever you want."

"And if I wanted to continue working here?"

The brightness in his eyes dimmed. "Cale is still AWOL."

She knew he'd disappeared with the dagger, but had expected he would have turned up by now. "You haven't heard from him?"

"Just a quick note that said he had something important to take care of and he'd be back when he could."

Kennedy pushed up on her toes and brushed her lips across his, hating the worry she read on his face. "Then I guess we should make sure this place is still up and running when he gets back, huh?"

A slow smile tugged at the corners of his mouth. "Sounds like a plan."

"Of course, I expect a hefty raise."

"Naturally," he murmured against her lips. "Any other negotiations we need to get out of the way?"

"Just say the magic words and I'm all yours."

"Pretty please," he offered.

"Nope."

"Let's get naked?"

Laughing, she shook her head and locked her arms around his neck. "You're getting warmer."

With an arrogant look, Tristan scooped her into his arms. "How about hocus-pocus?"

Primal Attraction

Chapter One

Here, kitty, kitty.

Sorcha resisted checking the time display on her cell phone. The one and only time she'd taken her finger off her crossbow while tracking a target she had ended up eating dragon scales. Not her best moment. Forget the laughs she'd given every other huntress when her so-called best friend blabbed about the whole disaster.

She scanned the area again, paying close attention to the shadows that stretched across the parking lot below. Cats were damn quiet, the hardest of the gargoyle clans to track when in their animal form. With a two-hour window left to catch her regular girls' night, she wasn't about to waste a second by missing the first flicker of movement.

If Callaghan was on time—and the information she'd been given said he was fairly predictable for a cat—she'd be able to return whatever artifact he had in his possession to Rhiannon before catching up with the girls. The goddess had a serious problem with immortals selling any piece of Avalon, let alone selling it on the human black market.

Since Rhiannon's stance on that had been made painfully clear to all immortals, Callaghan had signed his own death warrant as far as Sorcha was concerned. She didn't know who he was meeting, didn't particularly care. Humans were off limits even to her, unless they were a threat to Avalon.

A fleeting melody hummed on the air, sounding suspiciously like Madonna's "Like a Virgin".

Damn it, Nessa.

Promising herself she'd hit her best friend later, Sorcha turned her phone off. Her friend's addiction to texting—and worse, her insistence that Sorcha needed a new phone so she could text more efficiently—was going to get one of them killed. She should have guessed Nessa had screwed with the settings on her phone when the huntress had used it earlier.

Not that she'd hold it against Nessa for too long since her friend hadn't known she would be tasked with taking out a rogue after they'd met up. Usually immortals were closely scrutinized before the kill order went out. That Rhiannon had skipped that step this time meant Callaghan had gotten in way over his head.

A bank of clouds drifted across the moon, deepening the shadows below. The one lamppost in the small university parking lot had been vandalized at some point, leaving chunks of glass littering the concrete below. Not that she needed help seeing. The cat was the only one in the area whose night vision could rival hers.

Movement beneath the trees lining the far edge of the parking lot caught her attention. The outline of a man edged toward the only car left in the lot. Even without a backpack or briefcase in tow, she wouldn't have mistaken him for a student or professor. His movement was a little too...predatory.

Callaghan. A smile caught the corner of her mouth.

The gargoyle stopped, scanned the area.

Smart kitty, though she'd prefer him a little closer before she took her shot. The arrow would slow him down, give her time to finish the job, but she wanted the shot to count.

He took another few cautious steps, then returned to his smooth strides.

A soft breeze whispered across her face, and she tensed. So did Callaghan. She'd chosen the spot to stay downwind, lowering the odds he'd catch her scent before it was too late. At best he should only sense another immortal was close by. Unless he had reason to suspect a huntress had been dispatched.

She could almost feel the wariness creep over him, had seen more than a few rogue immortals recognize the moment they'd made their last error in judgment. Instead of retreating however, Callaghan cocked his head. He remained motionless for so long she wondered if he was lost in thought.

Take the shot.

Sorcha pulled in a soft breath and held, letting the quiet

steady both her heart and hand. Not yet. She needed to—

Callaghan's head snapped in her direction, his gaze seeking and landing on her as though he knew exactly where she was.

A flash of familiarity grabbed hold of her stomach and wrenched hard. Hard enough to catch her off guard. Her finger squeezed the trigger on her crossbow.

Callaghan jerked, his eyes those of a feral cat, rage imprinted on his human face as he ripped the arrow out of his arm and turned, fleeing toward the cover of trees.

Sorcha didn't move. Her gaze locked on the arrow lying on the pavement like a snapped twig.

She'd missed? She never missed. The poison-tipped dart should have embedded itself in the traitor's heart, slowing him until she could reach him to deliver the killing blow. If she wasn't looking at the arrow he'd torn from his arm—and that sure as hell wouldn't have tickled—she wouldn't have believed it.

How in hell had she missed?

The question buzzed around in her head, slowing her reaction time, and the second she realized it, she flattened her palm on the roof ledge and dropped over the side of the building. Her ankle turned over when she landed off balance on the grass. She'd underestimated the length of the drop.

Another mistake.

Annoyance bubbled beneath the steel-edged determination to finish her task, and she sprinted after him. Once she got close enough to see him, she'd be able to flash closer and use her sword. Even if he'd shifted into his cat form, he couldn't run faster than she could travel.

Sorcha burst through a clearing of trees and skidded to a stop as the clouds hiding the moon drifted past, brightening the small field.

Callaghan stood opposite her, still a man, still unarmed.

Not real bright, was he? Although surprised, she didn't stop to wonder why he hadn't at least armed himself, or stranger still, why he hadn't shifted into his cat form. She lifted her crossbow to fire another arrow.

"Sorcha?" Her name left his lips on a cracked whisper.

Her finger paused on the trigger this time. He knew her? How? Huntresses weren't exactly welcomed by other immortals, and making the effort wasn't worth it considering all huntresses were cleansed every hundred years, wiping out their memories.

Although she retained memories from her human life before becoming a huntress, she understood that each cleanse was the only way Rhiannon could guarantee those she'd gifted with godlike powers would never rise up against her.

Sorcha had never once regretted the price of being saved from her life as a slave. If she hadn't accepted the goddess's deal, she would have died at the mercy of Morgana's soldiers.

Avalon's most powerful sorceress didn't care how savage her armies were if it increased her empire, and having been a victim long enough, Sorcha would have agreed to anything to have been spared the kind of death those men had planned for her.

Countless immortals paid obscene fortunes to be cleansed and start over. For Sorcha, it was all part of the huntress package. Even if Callaghan did know her, she still had a job to do.

So squeeze the trigger already.

She searched his face, knowing she didn't recognize the brilliant blue eyes that bored into hers. Nothing about his dark hair or the shadowed jaw clenched tight struck her as familiar, and yet...

Her gaze landed on the scar on his chin. He would have gotten that before he reached maturity or it would have healed. From fighting as a cub maybe.

He took a step in her direction, and her finger tightened on the trigger.

"I saw..." He cocked his head, confusion and shock drawing his brows together, making him appear almost vulnerable. "I saw you die."

Die? Sorcha shook her head. "I think you've got me confused with someone else." A mortal obviously. Gargoyles had a higher tolerance for humans than most other immortals.

"Let me see it." She'd planned on searching his body for the item he intended to sell, but if he didn't have it on him, it would be more work to track down after he was dead.

"How did you...where have you...you're okay? You're alive?" His voice grew rougher with every word.

An enchantress. If Callaghan was high from banging one of the Lady of Lake's daughters that would certainly explain why he wasn't right in the head. A definite advantage for her.

He took three steps in her direction. She fired another arrow at him. This one caught him in the thigh. He snarled, his claws bursting from his fingertips.

Knowing just how fast gargoyles could shift, she sidestepped to keep her distance. "Easy, tiger."

He blinked, his hand stopping short of ripping out the second arrow, and then grinned at her. Actually *grinned* at her.

Well, that was a first. The poison usually made them a little drunk and whole lot slower. But amuse them? Not so much.

"You called me tiger."

"Don't take it personally. It's just—"

"A figure of speech," he finished. "I know." His smile deepened, a sexy, breath-stealing smile that tugged at her stomach.

Hell, she felt it all the way to her toes and every place in between that hadn't warmed in way too long to think about now. Not when she was supposed to do her job and take him out.

Callaghan shook his head, the fading smile replaced by an expression of such sheer longing she almost backed up. "You're not dead."

"And you're looking to change that, I suppose?"

His frowned. "You know who I am, right?"

She nodded, cutting him off. This was always the part where they tried to bargain their way out of death, even name drop as though she had anyone to fear except Rhiannon if she failed. "Cale Callaghan. Owner of a bar called Pendragon's and traitor to Avalon."

"Traitor?" He sounded just stunned enough she almost believed he didn't have a clue what she was talking about.

"Do you have it on you?"

His face went carefully blank, and the breath she hadn't realized she'd been holding unraveled in her lungs. Gods, had she really expected him to be innocent?

"You do," she guessed, watching a fine layer of sweat glisten on his forehead. The poison had started working. Not lethal but it came with one bitch of a headache.

"You're here for the dagger?" The last syllable slurred a little, but he still hadn't shifted. He had to know his cat form would be more resistant to the poison, and yet he remained a man.

Why?

Callaghan swayed on his feet, his eyes drifting shut, only to snap open a second later. "I don't understand."

"You broke the rules."

"You're not dead," he repeated, his gaze losing focus.

"Nope." What the hell had that enchantress done to him? Again she waited for him to shift, to attack, to defend himself. Something.

"I thought...all this time..." He frowned. "You sure you're not dead?" He stumbled, caught himself.

His visible struggle to concentrate might have been cute at any other time or place. And if she didn't have to kill him.

So get on with it already.

Sorcha lowered her crossbow, reaching for the sword secured inside her jacket. Beheading and fire were the only ways to kill another immortal, and fire was much too unpredictable to rely on.

"Gods, Sorcha. You're here, really here." He moved toward her, his stride suddenly not the least bit hampered by the poison.

Son of a bitch.

She gripped the hilt of her sword, but it somehow snagged on the inside of her jacket—a first—giving Callaghan just enough time to get a hold of her.

With only a heartbeat to brace herself for a crushing blow, she should have flashed herself out of reach. How many times did a girl have to miss her mark in one night before she got her head on straight?

His arms wrapped around her, and she anticipated the sound of her own bones crunching. A sound that never came. The arms sliding around her and tugging her hard against his chest didn't hurt her at all. Strong and solid, they cradled her as though he was afraid she would break into a thousand pieces.

Huntresses didn't break, and they certainly didn't let their targets—

His lips drifted across her forehead, and she went perfectly still. He rubbed his face against her hair, whispering her name over and over.

He really thought he knew her. When his arms tightened around her and his voice turned hoarse with emotion, she almost wanted him to know her. An idiotic thought, but knowing that didn't stop her heart from quickening as he sank his fingers into her hair, tipping her face up to look at him.

She gripped his arms, ready to drive her knee between the gargoyle's legs. And she would have if his didn't buckle at that precise moment. His possessive grip kept her close as he slid awkwardly to the ground.

That smile was back on his lips, slow and hot and doing crazy things to her stomach. Not until she squeezed her fingers did she realize she was the one keeping him on his knees so he wouldn't topple over. Something was seriously wrong with her. Was she really that hard up for sex that she could feel herself getting wound up for a man she'd come here to kill?

"Why are you looking at me like that?" He dragged his thumb across her jaw in a slow, sweeping arc.

"You're confused." And she was going to be a laughingstock for letting a target put his paws all over her, and worse, for liking it.

"No." The absolute certainty in his voice burrowed through her chest. "You're Sorcha, daughter of Alaios and Maurya. Slave-born and granted immortality by the goddess Rhiannon."

So what if he had known her—intimately judging by the way he cupped her cheek. He was still a rogue, a traitor. "You forgot the most important part. Huntress."

His blue eyes narrowed. "No."

"See, you don't really know me." He couldn't have. Maybe they'd hooked up a time or two for some really great sex, but if he had known her well enough to be more than one of her rare one-night stands, then he would have known what she did, who she was.

"I know you," he insisted, tightening the fingers he'd buried in her hair, but not to the point of pain. "And you know me."

"Sure I do, tiger." Better to keep him calm until she could work her sword free.

"But I can't give even you Constantine's dagger."

Her heart stopped. "You have one of the daggers? One of *the* daggers?" And he'd been about to sell it to a human? So he was reckless *and* out of his mind.

The six mystical daggers handcrafted by King Arthur's heir, Constantine, were the most sought after weapons in Avalon. It was believed, when reunited, they would lead to Excalibur. The sword was prophesized to awaken Arthur so that he could finish the war begun centuries ago. The war that suffered a significant setback when he'd died fighting his nephew and half-sister Morgana at the battle of Camlann.

Every immortal in Avalon—hell, even the remaining humans enslaved by Morgana—wanted that sword. Bad enough to kill to possess it.

"I do know you, Sorcha," Callaghan insisted, ignoring her question as his hand fell away from her face. He leaned in, nuzzled her cheek.

Her eyes slid closed. The traitor smelled much too good, too—

His lips teased her ear, his breath hot against her skin, and just when her next breath wedged in her throat, he murmured, "You're my mate."

"Hell no."

No? Cale frowned, his thoughts slipping away from him before pain exploded up his leg.

Fuck!

He hit the ground hard enough to knock his teeth together. Hard enough to jam the arrow deeper into his leg.

Cursing, he forced his eyes open, grateful for the fire burning through the layers of muscle where she'd shot him. The pain was the only thing that made him doubt he was dreaming. He should know. He'd dreamt of Sorcha being alive every night for the first decade after he'd lost her.

But he hadn't, had he? No sorcery or Fae glamour could fabricate the bone-deep certainty he was looking at his mate. The cat sure as hell knew, recognized her as his even when she stared at him like he was a stranger.

She sat opposite him, the sides of her long brown hair tied back to keep it from falling across her face, her eyes—one brown, one green—wary, her lips moving, though he couldn't understand what she said.

He squinted, watching her mouth work soundlessly. Hell no? He tried concentrating again, but the effort only made the vicious throbbing in his head worse. Something about hell and maybe…tiger?

The animal inside him growled at the familiar insult even as Cale's urge to smile cut through the agony in his leg.

"Stop that." Sorcha scowled at him. "Should have dropped you on your damn head," she muttered, crouching over him and patting him down.

"Stop what?" He caught her hand, laced his fingers through hers. The warmth of her touch instantly soothed the cat's need to get closer.

"Stop *that*." She tried jerking free.

He brought her hand to his face, leaned into her palm and closed his eyes. For a moment the last eighty years fell away and the hollow space in his chest was no longer eating everything up. "Gods, I've missed you." The words nearly lodged in his throat. "So much."

Her hand trembled against his cheek, then she wrenched it away from him. "I don't… I'm not whoever you think I am."

The cat snarled at the denial. Why didn't she recognize him? And how had she survived? He'd watched the fight, too far away to help, too far away to reach her before she'd been caught in the middle. One minute she'd been right there and then next she'd been gone, and his world had been ripped out from beneath him.

She shouldn't be here, so alive and warm and…reaching for her sword?

"Where's the dagger, Callaghan?"

He raised himself up on one elbow and even that much exertion left him shaking. What the hell had she done to him? During their short time together she'd joked about killing him for being a pain in the ass, but he'd never believed she was serious.

"Did you already sell it?"

He forced his gaze from her lips to her eyes. "Sell what?"

She sighed. "The dagger." She said it slowly, dragging the syllables out as though he was too thickheaded to follow her. "You have one of Constantine's daggers."

Had he told her that? He tried to remember, but from the moment he'd caught her scent in the parking lot— "You shot me."

Sorcha shrugged. "You're not dead yet."

"What happened to you?" Why didn't she know him and why the hell had she shot him—twice? More importantly, why was she dragging the tip of her sword down the front of his shirt?

"Sorcha?"

A flicker in her eyes, something akin to regret.

Shit. He rolled to the right a heartbeat before she drove her sword into the ground where he'd been. The cat ripped at the edges of his mind, wanting out. It took everything in him to fight the shift. He knew he'd lose her the second he did.

Locking his arm around her legs, he jerked her off her feet, rolling to trap her beneath him. He hadn't counted on her closing her hand around the arrow. Howling, he felt the bones in his hands realigning as his claws burst free again, digging into her soft flesh.

"Don't," he growled. Damn it, he couldn't fight her and the need to shift at the same time.

Surprisingly, she stilled beneath him. He sucked in a deep breath and then another and another. His claws retracted, but he didn't ease up on his grip, guessing the second he did she'd use the sword still clasped in her hand.

Her chest rose and fell sharply, her bored expression at complete odds with the flush of color on her cheeks and the legs she'd wrapped around him. If she was planning to use some kind of wrestling move to dislodge him, she was taking her time.

Cale shifted his weight to ease the pain in his leg, and her thighs tightened around him. Need, sharp and unbelievably sweet, slammed into him. All the heat in his body arrowed straight for his groin.

It didn't take her long to feel the full impact of him being without his mate for nearly a century.

Her eyes widened. "Oh, you did not."

"Get hard? Yeah."

She twisted beneath him.

He groaned, unsure if the pain or his arousal would do him in first. "That's really not helping."

"Get. Off. Me," she hissed.

He cocked his head, hoping he'd heard her wrong. "Get you off?" Because even with an arrow stuck in his leg and his head pounding and increasingly fuzzy, he was certainly up for trying.

Her face lost some of that pretty pink color. "That is *not* what I said."

"But you were thinking it," he countered. Her face might not betray her arousal, but her scent certainly did.

"I should have taken your head when I had the chance." She didn't sound as convinced as her murderous expression would lead him to believe.

"You really want me dead?"

She didn't need to think it over. "It's nothing personal."

"You sure about that?" His gaze dropped to her mouth. Where she was thinking of sticking her sword didn't seem nearly as important as kissing her. Kissing her and finding out how well his memories held up to the real thing.

"What are you doing?"

He couldn't decide if she sounded a little breathless or if that was just his imagination. "Getting personal." He traced the edge of her jaw with his thumb, then moved on to her bottom lip.

Gods, she was beautiful.

Eyes growing heavy, he rubbed his cheek against hers, sliding down to meet her lips but not quite making it. His mouth drifted over hers, a teasing brush of warm, soft lips that lingered long after he tucked his face against her throat.

Cale's last thought before giving in to sleep was that he'd make it up to her, make up the years they'd lost and then some.

Assuming she didn't bury her sword in his back first.

Sorcha didn't move for a long moment. She could barely breathe with over two hundred pounds of unconscious gargoyle pinning her down.

"Hey." She trailed her finger along his jaw then realized she should jam the hilt of her sword into his side instead if she wanted him awake.

And she would have if he didn't look so damn cute snuggled up against her. Traitor or not, the cat was certainly easy on the eyes, easier still when he wasn't looking at her like she meant something to him.

When her neck threatened to cramp from angling her head to study the way the strands of his dark hair fell across his forehead, Sorcha cursed under her breath. She unwrapped her legs from him, trying not to imagine Nessa's freakish cackling if the other huntress were to find her like this.

She purposely nudged the arrow in his leg, not feeling the least bit guilty when he grunted but didn't open his eyes. Although caught off-guard by the situation, she hadn't forgotten why she was here.

And the tightness in her stomach when she pushed against the arrow again was clearly because the beast was squishing her. This time he didn't make a sound.

"Heavy sleeper, huh?"

Her voice didn't rouse him any more than the pain, for which she should probably be grateful. Did she really want him to wake and pick up where he'd left off—with his mouth on hers?

Don't answer that.

She flashed from beneath him to beside him, refusing to think about why she'd waited until now to do it. With a last brief glance to be sure he was still out cold—she wasn't in the mood to be taken by surprise again—she finished checking him for the dagger.

It wasn't on him.

Pushing to her feet, she paced away from him. Maybe she hadn't heard him right. Maybe the dagger he'd mentioned was just another piece from Avalon and not one of Constantine's. Arthur's heir had disappeared after the daggers' creation, triggering the millennia-old search for the mystical weapons.

Arthur's mother, Rhiannon, still mourned her son's fall and was known to strike deals with any immortal who claimed to know the location of the daggers. The goddess already had one in her possession.

But while Rhiannon expected Sorcha to do her job, she would also expect her to do whatever was necessary to get her hands on any of the remaining daggers. As far as the goddess was concerned, the only thing worse than waiting for Arthur to wake was the thought of Morgana getting her hands on Excalibur first.

It was bad enough the sorceress had taken over Camelot since Arthur's defeat. Sorcha shuddered to think of what she'd be capable of once she got her grubby hands on Excalibur. These days most immortals tended to give the sorceress and Camelot a wide berth, Sorcha included.

Under Arthur's rule, Camelot had been considered one of the few neutral territories in Avalon. He and his knights had kept any warring clans under control within Camelot's borders. The same couldn't be said for Morgana since she'd claimed Arthur's throne. There would be no avoiding her if she claimed Excalibur. Morgana hadn't exactly made her ambitions to rule all of Avalon a secret.

Not even Arthur or the gods themselves had exercised that kind of control. Rhiannon's huntresses were the extent of the gods' involvement in immortal affairs, and even they were limited to policing immortals that broke the rules—namely exposing the existence of Avalon to humans.

Unfortunately, Sorcha had witnessed Morgana's brutality enough to know the sorceress would eagerly welcome anyone who would challenge her, if only to enjoy striking them down with Excalibur.

Killing Callaghan without learning whether or not he actually had one of Constantine's daggers would be a bad move. Seeing as how she'd made enough of them tonight, starting with missing his heart with the first arrow and ending with the way she'd wrapped her legs around him, enjoying the feel of him pressing her into the ground...

She craned her neck to check out her back. Why did her grass-stained ass suddenly feel worse than a puritan forced to wear a scarlet A?

"Sorcha," Callaghan breathed, and her heart skidded in her chest.

She closed her eyes and took a step backward before she did something stupid—like sit down beside him until he woke up. And what would happen when he did? Would he go back to insisting she was his mate?

Gods, she didn't even want to think the word, let alone hear him say it.

Keeping her gaze trained on him, she circled him slowly. How long would it take for him to sleep off the poison? Minutes? Hours? She'd never used it on anyone she didn't take out.

Maybe days if she didn't get the damn arrow out of his leg to help the healing along. She'd be better off taking her chances with the cat fully healed and coherent than waste time trying to wake him up like this. She might even get lucky and find him too furious with her for causing him more pain to make puppy-dog eyes at her.

Grinning at the offense he'd probably take to being compared to a canine, she gripped the end of the arrow. Better to push it all the way through than rip it out. Knowing that, she still found herself holding her breath as she forced it deeper and out the other side.

At least the poison had been good for keeping him unconscious, though she doubted he'd thank her for that. Cats could be so damn fussy sometimes. Few people appreciated how valuable a good poison was to a huntress. Sure, they were usually the last immortals added to the guest list, but few others stepped up to take care of the rogues that threatened to expose them all.

Sorcha tossed the arrow aside and checked the wound. It didn't take long for the bleeding to stop. Good. She would've really hated to waste a perfectly good T-shirt on patching the traitor up.

With nothing but time on her hands, she rocked back on her heels, studying him. In another time and place she might have made a play for the gargoyle, happily spending a few hours letting him put those wide shoulders to good use—holding her thighs apart. If he was half as good with his tongue as he had been with his lips earlier, he might have been worth seeing more than once.

"You didn't text me back."

Sorcha straightened and spun around at the sound of Nessa's voice, somehow managing not to draw her sword at being snuck up on. "I've been a little busy."

Nessa glanced past her. "Aren't you supposed to get them naked before you have your way with them?"

"He's a target." Sorcha gave her friend the CliffsNotes version of the last hour, keeping her own unprofessional response to the gargoyle to herself.

"So let me get this straight." Nessa sat next to Callaghan—a little too close—and leaned back on her hands. "You didn't kill him."

"No."

"He tried to kiss you."

Did kiss her, but Sorcha didn't clarify that point. Nessa was already looking at her like she'd lost her mind. Plus, if tongue wasn't involved, it wasn't really a kiss, right?

"And then he passed out?"

"Yeah." And he could wake up any time now so they could get on with it. At this rate the sun would be up and she'd be stuck babysitting a statue all damn day.

Rhiannon had been furious with the gargoyle clans when Arthur had fallen in battle and cursed the shape-shifters to be trapped in stone during the day.

"So you still don't know if he really has the dagger?"

"Nope."

"Is he cute?"

Sorcha stepped between her friend and Callaghan. "Is now really the time to be worried about what he rates?"

"Aw come on, Sorcha. He must be damn close to a ten if you let him kiss you—"

"I did not *let* him."

"But you didn't stop him either, huh?" Nessa gave her a smug look.

She released a frustrated breath. "Could we just focus on the important part for a second?"

"Finding the dagger?" When Sorcha nodded, Nessa stood and reached for her sword.

Whoa. "Whatcha doing?"

"Chopping off his hand." The other huntress motioned toward Callaghan as though the next move was obvious. "They always talk when you cut off a limb or two."

"Nessa," she warned.

"It's not like it won't grow back."

"Forget it." To think if she'd returned that damn text message, she wouldn't have to deal with her friend right now.

"Are you feeling okay?" Nessa scrutinized her as only a best friend could get away with. "You weren't drinking Sybil's homemade wine were you? 'Cause I told her that stuff was potent enough to wipe out a small village."

"No." Her gaze slid to Callaghan and she massaged the back of her neck. "It's just... complicated."

Nessa's eyes narrowed suspiciously. "Complicated how?"

"He thinks—" she blew out a breath, "—he thinks I'm his mate."

She waited for Nessa to laugh. Instead her friend crouched down to get a closer look at Callaghan. A weird look crossed the other huntress's face.

"What?"

When Nessa lifted her head, her lips curved in a pout. "You sure I can't cut off his hand?"

Chapter Two

Cale was dead. Dead or dying. Hard to tell when his head felt like it was hanging on to his shoulders by a thread. He nearly raised his hand to confirm his head was still attached, but stopped at the sound of voices close to him.

It took a minute to hear them over the rushing in his ears.

"You sure I can't cut off his hand?"

The hand still very much attached to his wrist? He wiggled his baby finger to be sure it was.

"How else do you suggest coercing him into handing over the dagger?" the same voice asked.

Of course this was about the dagger. He'd known other immortals would come looking for it. He'd just assumed his family would have had it in their possession longer than a few hours first.

They could damn well take his hand. He wasn't giving up the only thing that could free his brother. Cursed by a fledgling sorceress over a century ago, his brother had been trapped in his gargoyle form and the dagger was the key to breaking the spell.

Footsteps moved away from him as a breeze stirred the grass near his face, bringing with it a familiar scent.

Sorcha.

The cat growled possessively. Out of habit he started to remind himself she was gone, only to have his most recent memories push to the forefront of his mind. That he managed to remain motionless when his mate was only a few feet away was a testament to his restraint—that and the crushing migraine.

He mentally replayed everything he could remember, unable to stop coming back to the part where she'd shot him.

Twice. Somehow he figured it wasn't necessarily a good sign that she hadn't gotten around finishing him off.

Not when there was still talk about cutting off his hand. He didn't know whether to be relieved or not when the conversation turned back to the dagger. Sorcha he could handle, even if she still had a weapon within reach. But the other one? Not a chance. Holding his own against one huntress would be hard enough. He wasn't about to fuck everything up by playing the macho card. That was his brother Tristan's style, not his.

Though he loathed leaving his mate when he'd just learned she wasn't really dead, he hadn't imagined her not recognizing him or her complete ignorance about their past. She didn't remember him, didn't know they were mated. And somehow he doubted her friend was going to send them on a second honeymoon if he tried to explain anything to her. She was still hung up on severing parts of his body.

What the hell kind of people had Sorcha taken up with and what had they done to her?

Just two of a million questions he needed answers to. Answers he wouldn't get playing opossum. Still, he had something Sorcha wanted. Something she would come looking for. But even that certainty didn't come close to easing the cat's clawing instinct to stay with its mate.

"I think your kitty is awake, Sorcha."

Even hearing a sword being unsheathed, he waited. His mate's scent tangled him up inside, proving she was real, that she was as aware of him as he was of her. Painfully, achingly aware.

He needed to go. He knew it and yet he didn't move. How could he leave her again? He needed to stay, hold her until she remembered him, until he knew what happened and how to fix it.

He raised his head and that same unexpected, cut-off-at-the-knees shock slammed into him all over again. His mate was truly alive.

The very same mate who was staring at him like a lethal hunter who'd just bagged the biggest trophy of the season.

Damn it!

Cale shoved himself to his feet, not prepared for the agony that ripped through his head. His stomach twisted hard, threatening to empty its contents of half-stale nachos and peanuts from Pendragon's at his feet, and then he was shifting as the animal inside him broke loose.

His vision transitioned first, sharpening as his bones realigned beneath layers of muscles and fur. The pain in his head retreated to a more tolerable level, but the wound in his leg would slow him down.

He didn't let that stop him from tearing into the trees and leaving Sorcha behind—along with his now-shredded clothes.

"Nice ass," Nessa quipped, cocking her head as though she could still catch a glimpse of Callaghan's human backside instead of the cat's as he vanished into the woods. "Well," her friend began, "you two have fun."

"That's it?" Sorcha didn't know whether to be worried or relieved her friend was taking Callaghan's exit as her cue to leave.

"If you're looking for wisdom, I'm fresh out of fortune cookies, sorry. Sybil fed them all to her dragon." Nessa snorted. "I swear that girl has no taste in men."

"I doubt a fortune cookie is going to lead me to the dagger."

Nessa winked. "Never underestimate the power of Asian prophesy, young grasshopper."

"I'd sooner put my faith in a psychic hotline."

"So." Nessa nodded in the direction the large black cat had disappeared in. "Do you have a plan at all?"

"Not really." If she was smart, she'd just go with Nessa's suggestion. Too bad she wasn't up for getting any more blood on her hands for what was left of the night.

Nessa turned to leave, paused. "Just be careful with this one, okay?"

Sorcha had to dig a little deeper than usual for a smile. "I'll be fine. I know better than to turn my back on a half-crazy cat." Or anything else for that matter.

"It's not your back I'm worried about."

The other huntress vanished before Sorcha could bring herself to ask what prompted the warning.

Just as well. She really didn't need to hear anything that might suggest Callaghan didn't have nearly as many loose screws as she wanted to believe.

Sorcha was waiting for him when he stepped out of the shower less than an hour later. Cale had caught her scent a moment before shutting off the overhead spray. Although he knew the frosted glass distorted her view of him, he felt the hot weight of her gaze as though she stood next to him.

Not until he turned around did the panic take hold. The same paralyzing fear that compressed his heart the day he'd looked across the cavern in Avalon's catacombs and watched her fall under a wraith's sword. A moment later the bastard had kicked her body over the edge, into the fire pits.

She'd been gone long before Cale had sprinted across the cavern floor, long before she'd disappeared into the flames. He'd prowled the edges of the fire pits for weeks after that, part of him waiting for her to come back, the other part—the darkest—thinking about following her over the edge.

But he hadn't. He'd dragged himself out of there and every step had felt like he was abandoning his mate.

Leaving her in the woods earlier hadn't felt so different from those days or the ones that followed. For months afterward he'd think he glimpsed her face in a crowd, or he'd roll over in bed only to find she wasn't curled around him and hogging the blankets.

Watching her through the frosted glass now was like seeing her in his dreams, knowing it was her but unable to see her clearly anymore. And for the few seconds it took his hand to relax enough to push open the door, he dreaded that she would vanish before his eyes.

No matter how certain he'd been that she would track him here, his knees damn near shook with relief that she'd come. For that reason alone he counted to ten before pushing the door open and stepping out.

Sorcha sat on the edge of the vanity, legs crossed, palms down on the granite countertop. She'd changed into a short black skirt and a red T-shirt that read "Want Some?"

Cale wanted a hell of a lot more than some and it only took a few moments for them both to realize it.

Her gaze slid down his body, lingering on his heavy arousal before taking its time coming back to his eyes. Everywhere her attention lingered made him ache to feel her hands trailing down his chest and wrapping around his cock.

He could think of nothing better than stepping between her thighs and making it happen. That and kissing her. His tongue sliding into her mouth and dragging out one of those deep-throated moans that drove him crazy.

Sorcha arched a brow, her pointed gaze slipping past him to the stack of towels folded neatly on the shelf.

He shook his head, too content with thinking about stripping her down and getting her wet—with or without using the shower—to move.

She simply shrugged when he didn't reach for a towel to cover up. He wanted her to look, wanted her to know exactly what being this close to her did to him. Most of all, he wanted to see the rise of color in her cheeks as her own arousal increased.

She crossed her arms, and he'd bet Pendragon's that it was to hide how hard her nipples were. "It's sunrise."

"And?"

"Shouldn't you be a few tons heavier by now?"

"No."

Her brow furrowed. "You're a gargoyle. All you cats, wolves and dragons turn to stone during the day. Part of Rhiannon's punishment for letting the big guy down."

"Rhiannon punished every immortal involved in the fight for Camelot. Not just the gargoyles." The wraith Cale always believed had killed Sorcha had once been a Knight of the Round Table. Not even those most loyal to Arthur had escaped Rhiannon's fury after her son's defeat.

"That still doesn't explain why you're not hanging off the edge of a roof somewhere looking all gothic and toothy."

"Unless severely wounded, mated gargoyles can control the shift to stone."

It took a few seconds for her to catch on. "I am *not* your..." she broke off, scowling.

"Mate?" he provided. "Is that what you're trying *not* to say?" He closed the distance between them, careful not to move too quickly.

She looked more bored than threatened by his proximity but for the faint hitch of her breath when his thigh bumped her knees. Innocent enough, the brush of skin against skin twisted his insides up.

Holding her gaze, he leaned in and breathed deep, letting her scent wrap around him.

"Contrary to what you might have heard, I'm not big into sniffing."

Cale grinned. Whatever had happened since he'd lost her, it hadn't changed her sarcastic nature. Since she didn't push him back or ease away from him, he decided to push a little harder. Whatever it took to help her remember.

He wrapped the ends of her hair around his finger. It wasn't enough to satisfy the cat's need to touch her, and it certainly wasn't enough to satisfy the man's need to piece together how she'd come back to him, but it was something.

She glanced at the strands coiled around his thumb. "Are you trying to groom me?"

"Trying to kiss you actually, just working up the nerve." He waited for her to tell him to back off, and when she remained silent, he nuzzled her hair. "You're not armed, are you?"

"Worried my sword is bigger than yours, tiger?"

He laughed, the sound of it taking him by surprise. How long had it been since he'd had a reason to really laugh? Too long. "Isn't there a saying that size doesn't matter?"

"That's just what human women say to men with fragile egos."

"Do you have a comeback for everything, mate?"

Sorcha tensed, leaned away from him. Her eyes searched his. "Don't look at me like that. I'm not the one you lost. I'm not *her*."

"You're not you?"

"I don't know why you think..." Her voice trailed off as she stared at his chest. Her fingers curled around the pendant he wore. "Where did you get this?"

He glimpsed uncertainty in her eyes for the first time, and some of the pressure on his chest started to ease. "You gave it to me."

She shook her head.

"It was—"

"My brother's," she finished. She turned it over in her hand, tracing the fine lines carved into the back of the stone.

The more she tugged the chain to get a better look, the closer he came to her mouth. It took much too long for her to notice.

She raised her head in small degrees, as though she knew exactly how close his mouth was. Her bottom lip whispered across his, and his eyes slammed shut. He tightened his finger around her hair, grappling for control, and failing. She'd never been intimidated by him before, but he couldn't tamp down the fear he'd chase her off if he pressed her back against the mirror and took her mouth the way he needed to.

Screw it.

Sinking one hand into her hair, he slanted his mouth across hers, skipping slow and soft and jumping right into hard and hungry.

One of them groaned and then something smashed to the floor. He was too busy pushing deeper between her lips to care. Sweet and damp, her tongue slipped across his, and then she was sucking his bottom lip.

Sweet Avalon.

She leaned back, her hold on the pendant dragging him closer. And when she wrapped her legs around him, fitting him snug between her legs, his cock pressed against her sex.

All coherent thought evaporated with a single rock of her hips.

"Again," he growled, flattening his hand on the mirror behind her for leverage.

Sorcha smiled against his mouth. "Been awhile, huh?" She didn't give him time to answer, or even *think* of one. Her hand slid down his chest. One lone finger traced a snaking path to his groin.

"What happened to trying to kill me, huntress?" He intentionally emphasized the last word. As much as he wanted to think she'd come here because of him, because she felt their bond even if she didn't remember him, he knew better. She'd come for the dagger.

He had no problem using that to keep her close. After spending the last eighty years without her, he'd do anything to hold on to her. Anything but give her the dagger. Not until he figured out how to use it to free his brother first, and not until she remembered their past.

"There's more than one way to take a man out at the knees." Sorcha's smile turned wicked as she curled her fingers around his shaft.

His eyes slid closed, his breath hissing out. "Is that your way of telling me I might not survive this?" He swore the soft tug of her palm, which pumped him slowly from base to tip, sucked all the blood in his body right to his cock.

Her fingers teased across the head, playing with him. She'd always known the exact way to work him over, and apparently nothing had changed that.

"Too early to tell."

He cupped her cheek, clenching his jaw at the way she continued to stroke him. Part of her plan, the cool reasoning in his head insisted. Not that he cared when his mate's hand felt so fucking good.

He jerked at her shirt, working it high enough to expose her breasts. So beautiful. He hooked a finger in the front of one lacy black cup and tugged it down. Sorcha released her seductive hold on him the second he flicked his tongue across her nipple.

"Oh," she murmured. Her nails raked his scalp, pulling him closer.

Sealing his lips over her, he sucked greedily. She cried out, the sound as spirited and unrestrained as she was. He tugged her harder between his lips, spanning his fingers across her back to keep her close. After eight decades alone, he didn't know if it was possible to get close enough.

Somehow she got her hand between them again and wrapped her fingers around him. A slow pump of her hand made him groan against her breast, then he nipped at her, making his way back up to her throat.

Something ripped when he yanked her skirt up, but she didn't protest and he didn't stop. Stopping was a bad, bad idea. Stopping would give her time to think, and they'd have time for that later. There would be time for everything later. Now he wanted to please his mate, make her moan his name over and over.

Sweet Avalon. She wasn't wearing anything under the skirt.

Sorcha covered his hand with hers, bringing them between her thighs. Already wet and slippery, she rocked impatiently against him.

Instead of plunging a finger into her sex—and he knew she was more than ready for it—he traced her damp seam. The scent of her filled his head, cranking his own arousal to the breaking point, and she'd barely touched him.

Finding the slick knot between her folds wasn't hard. Neither was watching her lips part and her eyes slide shut as he swirled his thumb over her clit.

She slapped one hand on the countertop, roped her other arm around his neck. "More," she breathed against his cheek.

He kissed her then, taking her mouth as soft and slow as his fingers stroked her sex. Teasing, feather-light strokes.

"That's...not...what I meant," she managed, pushing her tongue into his mouth in between her words.

"No?" Every time he circled her clit her breath caught, and every time he spread her wetness across the plump flesh she clamped her lips together and rocked her hips.

Damn she was hot. And sexy and strong. *His*. And he was hers, even if she couldn't remember that.

"Faster," she pleaded, biting his lip hard enough to draw blood when he didn't immediately obey.

He laughed, trailing down her jaw to her neck, laving the soft flesh before making his way back to her breasts. With the flat of his tongue, he teased her some more. He had spent too long with fuzzy memories to rush this.

Whimpering, Sorcha pressed her legs together, her inner thighs trembling around his hand. He lifted his head, watched her eyes squeeze tighter, her lips part on each hitched breath. He pushed a finger inside her, thrusting slowly.

"Yes," she whispered, and he covered her mouth with his, sweeping hard and deep, willing her to recognize the feel of his hands on her, the taste of his kiss.

The wet walls of her sex clenched around him, and he thumbed her clit. The faster he rubbed, the quicker her tongue dipped into his mouth.

"Wider." He nudged the inside of her thigh until she did as he asked. With more room to play, he added another finger, thrusting harder.

Her nails raked his scalp, and he pulled away. The protest that formed on her lips never made it any further. Not when she watched him drop to his knees. Sliding his hands under her ass, he tugged her right to the edge, bunching her skirt around her waist.

Sorcha's eyes never left his as he opened his mouth over her damp center. A flick of his tongue and she moaned. The hands she'd buried in his hair vanished, and she flattened them on the counter, using it as leverage to lift her hips.

"Still want to kill me, huntress?" he taunted, closing his lips over the plump knot and sucking softly.

Her head dropped back. "Only if you stop."

Not a chance, though he pushed to his feet a few moments later, right before she would have come.

"Hey—"

He cut her off with a kiss, sinking his fingers inside her again. She groaned, wrapped one arm around him. Again he waited until her breath came faster and she started pitching her hips harder to meet each thrust of his fingers.

Just when he felt her caught on the edge, he withdrew, going down to run his tongue up her damp cleft. The sound that left her lips—part whimper, part hiss—was like a scorching brand on his cock.

Cale nipped at the inside of her thigh. "Gods, you make me want inside you."

She trapped her lip between her teeth, and he knew he had her back on the edge. Still he circled her clit, tonguing the sensitive flesh.

"Almost," she breathed. "I need—"

"To remember me," he answered, though he knew that wasn't what she'd been about to say. "To remember us."

Back on his feet, he palmed her breast, plucking at her nipple with one hand, using the other to mold against her sex. "You must feel it." He caught her earlobe between his teeth. "Feel what it is I do to you."

"Cocky, aren't you, tiger?"

He grinned. "Nope. I just know exactly how to make you come."

"So do it already," she dared.

Deliberately slowing his pace, he eased back. "Or maybe I'll just stop."

Challenge glittered in her eyes, but he didn't give her time to voice any threats. Kissing her, stroking into her mouth the way he wanted to drive himself between her thighs, seemed like a smarter move.

Sorcha moaned against his lips, arching her sex against his hand in search of release. Certain she hovered right on the edge, he kissed his way down her body, sucking her nipple into his mouth on the way.

So softly he barely heard her, she murmured, "Please."

Pushing two fingers inside her, he pumped quick and fast, withdrawing just long enough to drag his tongue up her folds and pull her clit between his lips.

She tensed in his arms, her fingers sinking into his hair as she came. As she sagged in his arms, Cale returned to her mouth, lingering over each brush of her lips as though it would be enough to bring her back to him.

Much too soon, she broke away, and he growled. His protest was short-lived when she tucked her face against his throat—and whispered his name.

Like being tossed from a Jacuzzi into a cold spring, every muscle in Sorcha's body went rigid before she tried to brazen her way through the slip.

And it was a slip. Nothing more. So she'd gotten caught up in the moment. The cat was good with his mouth. *Damn* good. That didn't make calling him Cale a big deal. A big deal would be buying into the whole mate thing when any traitor with his ass on the line would lie through his teeth to snag a get-out-of-jail-free card.

She planted her hand against his chest, then made the mistake of looking at him before she tried shoving him away. A fierce mix of desire and longing burned in his eyes.

Her heart thumped faster. Men didn't look at her like that. Not like they'd kill for just one more kiss. Not like she mattered.

She shouldn't have come here. Not alone, anyway. Callaghan might have one less limb by now if she'd brought Nessa along, but at least there wouldn't be a part of her wondering if there wasn't something to what he was saying. Of course, if she'd brought Nessa along, she might have stopped him when he curled his fingers around the back of her neck and angled her face up.

Like before, there was time to put the brakes on. Time to flash her ass out of there as he coaxed her forward to meet his mouth. She couldn't even use the excuse that she let him get so close because she could easily snap the cat's neck if he tried anything. He wouldn't hurt her.

How do you know?

There wasn't time to answer the voice of reason that

sounded further and further away. Sorcha was too busy watching his mouth, dragging in a breath before his lips slid deliciously across hers.

The kiss wasn't at all what she expected. The dangerous predator had curbed his need to dominate, taking her mouth so softly she could barely feel it. Why then did the backs of her knees tremble, and instead of locking her arms around his neck, why did she clench her hands into fists?

It couldn't have anything to do with being afraid that reaching for him would make it that much harder to let him go when the kiss ended.

Shit.

Shoving hard, she pushed him away. He hit the wall with enough force to dislodge the towel rack, sending a patterned hand-towel set to the floor.

"You have flowers on your towels," she pointed out, slipping off the counter and adjusting her skirt when he glanced at the floor.

"So?"

The only men she knew who used flowers anywhere in a bathroom were either gay or living with women who did the decorating. An unfamiliar tug of emotion pulled at her midsection. "Didn't figure you for the type to get in touch with your feminine side."

He gave her a lazy smile, then took a step toward her. "I'm not really interested in talking about my sister's taste in décor right now."

His sister? She remembered from her information on him that he shared the mansion with his siblings. Something on her face must have given her thoughts away because his smile widened.

"Good to know you're still the possessive type."

She arched a brow. "Possessive? Hardly. Though I do find it amusing that a cat, whose race is known for keeping their women barefoot and pregnant, could call anyone else possessive."

"Tell that to the enchantress you tackled for sitting in my lap during a birthing ceremony."

Sorcha couldn't help it. She burst out laughing. A huntress represented death in most immortal's eyes, making a celebration of life the last place she'd be welcome. Let alone to brawl with one of the Lady of the Lake's skanky daughters.

"Don't believe me?"

"Sure I do." She snorted.

He nodded to the S-shaped scar on the inside of her arm. "That's what she did to you when you sliced off a chunk of her hair."

As pissed as an enchantress might get if someone was stupid enough to screw with their cherished locks, Sorcha couldn't decide what sounded crazier. That she'd ever come to blows with another female over any man, or that an enchantress would stop giving come-hither glances to any nearby male long enough to do some actual damage.

"Nice try, tiger. But I got this before I was granted immortality in exchange for eliminating Avalon's traitors."

The traitor remark didn't even earn her a scowl this time. Callaghan crossed his arms. "The mark you got with your immortality is on your lower back, right above your ass."

Okay, so the scar wasn't from Rhiannon, but that didn't mean she hadn't gotten it right before she died and just couldn't remember. Immortals didn't scar unless mystical weapons were involved, and the odds of a make-love-not-war enchantress carrying around something like that were about as high as Sorcha wasting even another moment thinking about her human past.

He took another step closer. "I believe you called her a shameless hussy at the time."

Well that did sound like something she'd say. Not that she was convinced. "If an enchantress did this, it wouldn't have been because I was jealous."

"It was rather arousing actually."

Sorcha eased back a step, keeping a healthy distance between them. "I don't think I'll ever understand why men find two women fighting so appealing. Must have something to do with all that testosterone and a lack of imagination."

"You fighting her wasn't what turned me on."

She strolled past him, doing her best to ignore how *turned on* he was in the present. "Doesn't seem to take much with you in my brief experience."

He ignored the barb and snagged her wrist. The warmth of his grip seared her to the bone.

"What made me so damn hot for you had nothing to do with the enchantress." His gaze dropped to her mouth. "It was the first time you'd shown that you considered me your mate."

"You know, you should probably stop confusing me with your dream girl. Now that your hands aren't between my legs, it's bound to get on my nerves sooner or later." Hopefully sooner.

Callaghan growled, his eyes more cat than man. His fingers tightened possessively. The nutcase—insanely gorgeous nutcase, she corrected—was actually going to kiss her again.

She couldn't make up her mind if that made him desperate or just determined. Either way she needed to stay focused.

In a heartbeat she gripped the knife she kept tucked in her boot, and pressed the tip of the blade to his throat. "Don't."

"Sorcha," he warned.

Forget desperate and determined. He was undoubtedly suicidal. Why else would he ignore the stab of the blade to cover her mouth with his?

She started to lower the knife, the sweep of his tongue across hers much too intoxicating. He slid an arm under her knees, lifting her up.

Something slick trickled across her fingertips. She sighed. "You're bleeding on me."

"You cut me."

"Your fault." Most of what had happened tonight was. "Where are we going?" Her voice came out on a whisper. She couldn't manage more than that when he nipped and sucked at her neck.

"Bed." He rocked up on the balls of his feet, pushing his rock-hard cock against her bottom. "It's not really fair to leave me like this, is it?"

"You'll get over it." Knowing it was give it up or get out, she did what no huntress had ever done when faced with a formidable adversary.

She flashed her ass out of there.

Chapter Three

"Come again?"

Cale smiled, relaxing onto the worn stool at the counter. Only a few immortals frequented this particular tavern in Avalon, and the man—or wolf, depending on his mood—opposite Cale liked it that way.

The minute Cale had used the mirror that served as a portal and crossed through the veil separating Avalon from the human world, he'd felt some of the tension drain from his body.

He hadn't been crazy about leaving a note for Tristan, who still blamed himself for taunting the sorceress who cursed their brother, and felt even worse for taking the dagger without offering an explanation. However, leaving it behind hadn't been an option. In all likelihood, Sorcha would be back to search for it.

The cat growled again, anxious to track her. Cale could barely concentrate with his animal half riding him hard to find her, as it had been doing since she vanished out of his arms hours ago.

Nate waited, albeit impatiently from the way the tavern owner idly spun his glass around, not caring the remaining ale spilled over the sides.

"I want to know how I'd go about tracking down a huntress," Cale repeated.

He knew he didn't have to look for or even find Sorcha. She'd come looking for him when she remembered he still had the dagger, but waiting was impossible for both man and cat.

"A huntress?" Nate lowered his voice, probably so he wouldn't spook the rest of the patrons. "What in sweet Avalon could you possibly want with one of those crazy bitches?"

"Need to settle some unfinished business."

Nate's smile slowly faded. "You're serious." He shook his head. "Are you already on her bad side or just looking to make the list?"

Cale shrugged, but didn't comment further. Chances were his old friend would look at him like he'd lost his mind if he mentioned Sorcha wasn't really dead. He wasn't any closer to having an explanation for it yet himself and doubted Nate would believe it without seeing her with his own eyes.

He barely believed it.

"You know they're pretty notorious for biting a man's head off during sex, right?"

He laughed. "I think you're confusing them with a praying mantis."

"It's all the same when you don't come out whole from the experience." Nate shuddered. "But if you're dead set on finding one, then I think I might know someone who can help."

"I figured you would."

Unless Cale was close enough to catch her scent, trying to track Sorcha to her lair on Avalon would be useless. Only an oracle could help, but few immortals born with the clairvoyant skills he required were easy to find.

Probably something to do with Morgana hunting them down. The sorceress would exhaust any means of being the first to find Excalibur. Arthur's defeat wasn't enough of a victory for her it seemed, even if she'd lost her own son and ally, Mordred, during the last battle.

But unlike the goddess Rhiannon, who sought Excalibur for Arthur, Morgana never made it a secret she sought the weapon as a means of attaining more power. More than just Camelot would be as her mercy if she got her hands on an oracle.

Nate cocked his head, then whistled. "The huntress wants to kill you, huh?"

Cale's eyes narrowed suspiciously. Nate hadn't arrived at that conclusion without a little telepathic help. He stood and leaned over the bar, scanning the floor at Nate's feet. "Where's the pup hiding?"

"Hmmm?" Nate followed the not-so-innocent sound with a long chug that finished off his ale.

Turning, Cale spotted the toes of two scuffed shoes poking out from the end of the counter. He thought about trying to sneak up on her, but the pup had probably glimpsed that he might try it.

A pile of wayward black curls popped up first, followed by a set of eyes that mirrored Nate's. A ragged teddy bear hit the counter next.

"She's pretty for a girl." Arden pulled herself up on the stool a couple down from Cale.

Knowing the precocious seven-year-old meant Sorcha, he grinned. "I know."

Nate gave his niece a meaningful look without indicating the surrounding immortals.

Arden shrugged. "No one here will tell."

"That you can foresee," Nate quietly reminded her.

As far as Cale knew, Arden couldn't see her own future very clearly, both a blessing and a curse, according to Nate. Still, her gifts had forced her to mature much faster than other wolves her age.

Eyes far too wise, Arden pursed her lips thoughtfully. "You should wear some armor."

"Don't ask," Nate suggested, guessing Cale wanted more details. "It's probably just a feeling."

Sometimes Cale wondered which of the pair was the actual oracle. He nudged the pup with his arm. "So you think you can help me find her?"

"Well..."

Cale recognized the calculating expression on Arden's face. She had definitely inherited her uncle's trait for negotiating. "What's it gonna cost me?"

Too late, Nate made a cut gesture across his neck.

"A trip to the zoo. A human one."

Nate sighed.

She grinned at her uncle, then dialed up that pup charm. "And I want to go to the next Ava-fest."

"No," they both said in unison. The annual week-long party at Pendragon's was frequented by too many immortals to expose her, even if she could see trouble coming.

Arden rolled her eyes. "Okay, just the zoo. But can I get some of those mouse hats with the ears? Uncle Nate too?"

"That's Disney World," Cale corrected.

Her eyes brightened. "We can go there too?"

Nate glared at him. "She would have done it for free, you know."

"Yeah, but then I'd miss seeing you play Mouseketeer."

Get the dagger. Get out.

Sorcha repeated the words to herself for the hundredth time since she'd left Callaghan. It was also the last thought on her mind when she finally flashed herself—sword in hand—from her villa in Italy to the traitor's mansion.

And found the place empty.

She turned around in the middle of the room, half anticipating an oversized black cat to prowl through the door. When the seconds eased into long minutes and she remained alone, she tried to loosen some of the tension embedded deep in her muscles. She'd been wound tighter than Nessa's Slinky since their encounter hours ago.

Usually thinking of her friend's endless amusement with a toy that's only claim to fame was that it could travel down stairs on its own, made Sorcha smile. Not this time. Her mind was too hung up on what had transpired between her and Callaghan in the bathroom earlier.

Leaving hadn't been the best choice, but it had been the smartest. She'd enjoyed the cat's touch far too much. Every second spent that close to him meant one less getting the dagger for Rhiannon.

And she'd needed to remind herself of that—without the man's hands on her—almost as much as she'd needed a drink earlier. But unlike most immortals, wine was the only alcohol she could stomach without throwing up. She'd rather chew glass dipped in battery acid than spend even a moment on her knees heaving her guts out.

Although sipping a glass of wine after she'd left Callaghan had given her some much needed space and time to ponder her target's weaknesses, it had also apparently given the traitor time to split. She shouldn't have stayed away so long, and yet she'd known just how close she'd come to giving in to every last naughty urge the cat had awakened inside her.

But no matter how confident she'd been during her little happy hour that Callaghan truly believed she was his mate, she shouldn't have assumed he would stick around. Though he had to know she'd be able to track him with little effort.

Maybe getting hands-on with the cat hadn't been such a bad idea. The better she knew her targets, the easier it was to track them. Given their brief but insanely intense time together, it should be good enough to get her within eyeshot.

After taking some more time to make sure he hadn't stupidly stashed the dagger close by—she wouldn't be that lucky anyway—Sorcha easily called Callaghan's image to mind. His brilliant blue eyes blazed in her memory, and her stomach bunched into warm, tingling knots.

When she didn't immediately get a feel for him, she realized he must have fled to Avalon. Didn't he realize that only made her job easier? Many traitors and rogue immortals wisely chose to hide in the human world, taking advantage of the thousands of cities with dense populations to disappear in.

Avalon didn't offer the same kind of anonymity, although certain magical protections made some places much harder to track through. Thankfully only the most desperate rogues chose to hide in Korrigan territory. The lethal fairies were known to charm and ensnare any immortal that crossed their path.

Sorcha flashed back to her villa, standing directly opposite a floor-to-ceiling mirror. A handful of softly spoken words rolled off her tongue and her reflection shimmered, awash in a silvery rainbow that slowly retreated.

The colors in the meadow on the opposite side of the veil always looked brighter, and she knew the sun would feel warmer, the breeze fresher. Like walking through cobwebs, the veil slipped over and away from her as she emerged on the other side.

The cat's image remained on the forefront of her mind—proof she thankfully had her priorities aligned—and she flashed to...her lair?

Frowning, Sorcha immediately recognized the small dwelling she'd made at the base of a sheer rock wall. So much for her priorities guiding her to Callaghan. She closed her eyes to concentrate and try again.

Footsteps sounded behind her.

Knowing instinctively it wasn't another huntress—and no

one else visited her here—Sorcha whirled around. Her sword moved in a fluid extension of her arm, catching the intruder across the stomach.

He fell back against the wall, gripping the doorway behind him for support.

Her gaze darted from the blood on the hand he pressed to his abdomen to his face. Her lungs shut down, trapping her last breath in her chest.

"Cale?"

No.

The dull clang of Sorcha's sword hitting the ground echoed in her head long after she reached out to catch Cale. And then she was on her knees next to him—again. She couldn't remember the last time she'd so much as blinked when a traitor hit the ground, let alone dove to catch him.

"You idiot," she snapped, her gaze darting from his face to his stomach and back. His eyes were closed. Her gut twisted. "You can't just sneak up on a huntress like that." She couldn't decide which one of them was stupider. So fucking stupid.

She gripped the end of his shirt and the soft material bunched and rippled in her hand. She cursed the wobbling fabric then realized it wasn't the material shaking, but her hands.

Too much wine. Right?

Sorcha didn't give herself a chance to answer. She focused on gently peeling back his shirt. Why hadn't he moved faster? Weren't cats supposed to have excellent reflexes? Why—

His hand slid over hers, his fingers warm and reassuring.

"Cale?"

His eyes fluttered.

"Cale." Sharper this time.

Slowly, his eyes opened, though his gaze took forever to reach her face. She could have run the perimeter of her lair twice in the time it took, and when his eyes finally found hers, her heart skidded to a stop.

There it was again, that soul-deep look, like she was the center of the cat's universe. No wonder women tripped over themselves to find a mate. If this was what it felt like...

He tried to move, grimaced. The pained expression on his face cranked the tension back up her spine.

His hand tightened on hers. "Your sword is definitely bigger." A much too sexy grin curved his lips.

"Are you out of your mind? Stealing and betraying isn't enough, now you have to go *looking* for trouble? Unbelievable." Even more unbelievable was how she kept finding herself at the center of his screw ups.

"Could you—" He tried lifting his head off the floor, winced. "My head is killing me. Could you help..." He trailed off, cursing under his breath.

"I didn't stab you in the head." Though if she had, like maybe a few hours ago, she wouldn't be sitting here feeling *guilty*. Still, she glanced around for a pillow, and seeing none within immediate reach, she moved and carefully rested his head in her lap.

Callaghan stared up at her, his brows drawn into a pained line. "Why *did* you stab me?"

If he was hunting for an apology, he was wasting his breath. "You were trespassing."

"Guess I missed the sign warning me to stay off the property."

"What are you doing here? Shouldn't you be trying to navigate Shanghai's sewer system by now?"

"Is that where immortals hide out these days?"

"Only the ones smart enough to run." She watched the slide of his thumb across the back of her hand. Each feather-light pass seeped a little deeper into her skin.

Already edgy enough, Sorcha flicked his hand off, returning her attention to checking the wound.

"That's four times, by the way."

She didn't meet his gaze. She'd gladly examine a thousand festering wounds rather than lift her head and find those incredible blue eyes of his trying to see into her head. Since he'd come closer than most, she had even more reason to keep her head down.

"Four times that you've called me Cale," he clarified.

He just couldn't leave it alone, could he? "Well if that isn't your name, I guess I came after the wrong guy. Oops."

That she didn't rip the shirt up to see the damage at this point—which he so deserved for just waltzing into her place like he had a right to be here—was a testament to her determination to forget what being this close to him did to her.

She leaned forward, and her breast grazed his cheek. Her eyes snapped shut, but she kept moving, dragging out the decadent friction, inch by slow inch. Her next breath trickled out, as though her lungs knew that working too fast and hard would betray how turned on she was.

The cat grunted softly.

Okay, so maybe he knew exactly how turned on she was. Didn't mean a thing. Certainly not when she got his shirt out of the way and found—chainmail? More specifically a small slice in the thin armor that had protected him far more than she'd realized.

"You're faking?"

He craned his neck to see. "Feels worse than it looks."

She jerked at the armor, exposing the minor flesh wound. "It's just a scratch."

"Well that should make you feel better."

Sneaky son of a bitch. "You tricked me." Stealthy *and* cunning. She might have approved of the cat's methods if she didn't hate how knowing he wasn't seriously injured actually made her feel better.

"You were the one who stabbed me."

Sorcha shoved him off her, satisfied when his head thunked on the floor. "Maybe a second time will actually get the job done." She reached for her sword.

One solid arm caught her around the waist, flipping her on to her back. Fully recovered from his *scratch*, Callaghan hovered above her, one hand flattened on either side of her body.

She couldn't even lie to herself about not liking the way his eyes had gone all cat on her. Knowing she could push him to the edge of losing his cool helped make up for how much she wanted him to kiss her. The worst of it was how little she cared that kissing him complicated her life.

Complicated everything.

Not that she'd made up her mind to actually let him, but the memory of earlier had her gaze sliding down to his mouth. That fluttery feeling was back in her stomach, making her skin hot and her insides ever hotter.

"You never told me what you're doing here."

"It isn't obvious?"

She shook her head, watching as his head lowered. Or was that her arching up? Either way, she snared his shirt, closing the distance.

Except right before his mouth opened over hers, he had to go and fuck it up.

"I'm here to make a deal."

I'm here to make a deal? Fucking brilliant. Why not just remind her with a slide-show presentation that she'd started out wanting to kill him?

Smooth. Real smooth.

Cale watched the faint pink on her cheeks deepen to a red. Not good. If he wasn't familiar with that flash of telling color, followed immediately by a lack thereof, he might not have anticipated the arm she clocked around to deck him.

As it was, she nicked his jaw hard enough he bit his tongue. Better that than the full force behind the punch he barely avoided. He could do without his migraine sliding from tolerable to down right incapacitating.

"What I meant to say," he corrected, "was that I have a compromise."

"I don't negotiate with traitors."

There she went with the traitor crap again. "You keep calling me that. Why?"

"Do all gargoyles have such short memories or just you cats?" She snapped her leg up and around, hooking his upper body.

The move should have shoved him off, but for some reason she didn't carry through. So he used his weight against her leg, pushing down as though he were helping her stretch—and not thinking about how he fit so damn good against her. "I think I'm pretty good at remembering the stuff that counts."

"Like our supposed past? If I had a sword for all the traitors who've tried convincing me not to skewer them for betraying Avalon to the human race, I'd have an armory large enough to take down Morgana by now. Though you have been more creative than most."

"Betray Avalon how?" Denying it out right would only make her more convinced of his guilt.

"Did you really think you could sell one of Constantine's daggers to a human and no one would know?"

Sell the dagger? Is that what she thought he'd been doing when she came after him? Not bloody likely. Though now didn't seem like a good time to mention the lead he'd been following that night in hopes of unlocking the dagger's magic to free his brother.

Instead, he felt compelled to point out the obvious. "If you're so convinced I'm a traitor, why haven't you skewered me yet?"

She gazed pointedly at his already healing wound.

"Scratches don't count." Certainly not when she'd shifted her leg to hug his waist instead. If she wanted her distance, he knew she could have kicked him off. Mate or not, he wasn't stupid enough to believe a huntress couldn't kill him in a heartbeat if she wanted to.

"You're wearing chainmail. Why?"

He went with the first response that didn't involve giving away his connection to an oracle. "What, traitors don't take precautions?"

She smirked. "Only the guilty ones."

"You still haven't answered my question." When she remained silent, he grinned. "You want to know what I think?"

"That you've screwed one enchantress too many and don't know up from down?"

He shook his head, dipping down to nuzzle her cheek. "I think you can't bring yourself to kill me because you know there's something between us. Even if you can't remember what it is, you feel it."

Her lips parted, and he turned his face so their lips almost touched. Almost.

Then Sorcha's eyes narrowed and she vanished. He would have hit the floor if she hadn't reappeared instantly behind him, her sword across his throat and her hand gripping his hair, pulling him to his knees.

"Don't fool yourself into thinking I won't kill you."

"Then do it," he challenged, his voice deepening as the cat didn't take kindly to the threat. He caught her wrist and dragged the tip of her sword to his heart. "Just don't miss this time."

"It's not a good idea to push me, tiger."

She was the one with the sword, and he was pushing her? Not even close. "For a huntress, you're awfully sensitive, aren't you?"

"I've seen scarier immortals than you cry like little girls when they've been in your shoes."

"If you led them on the way you have me, I can see why."

The sword fell back to her side, and she stalked around to face him. "Led. You. On?"

Cale wasn't sure how she managed to sounded both stunned and supremely pissed off at the same time. And he suspected from the way the last syllable rose another octave she'd come close to screeching those three little words.

He cocked his head. "Isn't that your M.O.? Get close, maybe let them into your pants and then stab them in the back?" Okay, *now* he was pushing her.

"I've never let a traitor so much as lick his paws in my presence, let alone put them anywhere on my body."

"Until me."

She scowled at the reminder. "Where is the dagger, Callaghan?"

"Cale," he corrected, trying not to grin. The more she talked, the less she waved the sword in his direction. Both man and cat took that as a promising sign.

"You would die before sacrificing an opportunity to make a few bucks?"

Sobering, he shook his head. "I'd die to keep my family safe."

"You're not making any sense."

"The dagger was used to curse my brother. He's been trapped in his stone state for over a century and the only way to free him is to use the dagger." And possibly the sorceress who'd cursed him, according to a vague tip from Arden before he'd left Nate's.

Wary, Cale climbed to his feet. He might be willing to push Sorcha's buttons, but he also knew she was as much a predator as he was. Even before he'd known she was a huntress, he'd been incredibly drawn to her strength and independence. Still, any quick movements now could be interpreted as a threat.

"So," he continued, "you can make me cry like a little girl

all you want. I can't and won't tell you where to find it."

"Not a smart move—"

"But," he interrupted, "I will give it to you."

She arched a brow. "You won't tell me where it is, but you'll give it to me?" Skepticism dripped from her words.

"Assuming you don't kill me first."

Sorcha let out a frustrated breath. "I think I liked it better when your tongue was down my throat. At least I had no problem understanding that." She used one hand to massage the back of her neck.

She turned her back on him to sink onto a pile of thick cushions. More proof that she trusted him on an unconscious level whether she wanted to admit it or not. He doubted she would have ever left herself blind to an attack from behind by a rogue, even if she was half expecting one.

He gave her a minute then settled beside her, pleased when she didn't tense up. The eyes she'd closed moments ago slid open, and a fist squeezed his heart. He'd fallen for the warrior in her from the start, but he'd fallen hardest for the rare glimpses of a vulnerable woman who could tame both man and beast with a single, soulful glance.

Gods, he loved her. Even if the words would have made it past the sudden tightness in his throat, he wouldn't have dared utter them and risk extinguishing that look in her eyes now. She'd meant everything to him once and losing her had devastated him in ways he could barely fathom with her sitting right next to him.

Alive. Breathing.

He caught a long strand of her hair, twining it carefully around his fingers. It wasn't the lingering touch the cat craved. Wasn't the caress of skin against skin the man hungered for, but anything more might chase her off again.

She lifted her hand, tracing the shape of the pendant he wore. "I never took it off."

"Not until the day you gave it to me." The same day he'd lost her.

"My brother gave it to me."

Cale nodded. "He died trying to keep one of Morgana's slave masters from punishing you for stealing."

She didn't argue how he knew that. At least they were

making progress. Though having to tread carefully was killing him. When he found out who had done this to her, who had taken her memories away, there was going to be hell to pay. On that he and the cat were in perfect, merciless agreement.

"I was only ten." Sorcha let go of the pendant as though doing so would let go of the pain that came with the memory. "He knew I might not have survived the beating. I'd been so stupid to take the bread."

"You were starving and your mother was sick."

She glanced away but not before he saw the old pain flare to life in her eyes. "She never forgave me."

He slipped his palm beneath her chin, angling her face toward him. "She lost her husband and son within weeks of each other. She didn't know how to handle her grief."

Confusion shone in her eyes. "I've never spoken of my family to anyone and yet you know of them."

"You trusted me once. You can again, Sorcha. With your life." *With your heart.*

Indecision blinked across her face before she slowly shook her head. "I don't want to talk about us."

"Then you admit there—"

She straightened and swung one leg over his, sliding into his lap. "All I'm willing to admit is that one minute I want to kill you and the next, kiss you."

He got the impression she was frustrated with the latter more than anything. "I'm partial to the kissing myself." Especially when it involved her in his lap.

She leaned in, touched her forehead to his. Her soft exhale whispered across his cheek, and he ached to bury his fingers in her hair and coax her down to his mouth. He forced himself to be content keeping his hands on her hips and letting her call the shots.

"Partial to the kissing, huh? Surprise, surprise." Her nose bumped his as she lowered her head.

"But first we need…" His words went south, along with all the blood in his body when she caught his ear between her lips. "To come—"

She laughed, nipped him with her teeth. "I'll bet."

"—to some sort of arrangement." He groaned when she shifted to get more comfortable in his lap, grinding softly against his cock. "So I don't end up dead," he finished, tightening his hold and rubbing her up the length of his shaft one more time.

"It's inevitable."

Not in his mind. "After I use the dagger to free my brother, it's yours."

Her mouth hovered above his skin, her breath hot. "Yeah? What's the catch?"

"You stop insisting I'm not your mate for starters—"

"You're n—"

He pressed his finger to her lips. "You do know that stop means *stop*, right?"

She rolled her eyes, but didn't move to push him away or get up. Thank the gods.

"And?" she prompted.

"You let me help you remember me. Us."

Sorcha hesitated. "And how do you plan to accomplish that?"

Good question. Not that she needed to know he was pretty much winging it. He'd come here assuming he'd get a better handle on his plan when he saw her. Of course she'd thrown him off balance by stabbing him. "I'm sure it'll come to me."

Cocking her head, she searched his face. To determine if he was lying? "Why haven't you used the dagger to free him already?"

"We're still working out how to do that. We just need a little more time." As much as he wanted to free Cian, he couldn't move too quickly and risk losing their only chance, not with Sorcha involved.

"There's just one hole in your plan." Her gaze trailed down to his mouth. "What's to stop me from killing you after I get the dagger?"

He caught the waves of hair falling across her cheek and tucked them back. "By then you won't be able to live without me."

She laughed. "And defy Rhiannon's order to kill you? I'm not a huntress with a death wish."

"By then I'll have proved I'm not a traitor to Avalon."

"She'd be more lenient if you hand the dagger over now."

"But then I wouldn't be able to do this." He leaned in just

enough to open his mouth at her neck. “Or this.” Sucking gently, he pulled her soft skin between her lips. “Or this,” he murmured, sliding down to the deep V where her breasts pushed at the neckline of her shirt.

She leaned back, letting him move lower and rocking against him when he bit at the nipple jutting against her bra and shirt. A needy whimper hummed in the back of her throat. He gripped her hips harder, pulling her forward to rock against her sex. Planting his heels, he pushed up, fitting as snug as he could.

This time they both moaned, and he cupped her nape, dragging her back to his mouth. Just as his lips brushed hers and he ached to sink deeper, he paused.

“Do we have a deal?”

“You’d be a fool to trust a huntress.”

“I’ll take my chances.” Slipping his hands under her shirt, he unclasped her bra. “I’ve spent much too long without you. Besides—” he tugged her shirt up, and nudging her bra aside, he dragged his tongue across her nipple— “I think my odds are pretty good.” He slowly sucked the dark, hard tip into his mouth.

Eyes dark with desire, she held his gaze.

He gave her a lazy grin. “What, cat got your tongue?”

“Something like that.” She tipped his chin up, swept her tongue across his bottom lip before sliding inside.

A crackle of awareness snaked across his neck and he angled her to the side the moment he noticed they weren’t alone.

A few feet away a woman with long blonde hair stood with her head cocked thoughtfully. “So this must be that French torture method you were talking about, Sorcha.”

Chapter Four

Wonderful.

Nothing like getting caught with her pants down. Or her top up in this case.

Sorcha tried to climb off his lap only to find his grip on her hips unbreakable. A warning growl rumbled in his throat, his gaze locked on Nessa.

Instead of being annoyed, she felt strangely touched at the protective hold he had on her. She didn't need his protection but couldn't remember the last time anyone since her brother had offered it.

"She's a friend."

He didn't look convinced. "Your friend wanted to cut off my hand."

Nessa flopped back on the lounge opposite them. "Don't ruin the whole cute and protective thing by being a wuss about it now."

Sorcha tried again to get free, resorted to poking his earlier injury when he attempted to keep himself between her and Nessa. He loosened his grip enough that she could work free, but she didn't get any farther than beside him. Stubborn cat.

"Since you haven't been answering your phone, I figured I'd come looking for you. Should have guessed you had tamed the kitty-cat."

Callaghan growled again.

"Easy, tiger." Nessa grinned. "I'm not here to neuter you. I just need to borrow your girl for a minute."

Sorcha blinked. "His girl?" This coming from the woman who routinely said any man who tried staking a claim on a huntress deserved to have his balls handed to him on a platter?

"Mate," he corrected with a bump of his knee.

Nessa arched a brow, a curious smile on her lips when she looked to Sorcha to correct him.

Oh hell. Choosing not to say anything, she grabbed Nessa's hand and lured her toward the door.

Callaghan pushed to his feet. Had she really expected otherwise? Of course any normal male wouldn't have felt compelled to stick by her side when she'd already shot him with a couple arrows and sliced him with a sword.

Clearly he wasn't normal.

She stabbed her finger in his direction. "You stay there."

He crossed his arms, looking unimpressed.

Nessa laughed, glancing over her shoulder at him. "Maybe I'm not the one you should worry about neutering you."

Sorcha glared at her, then gave Cale another warning look. "If you've spent all this time alone, a few more minutes won't kill you."

He started to argue, but she glanced at Nessa, ignoring him. "Hilltop."

"Wait," he said, but she'd already flashed away.

A heartbeat later she joined Nessa at one of their regular meeting places. Her friend stood at the edge of the grass-covered cliff that overlooked the endless miles of dark water surrounding Avalon.

"He's definitely a ten."

She stepped up next to Nessa, studying her closely. "You called him tiger." She wanted to believe it was coincidence, but the flicker of something on her friend's face made the anxious feeling in her gut draw tight.

The same feeling she'd been doing her best to ignore since discovering Cale knew more about her past than she'd expected.

Nessa kept her gaze fixed on the horizon. "What?"

If she doubted her friend knew more than she was letting on, she didn't any longer. "You called him tiger. Why?"

Nessa shrugged. "Why not?" She glanced at Sorcha. "You getting a soft spot for the gargoyle?"

"Rhiannon wants him dead."

"What about you? You're not planning on going against—"

Sorcha didn't let her even finish that thought. "No. He offered to give me the dagger." Not that she planned on waiting him out. The sooner she got this over with, the better, and if that meant going along with him for now, she'd deal.

"In exchange for what, sex?" Nessa grinned.

"To let him help me remember our past."

The smile instantly fell from her friend's face. "I assume you didn't tell him that it would be impossible to get those memories back."

"You believe him?" It was one thing for her to wonder after the brief conversation about her family. But for Nessa to act like there was some truth to it... Sorcha closed her eyes, half anticipating her friend's response.

"I think the real question is what do you believe?"

"I have a job to do." It was the only truth she was willing to admit to. The only one she could face right now.

"So earn his trust and get the dagger." Nessa rocked back on her heels. "Though I still think it would have been easier to just cut something off."

"He wouldn't have given up its location."

"That's what they all say."

"He's different." And that was the biggest problem, and getting bigger by the moment. The only thing going for her right now was the fact that she didn't remember him.

Gods, she was really starting to believe it, wasn't she? At least that she and Cale had known each other well enough to have confided the darkest parts of her past. And then there was her pendant—which she really needed to take back.

Either he'd taken it from her somehow or she'd truly given it to him. The idea of him stealing it just didn't feel right, and she really wished it did. Better that than wondering how close they must have been for her to have entrusted it to him.

She couldn't imagine she would have let anyone claim her as a mate when her loyalty lay with Rhiannon. She owed the goddess everything, and for that reason alone, at the end of the day, she would do what she had to. Turning her back on Rhiannon would mean giving up her immortality, her strength, her skills and no one, mate or otherwise, was worth returning to a weak mortal for.

That concerned look was back on Nessa's face. "You don't

think he's guilty, do you?"

"He's either a very compelling compulsive liar, or someone wanted him out of the way."

"And I suppose you'd like me to find out who that might be while you play house?" When Sorcha nodded, she smiled. "Just so happens I already asked a few questions when I noticed you dragging your heels earlier."

Another first for Nessa. For the both of them really since Sorcha never dragged her heels when it came to eliminating a target.

"You didn't ask Rhiannon?"

Her friend snorted. "And tip her off that you're getting cozy with the cat instead of taking him out? Of course not. But I did hear that a representative of the McKibben clan pled a case with her recently."

What was it with her luck and gargoyles lately? "Why would a dragon clan be concerned with Cale?"

"On a first name basis are we?"

"Part of our deal," she lied to cover the slip.

Nessa gave her a knowing look. "Uh-huh."

Uncomfortable with leaving Cale alone in her place and giving him the opportunity to put his paws on her stuff, she tried to keep them both on topic. "The dragon clans haven't been interested in any other immortal faction in centuries."

Nessa shrugged. "Maybe they've realized they'll be as endangered as the remaining humans in Avalon if they don't take steps to prevent Morgana from moving into their lands."

"Do you know who it was from the McKibben clan that spoke to her?"

"No, but just so happens one was spotted flying above a human city after coming to blows with a cat. And it gets better. The cat who nearly shredded the dragon's wing? He's your mate's brother."

Doing her best to ignore the way Nessa said *mate*, Sorcha frowned. Cale probably didn't know. Seeing as time passed differently in Avalon compared to the human world, she'd guess he had probably crossed over before it happened.

"When was this?"

"Are we talking Avalon time or human time?"

Sorcha rolled her eyes.

Nessa nodded. "It's okay to admit you get confused. I do." Laughter shone in her friend's eyes. "I'd say a couple days in the human world since you're kitty went AWOL."

"How did you find all this out anyway?"

"Wraiths can be pretty chatty when they're wasted."

Sorcha wasn't even going to ask. A wasted wraith was about as common as a sober huntress during one of Sybil's luaus. Unlike being a huntress, a wraith didn't choose to be loyal to Rhiannon. She'd bound the former Knights of the Round Table to her for failing Arthur, hiring the blood-drinking mercenaries out to the highest bidder. Ignoring or prolonging the completion of a contract literally drove a wraith insane.

How Nessa even had managed to stumble across a drunken wraith would take more imagination than she possessed at the moment.

"So why was Cale's brother fighting with a McKibben?"

"Lucan didn't say exactly, but I got the impression it had something to do with him marking the cat's mate."

That would certainly do it. Any one who hired a wraith to target another immortal instead of dealing with it themselves was asking for trouble.

"Who's tracking the dragon?" Unlike the wolves and cats, the dragon clans couldn't get away with shifting anywhere near human populations. People tended to notice when gigantic mythical creatures took to the sky. UFOs could be explained away. Monstrous, scaly beasts with wings, not so much.

Nessa grinned. "As of now? You are."

By the time Sorcha returned to her lair, Cale had vanished.

He had, however, left behind a pile of clothes. For one long, hot-and-bothered moment she imagined him in her bed. Imagined all six-foot plus of him stretched out and tangled up in her sheets.

Waiting for her.

Entertaining that fantasy, however briefly, succeeded in jacking up her body's temperature until she felt the telling flush creep across her skin. The longer she stood there, the more acutely aware she became of how much she wanted him in her bed. The hours she could spend tracing the taut lines of muscle that defined his body.

But he wasn't there. He wasn't anywhere in her lair at all.

Bracing herself for the unexpected, she concentrated and flashed to his location.

She turned at the sound of rushing water, surprised to discover Cale had covered so much ground in such a short amount of time. The cat could run. The waterfall and lagoon were miles from her place.

Perched on a rock, she crouched to make herself as small a target as possible, and scanned the area. The heavy pounding of the waterfall might have made it difficult to hear him, but she could feel him watching her.

She waited for the hair on the back of her neck to prickle or that knife-edge awareness to dart up her spine. Instead, the tension in her abdomen gave way to a stampede of butterflies that might have knocked her on her ass if Cale hadn't prowled out of the trees at that exact moment.

The fluttering sensation was forgotten as Sorcha took in the cat's sleek, black fur, almost glossy in the sun. Two amazingly vivid blue eyes pinned her in place. The gleam of viciously sharp claws peeked out from his massive paws. She'd heard they were strong enough to take off an immortal's head with one powerful smash.

Despite that, she didn't fear him. Most immortals didn't incite any fear in her, but that didn't mean she was reckless. Which was why she instinctively inched her hand toward her closest weapon—the knife tucked in her boot. If everything Cale had said to this point had only been to make her lower her guard, this would be the moment to strike.

Whenever she'd been tasked to handle a gargoyle, she'd done her best to avoid a confrontation when they were in their animal form. It didn't matter that her abilities gave her the edge. Gargoyles were more unpredictable this way.

Nothing on Cale's furry face betrayed what he was thinking. He could be imagining the taste of her bones crunching between those massive jaws for all she knew.

"I don't taste anything like chicken. Just so you know."

He cocked his head, and she pictured Cale smirking at her.

Motionless, she watched the cat stroll closer. The occasional snap of his tail suggested the cat didn't appreciate her lack of trust. Simply by narrowing his eyes he gave the impression he was downright annoyed.

Tough.

He leapt gracefully to the rock next to hers, taking his time closing in on her. She lowered her hand, but made no move to touch him when he jumped onto the same rock. Her gaze again fell to the size of his paws. She was a little envious of the power in them, the inherent strength he'd been born with, unlike her.

"What are we doing here?"

He could have run in any direction, and yet he'd ended up here. Something told her it wasn't coincidence. The lagoon had been one of the reasons she'd chosen to make her home close by after her last cleanse. The remote location was a world away—literally—from the villa in Italy she used as a home base when tracking immortals in the human world.

In answer, Cale leaned in until his face was inches from hers. His eyes were a lot bigger this close. So were his teeth. She'd bet Nessa's Slinky that the deliberate display of teeth was just to screw with her.

"If you even think about licking me, I'll shove you into the lagoon."

A puff of air from the cat's nostrils sounded suspiciously like a snort. She opened her mouth to tell him she meant it, that she'd happily send his furry ass over the edge, only to be knocked on her ass when he nudged her hard with his head. The second she was down, he sprawled across her legs, trapping her.

Gone was the urge to reach for a weapon, replaced by curiosity and a little bit of awe. Not that she'd admit that to the cat. He was arrogant enough without knowing he was just as stunning to her like this.

"You're heavy."

He flicked his tail, then settled his head on his paws, watching her.

"That's probably *your* M.O. right? Stretch out on a girl's legs then pounce when they're too numb to run?"

He responded by butting her hand until she got the message.

She moved to stroke his fur, paused. "You don't have fleas do you?"

The heavy stare he leveled her with managed to effectively communicate his disgust a few times over.

"Just checking." And stalling.

Suddenly the idea of stroking his fur felt far more intimate than if he'd been a man and asking her to run a finger down his chest. Sex and all the trimmings could still be impersonal, even when both people were naked and exposed. This, the unwavering trust she glimpsed in his eyes, was anything but impersonal.

Sensing her hesitancy, he stood and rubbed against her, taking the decision out of her hands.

Warm. Gods, he was warm.

She turned her face as he curled around her, his fur caressing her cheek. Her eyes closed and she leaned into him, forgetting everything. Her assignment. The deal he'd offered. The dagger he still had in his possession.

Even the sound of the waterfall and the neighboring chatter of woodland creatures seemed further away. Keeping her face tucked against him, she ran her hand down his back, returning to his neck each time and stroking toward his tail.

Sorcha lost track of how long she remained that way, lulled by the throaty rumble that reminded her of a purr. Slowly, he sank down next to her as though he knew moving too quickly would disrupt the rhythm of her hand.

Stretched out on his side, he watched her through heavy lids, his tail thumping occasionally on the rock. Sitting there, her skin warming in the sun, lazily trailing her palm across his side, she felt herself relaxing, getting sleepy.

When her eyes slid closed for at least the tenth time in five minutes, she gave serious thought to lying back for a minute, maybe resting her head on—

Oh, he did not. She stared at her hand, the telling moisture on her skin a dead giveaway.

The damn cat had licked her.

She shook her head, and with a sigh planted her foot on the cat's side and pushed.

Claws scraped across rock, but it was too late. Gravity was on Sorcha's side and she couldn't help but flinch as he hit the water with a belly-flopping splash.

Grinning, she peered over the side and into the water. And kept looking. Where the hell did he go? She scanned the surface of the water, watching for the telltale ripple. Nothing.

Not being completely stupid, she took a step back—about two seconds before a hand shot out of the water to slap the rock. If she hadn't moved, he would have caught her around the ankle.

"Nice try." She took another step back, just in case.

Smoothing his hands over his face, Cale pushed his wet hair back. "That was a cheap shot."

She shrugged. "I warned you."

"Come here and say that."

"Not a chance." She'd sooner be hogtied, dipped in honey and left to face a starving grizzly bear than dip so much as a toe in the lagoon with Cale within reach. And naked no less.

Liar, liar, pants on fire.

Okay. So maybe her reluctance to get any closer stemmed more from her own paranoia than it did avoidance of Cale's perfectly sculpted body.

"You forgot how to swim too?"

"I know how to swim." Somewhat. Either way, she wasn't about to admit a weakness to anyone, least of all a target.

"You used to race me from one side of this lagoon to the other."

So he had chosen this place for a reason. "I doubt that." And not only because she could barely manage the doggy paddle.

He pushed off from the rock, heading towards shallower water. He turned, cutting through the water is smooth, sure stokes. Sticking to the rocks, she moved in the same direction, ignoring the slab of rock she occasionally stripped down and sunned herself on. She was too busy watching the water sluice down his solid frame as he planted his feet and turned to face her.

Hip deep, he held out a hand.

Much too preoccupied with thinking about those wet hands sliding under her clothes and peeling them off, it was a wonder she could form a single syllable. "No thanks."

Before her eyes, his gaze turned cold. "It's a good thing he's dead."

Sorcha froze in the process of taking a seat on the grassy shore. "Who?" But she knew. One look at Cale's face and his barely contained rage and she knew exactly who he meant.

"Your father."

Every time she started to think he couldn't say anything else to take her by surprise, he did.

"Yeah," he continued. "I know exactly how he tried to teach you to swim."

Teach her to drown was more like it. What else had her father expected when he pushed his eight-year-old daughter off the docks? Had it not been for her brother diving in when she hadn't surfaced...

Her throat grew tight as it always did when she stirred up memories from her human life. Perhaps if the memory of all the centuries since then weren't wiped out every hundred years, she might have made her peace with the past by now.

Crossing her arms, she studied Cale. "How is that you know so much about me, but you didn't know I was a huntress? Why didn't you know I was alive? What made you think I was dead in the first place?"

"I saw you die."

The emotion behind the words hit her hard and she had to look away. Whatever else Cale had done, he'd loved the woman he lost. You couldn't fake that kind of hurt, not the kind that lay buried in his eyes, pulling at her every damn time she held his gaze for more than a heartbeat.

When she had the courage to glance at him, she found she wasn't the only one who'd looked away. He studied the water that swirled around his waist, slowly raising his head.

One glimpse of the raw need imprinted on his face, and Sorcha felt more than her knees nearly give way. And it wasn't the savage, I-want-to-get-you-naked kind of need. She could have handled that. It was the kind of need that sucked you in and stripped you down, consuming you until you were left irrevocably changed.

The kind of need that made people fall recklessly, hopelessly in love.

How she knew that wasn't nearly as staggering as the certainty she'd felt it before.

Sweet Avalon.

She didn't move as he emerged from the water. Didn't break eye contact—couldn't have if she'd tried—when he crossed the shore to reach her. Her heart pounded as though she was powerless and surrounded by a legion of Morgana's bloodthirsty trolls instead of facing one man. Just one.

Had she felt this way before? Had he made her feel the same anxious mix of scared to death and delicious anticipation?

Yes.

She couldn't deny something about it tugged at her even though she had no memory to prove it. Thank the gods for that. Because when Cale slipped his hand around her nape and drew her up to meet his mouth, she didn't want the past to compete with this moment in time.

Everything about this felt different than earlier. The way his fingers curled around her neck, anchoring there as though it would keep him from losing her again. The way her legs, strong and solid, nearly trembled under the strain of keeping herself upright when she ached to fall into him.

Ached to take away the pain she saw in his eyes, to be the woman he remembered—if only just this once.

"Sorcha," he murmured, his lips teasing across hers.

"I'm here," she breathed. For now she was here, with him. She wanted to see what came next, to feel it, too much to even think about leaving.

"Don't—"

She opened her mouth over his, drowning out the words she couldn't hear right now—*don't leave me.*

If he said it aloud, she'd be tempted to agree to something that would hurt them both later. So she kissed him. Caged his face between her palms and rocked up, stealing his next breath before he stole another piece of her. He already had her past. Any more than that and she might not walk away whole. Might not walk away at all.

He slid his tongue across her bottom lip and swept into her mouth, snatching away all coherent thought. His arm snapped around her back, bringing her flush against him.

She whimpered, sucking at his bottom lip and luring him deeper. So deep she didn't register much of anything for a few minutes. Not why he tugged off her boots or where they were going when he lifted her up.

There was too much sensory information to process, from the electrifying kiss and the possessive grip he had on her, to his seductive, throaty growl when they broke away to draw a breath.

Not until her feet felt wet and her eyes snapped open did she realize he'd carried her into the water.

Something that sounded suspiciously like a squeal escaped her lips as she grappled for a better hold on him.

"You're okay."

Hardly. Okay would be sitting on the grass in the sun, not surrounded by enough flowing water to eradicate drought in the barren region. And certainly not with him looking at her like she was the very last bite of dessert when he hadn't eaten in weeks.

"I've got you."

She narrowed her eyes. "I'd feel better if you said that with a straight face." But even though her heart kicked against her ribs and she couldn't bring herself to look at the water for more than a second at a time, she knew he wouldn't let her go. If not for that unwavering certainty, she would have been across the lagoon and safe on shore already.

His grin widened, and she felt a little of her panic ease.

"I thought you said you could swim?"

It took a minute to register the playful taunt with his fingers lazily rubbing the side of her breast. Her nipples—already hard from the cool water—started to ache, eager for his hand to slide higher.

"That doesn't mean I want to." Or that her limbs wouldn't freeze up the moment she tried. She might not be able to die from drowning now, but that didn't mean it wouldn't seriously suck to find herself struggling at the bottom of the lagoon.

"This is where you conquered your fear."

Oddly enough that was one memory she wouldn't mind recalling right about now. "How did you do it?"

He shook his head. "Not me. You."

The deeper he waded, the more aware she became of the water inching higher. It already covered her ankles.

"I still have my clothes on."

"We can fix that," he said. But what she heard in his voice was, "*I'll* fix that." Somehow she guessed his plan didn't involve turning his naked ass around and heading back to shore.

"If you're trying to scare me—" Her voice cracked a little as the water rode up over her calves. This was insane.

He stopped and the mist from the waterfall cloaked them in

a fog shot through with slivers of color as the sun cut though the water vapor.

"Scare you? I doubt that's even possible."

Clearly, he hadn't been paying attention a minute ago when the thought of kissing him—or worse, not kissing him—had seemed pretty damn terrifying.

"You can hang on a little tighter if you want. I won't mind."

She snorted. "I'll bet."

They plunged deeper, another foot at least and she locked her arms around his neck. She also squeezed her eyes tight, which might have shamed her a little if she hadn't forced them open again to find his mouth so enticingly close.

She felt his attention drop to her lips, and her stomach back-flipped. It didn't take much to close the remaining centimeters and get another taste of him.

Incredible. Slow, sweet and all kinds of trouble, it was just...incredible. Was it any wonder she struggled to concentrate on what needed to be done when he caressed her mouth like he couldn't get enough? And when he caught the tip of her tongue and sucked it like that...

Was it possible to orgasm from just a kiss? The needy clenching deep in her core was damn near banking on it.

Something brushed her back and she realized they were behind the waterfall. The air was cooler, the shallow cavern behind them buffering some of the sound from the tons of water pouring into the lagoon.

"A cave?" She'd been to the lagoon countless times and hadn't imagined anything more than rocks lay beyond the falls.

"Grotto," he corrected.

The water grew shallower again, his footing surprisingly steady as he moved from the lagoon and into the mouth of the cavern. The thought of him losing his balance and them both falling back into the lagoon made her hold on even tighter.

"Breathing would be good," Cale choked out.

"Okay then." She let her arms fall back, far enough from the water now she could relax.

Cale growled until she clung to him again, and she laughed. Gods, it felt good. She laughed with Nessa and the other huntresses all the time, but this felt different. Deeper, like it touched places inside her nothing or no else ever had.

The intensity in his eyes slowed her laughter until their gazes locked. Heart thumping, she tentatively ran the back of her fingers across his shadowed jaw, seduced by the roughness. Seduced by everything about him.

She moved on to his mouth, and he kissed the tips of her fingers. Lighter than a breeze, the touch might have been more innocent than carnal if not for the hungry expression on his face.

For the first time she knew what it was like to be targeted by a true predator—one that wanted to devour every inch of her.

Cale's attention dropped to her mouth, and he leaned forward. At the last second, just when she felt her lips part in needy anticipation of his, his mouth brushed her ear. "This was our place."

Sensing it was important to him to pay attention to their surroundings when all she wanted to do was drag him down for a kiss, she glanced around the cavern.

A sound of surprise left her lips. "Wow."

Black sand blanketed the cavern floor, glittering like a diamond-filled night sky, shimmering brighter near the edge of the cave where a solitary burst of sunlight struck the sand. A handful of pools, fed by a run off from the waterfall above, rippled with a light current. At the edge of the cavern small streams ran over the sand in twisting paths that emptied back into the lagoon behind them.

"Just...wow," she managed again, wishing she'd taken the time to explore the area more thoroughly.

He passed the first pool and slowly waded into the largest one. "They're not too deep."

"Shouldn't you be telling me they are so I won't let go?" The water brushed her ankles, cool enough to notice, but not enough to make her shiver. That might have been impossible anyway with the heat from Cale's bare chest keeping her warm.

"Is the water really the reason you're holding on?"

Chapter Five

"Why else would I be?" Teasing him, she slid to her feet, surprised he didn't try to stop her. It only took a moment of standing in the thigh-deep water to figure out why he hadn't.

A slow, sexy smile curved his lips, and then he ran a claw down the middle of her shirt, tearing the fabric neatly in two. She barely had time to suck in a breath, the cooler air caressing her skin, before he pushed the shredded material over her shoulders.

"I liked that shirt."

Unapologetic, he made quick work of her bra. "I think you'll like this even more." Holding her gaze, he bent and swirled his tongue across her nipple.

She dropped her head back. It was too easy to sink her fingers into his hair as the hot walls of his mouth closed around her. Damn, he was good with his mouth. Every feverish tug pulled at the nerve endings coiling in her sex.

Wanting him closer, wanting every inch of him pressing against her, she wasn't above using her grip on his hair to get him there. Too bad he seemed intent on flicking the tip of each breast, making her squirm helplessly in her effort to seek some relief. And when he cupped her breasts, running his thumb across the nipple he hadn't pulled into the slick heat of his mouth, her need for him multiplied.

He took his time letting her slide free only to nip and suck her greedily back in over and over. By the time he finally released her, her body burned a thousand degrees hotter. She whimpered both in protest and then in relief when he dragged her flush against him and his cock nudged her.

Cale palmed her ass, moving higher to skim his fingers

along the back edge of her pants, dipping inside to sweep across her skin. Practically a tease. She grabbed his hand and brought it to the button on her pants.

The sound of his deep-throated laugh licked up her spine. "Let's not shred these too, huh?"

Taking her hands, he pinned them behind her back, holding them there with only one of his. "Are you trying to rush me, huntress?" He plucked at her nipple, brushing the pad of his thumb back and forth.

The longer he teased her nipple, bending every few seconds to lave the hard tip with his tongue, the sweeter the ache deep between her thighs.

"Just pointing out—" her breath caught as he sealed his lips around her and sucked "—you should have saved us time and taken these off earlier."

"Before you got wet you mean?" He got her pants open and slid his hand inside. "Or have you been wet since coming hard on the counter in my bathroom?" His fierce eyes dared her to deny the effect he had on her.

Sorcha tugged at his hold, testing him. He didn't give an inch, his grin widening at her half-hearted attempt. Of course he would be cocky about having her at his mercy, but that didn't mean she needed to like it. Didn't mean she needed to crave his touch so damn much or eagerly part her legs, making it easier for him to palm her sex.

She bit her lip, rolling her hips into him, willing him to stop torturing her by only sliding up and down her cleft. He softly circled her clit, sweeping across it in so soft a caress she clenched her jaw.

All at once, he eased back and herded her toward the shallow end of the pool. His foot tripped hers and she fell backward, bringing him down with her. She didn't care the fall sent cool water splashing over both of them, she was too busy sliding her hands up his back, getting him closer.

Raised up on his elbows, he stared down at her. Thinking to wipe the satisfied look off his face, she slid her hand between them and curled her fingers around his cock. She'd barely adjusted her grip, pumping softly, when he growled in pleasure.

She grinned. "I guess the cold water isn't having any effect on you."

"I could be lost in Morgana's shadow realm and I'd still be

hard for you."

"That so?" She pulled him from base to tip, felt him dig his feet into the sand to push against her hand.

"Never doubt what you do to me." He closed his fist around her hand, encouraging her to go faster.

His breath grew short, choppy, his hand falling away as she pumped him faster. "Don't stop," he pleaded, his voice rough and just a little bit savage.

His hips rocked with each slow shuttle of her hand, as though he couldn't help but grind a little harder against her.

"Fuck," he groaned, shaking his head. His fingers brushed hers under the water.

"You're not worried I'm going to leave you hanging again?"

Eyes dark with lust, he palmed her breast, his thumb alternately rasping across her nipple and tugging it to a harder, hungrier point. "I think you said I'd be foolish to trust a huntress."

"Others have made that mistake."

He clenched his jaw. "What others?"

"Down, boy." Ignoring the jealousy in his tone, she pumped his shaft until she knew he hovered right on the edge, then slowed down again. "I wasn't talking about sex." Her own voice turned breathless, her body twining tighter and tighter just by watching him get closer to climax.

His forehead touched hers. "We've been here before. Right here," he murmured, his jaw tight, his muscles straining.

"Did I have my hand wrapped around you then?" She deliberately slowed the rhythm. "Did I make you come?"

He answered her by tipping her face back and slanting his mouth across hers.

Power. Pure, raw sensual power buzzed through her system more potent than any victory against an adversary. Every ragged catch of his breath, every trembling slide of his fingers across her skin, heightened her own pleasure until she thought she might orgasm just watching him.

He broke from her mouth, sliding down her throat and almost sliding free of her grip in the process.

"Oh no," she chastised, tightening her hold enough to make him moan. She worked her fist faster.

He dug his fingers into the sand. "I didn't plan—" The rest

of his words were lost to a hoarse shout muffled against her neck, the tension slowly draining from his body.

Sorcha took her time letting go and he took his time lifting his head. Maybe she'd underestimated her skill because instead of seeing satisfaction in his eyes when he met her gaze, all she saw was blatant hunger.

Confused, she shook her head. "I thought you..."

"Came? Oh, I did, but it won't be nearly enough until I get inside, until you're right there with me."

Here? She didn't need to voice the question to know that's exactly what he meant.

Part of her didn't want to move except to lift her hips and let him get her pants all the way off. The other part was frozen at the thought of him comparing her to the woman he loved. Whatever had happened in the past, Sorcha wasn't her. Not the way he remembered her.

He dipped his head, his tongue tracing a hot path down her throat.

"Wait."

Never having flashed anyone besides herself and another huntress to a different location, she struggled to concentrate. It didn't help that she felt his arousal fitting tight against her already.

Focus.

A cool hard surface replaced the wet sand and she knew Cale had her pinned to the floor now. A smooth, polished floor so white it gleamed like a fresh snowfall in the afternoon sun.

She didn't have a floor like that in her lair.

Cale cursed, and her gaze slid to the half a dozen huntresses staring curiously at them, smirking.

Oh fuck. She'd flashed them directly into Rhiannon's throne room.

He wouldn't get out alive. If one huntress didn't have a problem with suggesting a little dismemberment to get the dagger, he couldn't imagine there would be anything left of him if a whole gang of them got in on the action.

"Sorcha," he prompted.

His mate's eyes widened, shock making her pretty mouth fall open. He took that as a sign she hadn't purposely hand-delivered him.

"I don't think I'm really dressed to meet a goddess, do you?" And there wasn't a doubt they were smack dab in the middle of a huntress meeting hall in Avalon, or worse—Rhiannon's throne room.

"Shit," she muttered, and then he felt the same charge of static race across his skin.

The hall disappeared behind them, replaced between one moment and the next with Sorcha's lair.

He exhaled slowly, his muscles relaxing even as he felt Sorcha's lock up.

Damage control. It didn't take a rocket scientist to see how wrong this could go in less time than it took for her to reach for a weapon. And she was certainly tense enough for it. That's all it would take to wipe out the progress they'd made.

He could have anticipated a dozen factors that held the potential to drive a wall back up between them. A group of cannibalistic females hadn't made the list.

Cale touched his forehead to hers. "Hey."

She turned her head, avoiding him.

He did the only thing he could do to get her attention. He bit her shoulder. Hard enough to pull her thoughts away from their impromptu detour, but not enough to break the skin.

Her gaze snapped to his. There. He wanted her eyes on him as he cupped her jaw and slanted his mouth across hers. Slow wouldn't get the job done, so he didn't hold back. Didn't give her the time to think about stopping him. He'd rather go back to huntress headquarters than put a halt to what they'd started in their grotto.

The second he pushed his tongue into her lush mouth and took the kiss deeper, he felt her indecision. Her spine went rigid, but her mouth softened beneath his. He palmed her breast, teasing her nipple.

"Later," he breathed against her lips. "Worry about it later. Right now I need you. And you need me."

He'd needed her long before this, but he couldn't guarantee he wouldn't go out of his mind if he couldn't lose himself inside her. He hadn't wanted it to be here, among the memories of her life as a huntress.

The only hope he had of reclaiming his mate lay in

triggering her memories. The lagoon had meant something to them, but he wasn't about to suggest she take them back. Not after their last side trip.

Lacing their fingers, he pushed her hands against the floor, exposing her breasts like a decadent meal he planned on devouring. Slowly. He caught her nipple between his lips and sucked.

Sorcha moaned and satisfaction curled through him, stroking the cat's need to dominate. He fought the need to turn her over on her belly and thrust into her from behind. Not yet. She wasn't ready. She might be wet for him, the scent of her arousal filling his head, but he needed her as desperate for him as he was for her.

Gods, she tasted good. So sweet and familiar and real. He let her slide free of his mouth, searching out the other dark nub. She moaned louder this time. Longer.

He released one wrist to get his hand inside her pants. Her panties—if that's what you could call such a thin strip of fabric—were all that stood between him and her hot flesh. He rubbed softly, and she responded by grinding against his hand.

Circling slowly, he slid a finger under the edge. Her nails bit into his skin where he still held one hand trapped against the floor. And then she was letting him slide up through her slick folds.

"Cale," she hissed when he drew the pad of his finger around her clit. The sensitive nub plumped up as he grazed it with every pass. "Please," she begged. "Please."

He pushed past her snug opening and slid deep. Sorcha shuddered, arched her back. Slower, he withdrew, spreading her wetness across her clit until she writhed beneath him.

Much too soon he was ready to explode, and she didn't even have her hand wrapped around his cock. He closed his mouth over hers, filling her mouth the way his fingers filled her sex. A lazy pump. A harder one. A deeper one.

She bucked her hips, her breath coming faster.

Keeping his mouth on hers and his hand between her legs—sweet Avalon, she was hot—he somehow coaxed her to her feet. They only made it a few feet, the two of them slamming up against the wall. He loved the way her nipples rubbed against his chest, and that sound she made when he bent to trap one between his lips.

Getting her pants down should have been easy if he wasn't constantly distracted by the soft bounce of her breasts and the slick heat between her legs. They staggered another few feet and he managed to strip her pants off.

By the time they reached her bed, he was hot all over. The need ravaging him, making his cock ache, had him pushing her back on the mattress and nudging her legs further apart.

Satisfied she wasn't thinking about anything but him, he took a minute to look at her. Thighs parted, chest rising and falling, her hair fanned out across the pillow like a gift from the gods. When his attention fell to the center of her, all soft, dark curls and glistening folds, he palmed his shaft, desperate to ease the ache for a second.

Sorcha watched him, the flush on her cheeks and breasts deepening. The sound of his name on her lips was like a siren's call, and he stepped closer. But instead of covering her body with his and sinking into her, he bent and pressed his face between her legs.

She cried out in pleasure, rocking her hips beneath him, letting his tongue slide deeper along her cleft. When he reached her clit and took a long, sucking taste of her, she yelled and fisted her hands in his hair, riding out her climax.

"Oh my." Barely breathing, Sorcha melted against the bed. Not even in her most vivid fantasies had she imagined a mouth capable of making her climax that fast. And he wasn't done yet.

Cale hovered over her, his cock bumping against the inside of her leg and setting off a scorching chain reaction. She spread her legs wider, lifting her ass to coax the full length of him to slide up her sex. They both moaned at the exquisite friction, and he lowered his head, stealing a kiss that rocked her inside and out.

Without breaking away from her mouth, he caught her hip, pulling it high enough so that he could fit his cock snugly against her. A heartbeat, then another, and another as he watched her, then seeming to know the second she couldn't take the wait a moment longer, he thrust inside her.

Clutching at her sheets, she arched up only to be pushed back each time by the sheer addictive weight of him pressing her into the bed. Every hard thrust kept her pinned, his hips pumping hard and fast, driving him into her over and over.

Forget breathing—there wasn't time anyway, not with the savage pace Cale set. Eyes dark and hungry, he rammed deep, one hand gripping her nape while the other dug at the sheets for leverage.

Drugged by the taste of his mouth, his possessive grip, the way their bodies fit perfectly together, she clutched him tighter, keeping him close. It all felt too damn incredible and much too right to sacrifice even an inch. Cale only succeeded in getting any space between them when he hooked her legs over his arms, sinking impossibly deep.

Crying out, she raked at his shoulders before letting her arms fall back, shielding her face. "More," she begged, not caring that she didn't beg anyone for anything. Ever. She needed him to give her more, to give her everything, and she would scream if she had to.

Wicked blue eyes bored into hers with a ruthless intensity that matched each thrust. Totally without mercy. Not for her body that welcomed the savage release building inside her, and not for her heart.

She closed her eyes, consumed by the staggering orgasm that made her forget she didn't know him. Because right then, with him locked deep inside her, he was a part of her.

Always.

As though he sensed her acceptance of their bond—however temporarily—he lost control, pushing them both up and over and into the sweetest oblivion she'd ever known. Even after he collapsed, his face tucked against her throat, his breath harsh and uneven, she didn't let go.

Didn't ever want to let him go.

It took hours. Hours of being curled up against him before Sorcha couldn't pretend that she hadn't made a mistake. And it wasn't sleeping with a target, though that wouldn't win her any points with Rhiannon.

No, she screwed up the second she'd started believing she and Cale had a history together, and risking everything important to her to spend a few hours indulging in a past she couldn't even remember.

She couldn't get back the time and memories she had willingly sacrificed to get as far away from her mortal existence as possible, and she didn't want them. Neither did she want to get any closer to Cale.

Already, she'd let their brief time together compromise her, and if he couldn't prove his innocence and hand over the dagger, he would be taken out. If she couldn't do it, another huntress would. His best bet was to give it up, the sooner the better. If he could be persuaded to do it today, Rhiannon might not believe Sorcha's judgment had been compromised.

Easing out from beneath the arm and leg he used to keep her close, she made it out of bed without disturbing him. His face was planted in the pillow, the sheet tangled around his waist, except for one corner that fell down his hip.

Without a doubt, tugging the sheet down would wake him. Tempted to do just that, if only so he would drag her back to bed and make her forget everything but him, she grabbed some clothes and slipped away.

By the time she pulled on pants and a shirt and retrieved the boots he'd left at the lagoon, she was much too keyed up for having slept as deeply as she had in his arms. Sex would certainly burn off some of her excess energy.

She discarded the possibility the moment it crossed her mind. Considering how much she'd enjoyed the last few hours, it was a bad idea. If she'd doubted their past before, the time he'd spent working her body over, driving her to such intense pleasure...

She took a breath and headed outside before she crawled back into bed and up his body. The longer she thought about straddling him and sinking down, taking him inside her, the harder it was to walk away.

Bottom line—there was no way he could have known how to give her that much pleasure right out of the gate. He should have fumbled around a bit, taking a little time to learn what made her rake at the blankets or scream his name to the point her voice grew hoarse.

But he hadn't. He'd known from the start what slow strokes would push her right to the edge, and how to drag out the pleasure until she was drowning in it, begging for him. Her mind might not know him, but her body did. And as easily as he could make her pant and writhe, she'd instinctively known what made him lose control.

She'd loved that best, watching him get closer and closer to giving in to the wildest, most primitive parts of him. He didn't hold back, wasn't afraid of getting rough with her. Men, even immortals, were intimidated by her more often than not. But not Cale.

Did that explain why she had never told him she'd been a huntress? Had she been afraid that if he knew the truth, he would have been more wary of her?

Not that it mattered. It obviously hadn't ended well between them for reasons she couldn't afford to think about. They had a past, but they didn't have a future. Regardless of their connection or their undeniable physical chemistry, she couldn't be anyone's mate.

"The gargoyle still lives."

Sorcha turned, the sword she'd grabbed on her way outside disappearing from her hand, along with the knife in her boot. Rhiannon never allowed anyone to be armed in her presence, routinely vanishing any weapons. Seeing as the goddess's closest ally, her own husband, had once nearly killed her, Sorcha couldn't blame Rhiannon for not trusting anyone.

Rhiannon's long red hair was pulled back in its usual braid and the gold arm band she wore that carried Camelot's crest gleamed in the early morning sunlight. When she moved, the scabbard of her own sword clinked softly against the delicate rope of braided chains draped around her waist.

"You wouldn't be the first you know." Rhiannon inclined her head in the direction of Sorcha's lair. "Other huntresses have fallen into bed with their targets." She strolled a few paces away, then turned, her expression sliding from understanding to resigned. "But they didn't forget what they had to do. Have you?"

"No." She had to force the word out.

"I hear you're tracking a dragon now. Should I take that to mean you do not plan on completing your first assignment?"

"I have reason to believe Cale was set up because he has an object of interest in his possession that the McKibben clan is after."

Telling the goddess what that object was right at this moment would be nothing short of a death sentence for Cale. Nessa might have been content with one of his hands. Rhiannon would tear him apart if she thought it would get her that much closer to Excalibur and awakening her son.

"And why would they involve us in their dispute with the cat if he didn't pose a risk to all of us?"

"I haven't figured that out yet."

"Your job is not to investigate. It's to carry out my orders."

"I understand—"

"Do you? Perhaps you'd prefer I returned you to that bloody battlefield where I found you wounded and unable to protect yourself from Morgana's men."

"No."

Rhiannon's face softened. "When you retrieve the artifact, bring it to the hall."

Sorcha nodded, her chest tight.

The goddess turned away, paused. "I never assign these tasks without being certain each of you is equipped to handle it."

It was more of an explanation than Rhiannon usually offered, which was none.

The goddess vanished, leaving Sorcha alone once more. Her sword reappeared on the ground a few feet away, but she made no immediate move to retrieve it. Her muscles were locked too tight and she hadn't made up her mind if the painful churning in her stomach was going to make her throw up.

She didn't want to kill him, and yet disobeying Rhiannon wasn't an option. Fury rose in her, hot and fast. Fury directed at Cale for knowing her. For making a situation impossibly complicated and refusing to give her the dagger.

But most of all she was furious with herself for getting sucked in so deep, so quickly. If she hadn't hesitated to force the truth from him, she wouldn't have disappointed Rhiannon. She wouldn't have taken so long to do her job.

She wouldn't have spent last night with him.

Sorcha sighed, her anger fading at the thought of what she might have missed out on if she'd remained the cool, detached huntress Rhiannon had dispatched.

A breath of movement whispered across the back of Sorcha's neck, and she spun, tossing her knife.

It stuck in the ground a few inches from Cale's bare foot. The man had pulled on pants but hadn't gotten around to doing up the top button. Given his lazy smile, the oversight had been intentional.

He picked up her knife, studied the blade before glancing in her direction.

She shrugged. "Guess my aim is off."

"Is it?"

She collected the knife from him, unable to avoid the fingers that brushed the inside of her wrist as he handed it over.

Like before, his touch pushed her heart into the next gear. She drew back before the yearning that took hold made her step into his arms. That spot between his shoulder and neck had to be the most perfect place to rest her head.

Turning away, she threw the knife. This time it struck the middle of a tree a few meters away.

"You never even hinted at being a huntress."

"Didn't you wonder how I could be immortal?"

He nodded. "You said you were rewarded for coming to the goddess's aid during a confrontation with Morgana."

An unlikely scenario, but not improbable. Though a long-ago pact with another god prevented Rhiannon from directly moving against the sorceress, the goddess had manipulated circumstances in the past to strike out at Morgana.

"How long were we together?" She asked to appease her curiosity.

"Six years."

A blink of time when you could live an eternity. "And not once did you wonder where I disappeared to?" She wouldn't still be a huntress if she hadn't continued to do her job after they'd met.

"You were rarely gone for long periods of time." He followed her to the tree, cringed when she jerked the knife free.

"It must have bothered you." Already possessive, she couldn't imagine he'd been okay when she'd vanished with little explanation, without knowing where she was.

"You were my mate, not my slave. I didn't demand extensive explanations for the absences or brood over it. I knew it if was important, you'd tell me."

She snorted.

Looking annoyed, he crossed his arms.

"Oh, come on. You expect me to believe that?" Throughout her short mortal life, she'd witnessed how controlling men were, had seen dozens of women succumb to their husbands' demands with few objections. Had witnessed their cold brutality when they were denied what they believed was there due.

Immortal males were even more territorial. She'd confronted enough of them to know that much. Enough to make her doubt Cale would have been so laid back about it.

"We argued over it sometimes," he admitted. "But it wasn't a big deal."

Didn't sound that way to her. Her expression must have mirrored her thoughts because he crossed his arms.

"Not at the time anyway. Knowing now what you were doing changes my perspective a bit."

"That's what I thought."

His gaze darkened. "So I'm not supposed to be concerned about my mate tracking down traitors and rogues?"

She opened her mouth.

Cale growled. "I swear to the gods if you're about to deny being my mate—"

"Whatever we were to each other has nothing to do with the present."

His eyes went completely cat on her. "The hell it doesn't."

"So what happened then? How is it you saw me die and yet I'm standing right here?"

Some of the anger left his face. "You were run through by a wraith's sword and when you hit the ground, he kicked your body into the fire pits."

A wraith? She wasn't chummy with any of the former knights. Like huntresses, they didn't play well with others. Then there was that whole drinking blood thing. Still, she couldn't imagine any risking Rhiannon's anger to attack her.

And the catacomb fire pits?

She held up her arms. "No scars." Which he must have noticed by now. Since the fire pits were mystically charged, she wouldn't have fully healed from those kinds of burns.

Cale caught her hand and she realized she'd all but invited him to touch her.

He rubbed his thumb back and forth across the inside of her arm. "I know."

She kept her gaze down. "When was this?"

"Eighty years ago."

She would have only been months, maybe even weeks away from her last cleanse.

"I keep running it over and over in my head," he said softly. "Trying to figure out how I didn't know you'd survived. I should have felt it somehow. Should have found you."

Unless she hadn't wanted to be found. But she didn't say that. Couldn't speak past the tightness in her throat. He was giving her that look again. The one that made her feel needed, cherished.

"Whatever happened, it wasn't your fault."

"I didn't protect you." He cupped her face. "I should have been there."

"I can take care of myself."

Leaning in, he nuzzled her cheek. "That doesn't mean I don't want to keep you safe. That I won't still try." His lips grazed hers. "I love you too much."

Sorcha's world ground to a staggering halt. A horde of Morgana's soldiers could have appeared out of thin air, swords waving and she wouldn't have been nearly as dumbstruck as she was right at that moment.

"I have to go." The words ran together as she stumbled back a step. A lot of steps. She closed her eyes. For the first time in so very long she knew she was in way, way over her head.

Chapter Six

Stupid. Unfuckingbelievably stupid.

"Wait." Cale searched his mind for something to say, something that would erase the panic that flashed in her eyes. "Just a minute. Please."

He couldn't think. Words, explanations, questions spun through his mind but he couldn't find the right thing that would make her stay.

She shook her head, her face visibly pale. "I can't... I need to go. I'll be back."

"When?"

"Soon. I'll need the dagger, Cale."

"I can't do that, Sorcha. You know I can't. Not yet."

"Rhiannon wants the artifact. She also wants you dead. If you're dead, you won't be able to help your brother." The reminder sounded rushed. "I'll be back."

The cat snarled, wanting to force her to stay. "Sorcha."

She shook her head. "I know you want me to remember you and the life we had together. I just... I have to go. Stay out of trouble and don't go anywhere."

And then she was gone.

He lashed out, his claws breaking through to slash the tree. He stared long and hard at the gouges in the trunk. He'd fucked up. Royally.

Even if there was a slim chance that hearing how he felt could help her remember, it didn't do a damn bit of good when it chased her off.

Cale pushed away from the tree, took a few steps without knowing where to go. How long would she be gone? More importantly, how did he keep that from happening again?

A familiar howl pierced the early morning air. He scanned the distant tree line. Unable to spot Nate right away, he headed west, toward the forest.

After getting enough details from Arden to track Sorcha, he'd been stunned to recognize some of the landmarks on the way to her lair. It couldn't be a coincidence Sorcha had chosen to make a home so close to the lagoon, a place they'd come countless times. A place he hadn't been able to return to for the last eighty years. Maybe if he had, their paths would have crossed decades ago.

Still furious at himself for not sensing she'd been alive, he shucked off his pants and shifted. The short run only fed the cat's determination to hunt down its mate. So much so that it took Nate saying his name a few times for him to focus on anything but tracking Sorcha.

"Well you're still alive," Nate said when Cale reluctantly shifted.

He gave their surroundings a more thorough inspection. He doubted anyone would be hanging around so close to Sorcha's lair, but he preferred not to be taken by surprise either.

"If you thought I was insane for encroaching on a huntress's territory, what are you doing here?"

Nate's eyes glinted, his wolf half surfacing at the reminder of where they were. "The sorceress who cursed your brother, I think I may know where to find her."

"Arden?" Cale had mentioned the situation to Arden before he'd left, hoping something might come of it.

Nate nodded. "But it was hard for her to pin down the exact time, so we need to leave now."

The cat snarled in protest, nearly drowning out the part of him that knew he couldn't let his family down. Tristan had been shouldering much of the blame for Cian's state from the beginning, but what kind of a brother would that make Cale if he let this kind of opportunity pass?

Sensing Cale's hesitation, Nate said. "We might not get a chance like this again if we don't go now."

He nodded grimly. "Where's the pup?"

"With my sister." Nate waited. "We need to leave as soon as possible," he added, transitioning seamlessly back to his wolf form.

Alert, the gray wolf watched him, waiting.

Cale glanced back over his shoulder. Sorcha could be gone for hours or return at any moment. There was no way to know. No way to know if she'd come back alone or with back up. She had to know he was serious about holding on to the dagger, leaving them at an impasse.

A sharp bark cut off his train of thought. Twice now he'd been forced to leave her side when he'd only just found her. That knowledge only intensified his guilt, made the cat want to dig in, stay.

Nate started in the opposite direction, circling back around when Cale didn't move to follow.

What if she needed him and he wasn't there? He'd lost her once. The wolf pawed impatiently at the ground, reminding him that according to Arden, their time was limited.

The pain in his chest made it increasingly harder to choose.

I can take care of myself. Sorcha's words echoed in his head. She hadn't died. Somehow, someway, she'd survived, and as much as it killed him to think of her returning to find him gone, he knew he needed to trust her instincts.

That didn't stop the indecision from flaring all over again the moment he shifted back to his cat form. Only snarling at Nate, who responded with an equally wary growl, managed to keep him from tearing through the trees to return to Sorcha's lair. The men's trust was the only thing that allowed their animal halves to tolerate the other.

Forcing himself to think about his family, the one thing he could do something about right now, he promised himself to return as soon as he could, and trailed after Nate.

"Where the hell have you been?"

Where hadn't he been was the real question as far as Cale was concerned—and he'd been asking himself that since leaving Sorcha's lair—but voicing it seemed impossible when he couldn't lift his head off the damn couch. Maybe if it didn't feel like a wrecking ball had nailed him right between the eyes.

Through slitted eyes, Cale watched his brother slam his office door, thankfully drowning out the music from the bar downstairs. Of all the places for Nate to dump him. His friend hadn't listened when he'd insisted on returning to Sorcha's, in between stopping to empty his guts every few minutes.

Damn Korrigans. One minute he'd been within striking distance of the sorceress, and the next he'd been flat on his ass.

So no sorceress. No freed brother. No Sorcha.

Oh yeah, he was batting a thousand tonight.

"You look like shit."

He didn't even open his eyes to look at Tristan. "You too."

"Briana and I've have been worried about you."

"How long have I been gone?" It was hell trying to keep track when time passed so much faster in the human realm than in Avalon, plus he'd lost days tracking the sorceress through Korrigan territory.

"Almost a month."

The cat prowled restlessly in his mind, demanding he get his sorry ass up and find his mate. That Sorcha hadn't tracked him down wasn't sitting well with either man or beast. The certainty that she'd be on his ass in a heartbeat had been a deciding factor when it had come to leaving her in the first place.

He tried to sit up, only managing to lift his head a few inches before nausea clamped down on his stomach.

Tristan frowned. "How long has it been?"

"Since I've gone to stone? Too long." And it couldn't be put off much longer. His injuries were too extensive and his mind too exhausted. Once the sun was up even his need for Sorcha, which was the only thing keeping him conscious at this point, wouldn't stop the inevitable.

"At least you didn't burn the place down while I was gone." He would have knocked on the table next to him if he could have reached it. He needed to save his energy anyway. He'd be leaving just as soon as he figured out how to move without the world tipping.

What the hell had that Korrigan done to him? One minute he'd had the sorceress cornered, and the next flashing red eyes had come out of the dark and he'd been treated to a vicious lashing. One he was vaguely aware of actually begging for thanks to the Korrigan entrancing him. If not for Nate, he'd probably still be the bitch's whipping boy.

He'd known the risks when they'd crossed into their territory, knew their magic stemmed from the darkest places in

Avalon. Korrigans even intimidated Morgana. At least that was the bedtime story cubs were told when they were too young to understand the risks Korrigans posed.

It was that fear that probably prompted the sorceress to hide out in their territory.

"The bar is fine. Can't say the same about you. At least tell me you managed to figure out how to use the dagger."

"Sort of."

"Where is it?"

He shook his head, forced his eyes open. Thankfully there were only two Tristans instead of five. Squeezing and opening his eyes again helped a little. "Where's Nate?"

"He just left. Said he figured you might try to off yourself if he'd taken you home instead of here."

"What?"

Tristan shrugged. "Something about going to see a huntress."

"Sorcha," he began.

"Shit man, you are messed up." Concern flashed across his brother's face.

"No." He made it to a sitting position, only having to swallow the bile that rose in his throat twice in the process. "The huntress is Sorcha."

"Oookay." Tristan poured him a drink and watched as Cale miraculously brought it to his lips without spilling any. "You need to be patched up and get some sleep."

Cale followed his brother's gaze to his bloodstained shirt. That explained the bitch of an ache in his side.

"What were you and Nate doing anyway? You've missed a hell of a lot in the last month."

Something in his brother's voice sounded different. He searched Tristan's face. "We were tracking the sorceress who cursed Cian. Arden thinks she's the key to freeing him."

The door to Cale's office opened and Kennedy poked her head in. The blonde bartender's smile quickly turned into a frown when she noticed the sorry state he was in.

"I thought the wolf was jerking my chain." She crossed the room. "This wasn't the work of a wraith I hope?"

Wolf? Wraiths? He shot his brother a troubled look. Last time he'd checked, Kennedy had been oblivious to the immortal crowd she regularly catered to downstairs. When had she—

Tristan's arm slid possessively around her waist.

Hell, he had missed a lot apparently. His gaze darted to Kennedy, his eyes widening. "Mated? You're human." He cocked his head thoughtfully. Or was she?

"Long story," Tristan began.

Something below drew Kennedy to the bank of windows overlooking the club.

Tristan scowled. "If Dolan is causing trouble—"

Kennedy snorted. "You'll what? Challenge him to another arm-wresting match?"

His brother shrugged. "You won't let me stalk him.

"Or pounce. Or chew."

"Or anything fun," Tristan countered.

Cale gripped the side of his head. "Maybe you two could do this later if you don't mind."

"And it's not Dolan that's making people nervous down there. A pack of wolves is harassing some brunette by the bar." Kennedy opened the door.

With so many immortals below, the air was ripe with exotic scents, but only one made the cat claw at the edges of his mind.

"Where are you going?"

Tristan moved forward to help when Cale staggered to his feet, determined to block out the pain. Block out everything but his mate.

Beyond his office lights pulsed from the stage, drenching those below in blinking shades of red, blue and white. Even with bodies crammed together and the music pounding out of speakers, he had no trouble spotting her.

One guy was already out cold at her feet. That probably explained why everyone within ten feet was giving her a wide berth. Everyone except the remaining wolves.

Judging by the empty pitchers on the table they'd collectively vacated, they were young and looking for trouble. By the time Cale made it to the stairs, the cat pulsed dangerously close to the surface. Breaking his own club rules and shifting wasn't a good idea at all, but if one of those wolves put a finger on his mate...

They looked ready to put a whole lot more than just a finger on her when he started shoving through the crowd. He growled in warning, and a few immortals backed up before he plowed them over. The last handful of spectators were too caught up in watching the wolves close in on Sorcha to pay any attention to him.

"Hey!" Tristan snagged Cale's arm. "Not a good idea, bro. You need..." Tristan's hand fell away, and he knew his brother had spotted Sorcha. "Fuck me."

One of the wolves said something to Sorcha. She smiled at the comment, and then nailed him in the jaw with a punch that shattered a few bones. Seeing their friend go down, the others moved in, snarling.

A bouncer would have stepped in to avoid the bloodshed by now, but even the closest one seemed reluctant to go near Sorcha.

Cale knocked the last person between him and the wolves aside. He was only a handful of feet from his mate when two more gargoyles hit the floor. The first ones down were already back on their feet, but Sorcha didn't even slow down.

She seamlessly rotated, kicking the wolf in front of her before jamming her elbow into the gut of the one who'd come at her from behind. When he doubled over, she pivoted and caught his head, smashing it down to meet her knee.

With four wolves struggling to get back up, the last one left standing might have made the smart call and gotten the hell out of there. Except some jackass enjoying the show shoved him right at Sorcha.

The wolf grabbed a pool cue from the culprit's hand. Not that he had it long. Sorcha snatched it from him on the first swing, then rammed the end into his stomach and snapped it around to knock him upside the head.

In ten seconds flat it was over and Sorcha stood in the middle of five guys who looked more like college frat kids unable to hold their liquor than deadly immortals.

Around them, nobody moved. Nobody breathed.

And then the same asshole who'd pushed the last wolf opened his fucking mouth. "Bar fight!"

All hell broke loose.

Three more immortals came at Sorcha, one managing to

slam her up against the counter before she brought her knee up between the bastard's legs. She'd no sooner turned from him before a meaty paw landed on her shoulder.

Gripping it, she turned, bringing the dragon over her shoulder.

All around her bodies collided, the sound of grunting and flesh striking flesh, riding on the air. Hell, even an enchantress dove from the bar to land on some Fae's back.

The crowded bar had taken her by surprise when she'd flashed here in search of Cale. She had almost given up on tracking him, fearing at one point that something must have happened to him when she'd left him at her lair. The time differences between worlds shouldn't have prevented her from catching up with him for so long, and yet he'd vanished.

She'd even suspected Rhiannon had learned of the dagger and returned in her absence to personally oversee its retrieval by another huntress. Constantine hadn't wanted any of the gods—though few bothered—to interfere with the daggers, and had deliberately made the weapons poisonous to them.

Only Nessa had prevented Sorcha from going to the goddess to make sure, and given the irrational panic that had her fearing the worst, it wouldn't have been a pleasant little chat.

"He'll turn up," Nessa had said. "He can't hide forever."

But he wasn't hiding. And he wasn't dead. He stood an arm's length away. His fierce expression locked on her.

Relief came first. Then anger. Anger she directed at herself for trusting him not to run. For worrying about him. For caring.

His gaze darted to the right, but she was already whipping around, the pool cue snapping in half across a Fae's head. It took another punch to knock him backward and he disappeared into the crowd that surged around them.

Two hands settled on her hips, but her body immediately recognized the touch.

"Outside," Cale growled against her ear. His chest crowded her back, his warmth instantly draining some of the tension in her spine.

A vicious snarl erupted from him and he twisted her around, away from the trio of humans too stupid to realize they could get themselves killed in here on a regular night, let alone during a full-on brawl.

"Quite the place you've got here," she yelled over the noise.

"It was before you walked in."

"They started it."

"And you finished it." The pride in his voice made her try to turn around to look at him.

A high pitched screech sounded and water erupted from the overhead sprinklers. The crowd that had been tearing into each other started breaking apart, many heading for the exits.

Behind her, Cale cursed, his hand never leaving the small of her back. More than once he shouldered past people looking to drag them back into the fray. He ushered her down a narrow hall. Water from the sprinklers made the floor slick. More than once she lost traction before they rounded a corner and he opened a door.

Voices sounded behind them, and they stepped out into an alley. Further down, more people spilled out from another exit, heading toward the street. Cale didn't let go of her until the last of the stragglers trickled outside and away from them.

"You disappeared on me."

He edged her backward, toward the wall. "Isn't that what traitors do?"

"So now you're guilty?"

"If you're still thinking about taking me out, I might as well be."

"You don't seem real concerned about that." If he was, he'd be trying to get some space between them, not moving in until she had only enough room to breathe.

Cale leaned in, his cheek dragging across hers. "Maybe you're just not as convincing when you're not armed."

"That can be arranged, you know."

"Or," he countered, "maybe it's because you're actually glad to see me, mate."

"In your dreams, tiger."

He laughed, the sound rich and deep and close enough she felt his lips graze her ear.

"Did you come here to retrieve the dagger from your hiding place?" Reminding him of what this was really all about was the only shot she had to make him back off.

"And here I thought *I* had a one track mind." He swept his thumb across the base of her throat, the wicked undercurrent in his voice making it obvious what track his mind was on.

He might as well have put his hand down her pants because the effect was the same. Her whole body got hot.

"Maybe you should talk to someone about that," she suggested, barely keeping her eyes open under the seductive caress of his fingers.

He laughed, the sound sexy as hell. "Like it would do any good. We both know where my head goes the second I catch your scent." He brushed her hair back from her face. "I've missed you."

One look in those baby blues and she knew he wasn't talking about their recent separation. And just that fast the last of her earlier anger and frustration was wiped out.

"How do you do that?"

He nuzzled her neck. "Hmmm?"

Her eyes slid shut. "How do you make me forget everything but you?"

"Do you want the simple answer, or the complicated one?"

"Simple." Everything else was complicated enough.

"We're meant to be."

She might have been able to brush his answer off if his voice hadn't deepened with emotion.

He touched his forehead to hers, his hand gently cradling her face. "*We're* meant to be." Then he swooped down to cover her mouth with his.

Not for all the daggers in Avalon would she admit how much she wanted to believe that. But that was the best thing about kissing him, when his arms slid around her until she fit perfectly against him, she didn't have to think or believe anything.

She just needed to feel.

With the brick wall at her back, his body slowly grinding against hers, feeling was so damn easy. And it only got easier when Cale wedged his thigh between hers, rubbing just enough to make her squeeze her legs around him in response to the soft ache deep in her sex.

The hand at her back peeled up her soaked shirt and slipped beneath. She shuddered at the warmth from his palm, moaning against his lips when he inched up and cupped her breast.

She turned her head, dragging in a deep breath in an attempt to calm her insides. Every cell in her body cried out from the closeness, the release.

The buttons on her pants gave way beneath his fingers.

Sorcha rocked up, willing him to—

He slipped beneath the edge of her panties, ran his fingers up her cleft.

Sweet goddess. She rolled her hips, making it easier for him to find the right spot. She whimpered. "There," she hissed.

"Spread your legs wider," he demanded.

Not wanting him to stop, she didn't even argue about this not being the time or place. There would be time for that later, after he made her come. After he buried himself inside her and fucked her against the damn wall.

Gods, she wanted that. Wanted it so much, she trembled from head to foot.

"Cale," she breathed. She nipped his bottom lip, and he groaned. Groaned and kissed her so hard and deep he might have bruised her mouth if she wasn't so busy sweeping her tongue across his.

A shout of pleasure rocketed up her throat as he pumped a finger inside her. Needing to be closer, she tugged his shirt up, wanting to feel skin against skin.

Cale hissed, and she drew back. "What's wrong?"

"Nothing," he growled, angling her head back to take her mouth in another drugging kiss.

Her fingers raked at his side. He tensed at the same moment she grazed a wound on his side.

"You're bleeding."

"That hasn't stopped us before."

She eased back as much as she could manage. "It doesn't count when I'm the one who made you bleed."

"You do know how twisted that sounds, right?"

She rolled her eyes. "You know what I mean."

"Sure. You've got the monopoly on torturing me."

Since one of them needed to be serious, she tried again. "What happened?"

"It happened when I was tracking the sorceress who turned my brother into a permanent rock. I only had a small window of opportunity."

Sorcha frowned. "So you didn't run?"

Cale looked amused. "Sorry, you'll have to come up with another reason to punish me."

"I don't need a reason—"

He bit her lip, his eyes gone cat.

She glared at him. "Don't play the dominate male with me."

"Right, I forgot—" he brushed his lips across hers, "—you eat kitty cats for breakfast."

"Ass," she murmured, struggling to remember what they were arguing over with his mouth drifting so lazily across hers.

A door banged open in the alley.

"There you are."

Cale caught her hand before it reached her knife. "My brother Tristan." He stepped back, giving her a second to adjust her clothes, and taking with him the only warmth she could feel when she was this drenched.

His brother wasn't alone. An equally drenched blonde hovered behind his shoulder.

"How?" The other gargoyle's gaze darted from Cale to her and back again. "You...I was there. You..." He shook his head then reached out and pulled Sorcha forward, wrapping his arms around her in a bear hug. "You're not dead."

Stunned, Sorcha slanted a helpless glance in Cale's direction. He hadn't let go of her entirely, and his grip on her hand tightened.

"At least some things are making sense now." Tristan stepped back.

"I'm glad they are for someone," the blonde said. She held out her hand to Sorcha. "Kennedy."

Cale's brother continued to stare as Sorcha shook hands with her. "How is this possible?"

"We're still working that out." For the first time in the last few minutes, Sorcha heard the strain in Cale's voice. He shifted his weight, signs of pain showing in his face.

"Now I get why you vanished. But—" he broke off looking at her, puzzled. "You do know me, right?"

Sorcha shook her head.

Inside, the fire alarm finally stopped screeching. "And to think we just got the bar back up and running." Tristan directed his comment at Kennedy.

She shrugged, not looking the least bit apologetic. "It was pull the fire alarm or let them tear the place apart."

Tristan sighed. "We need to go deal with the police and fire crews pulling up."

The pair gave a little wave and then she and Cale were alone once more.

"Couldn't bring yourself to tell my brother I'm on your hit list, huh?"

Sorcha frowned. "You might not treat this seriously—"

"Oh, it's serious." He turned, propped a hand on the wall next to her head.

"Where's the dagger, Cale?"

"Some place safe."

She planted a hand against his chest. "That's your only bargaining chip, you know that."

"I thought you didn't negotiate with traitors?"

"Stop it," she snapped. "It's the dagger or your head on a platter."

"So we're back to that. What happened to giving me some time?"

"Like the time you had to track the sorceress? It's out of my hands now." Using the dagger to bargain with Rhiannon was their only chance and a slim one at best.

His eyes narrowed. "So you're just doing your job?"

Sorcha ducked under his arm. "Yes." Because as much as she believed they'd shared something once, it was in the past. Even if she could convince Rhiannon to rescind her order to kill Cale, the two of them wouldn't be riding off into the sunset together.

He pushed away from the wall, his predatory strides tripping every internal alarm she had. "That's a shame."

She sidestepped to maintain some space between them. "Stop."

He shook his head.

"I'm not doing this. We're not doing this."

A grin curved his lips—cunning, seductive.

Footsteps echoed down the alley, but she wasn't dumb enough to take her eyes off Cale. Not when he looked ready to pounce. Every step was meant to get him strategically closer to his prey.

Her.

The fact that he appeared to enjoy her piecing that together only annoyed her. Mostly because there was no way she could be remotely turned on by him trying to corner her.

Of course, the flush of heat that started at her toes and swept upwards vehemently disagreed. Then there was the come-and-get-me smile that tugged at the corner of her mouth. And worse, the sinking sensation that she wanted to be caught.

Caught. Trapped. Pinned.

The more she thought about his body pressed up against her, the more aroused she became. Stomach-tight, pulse-jumping, panty-dampening kind of aroused.

"Come here." He might as well have skipped talking and tackled her. His words alone were enough to throw her off balance. Made her think of hot, naked bodies locked together.

His. Hers.

Noticing more than one shadow stretching across the alley wall, she risked a quick glance. At first she thought the four men approaching were the same gargoyles who'd pushed their luck with her inside.

Not wolves, though, she realized, dragons. The skin on the front guy's face flashed iridescent shades of crimson along his jaw.

A pissed-off dragon apparently, one struggling not to shift. At her current rate, she should probably expect a couple of Fae to try tag-teaming her tonight too.

Only one of the four guys spared her more than a dismissive glance, their collective attention focused on Cale. If they'd been inside earlier, they'd obviously missed her at the center of the brawl. Otherwise they wouldn't be ignoring her entirely.

The smart dragon in the bunch watched her as she edged toward Cale.

"Get lost, bitch." This from the lead guy.

Cale snarled, but she saved him from the protective crap by moving close enough he at least wouldn't injure himself further trying to position himself in front of her. She knew he'd try even if she was more than capable of handling anything these four could dish out.

The longer she looked at Cale, the clearer it became he was

worse than she'd believed when she found the wound on his side. It was just a matter of time before the dragons realized that and tried to take advantage of any weakness.

She turned her attention on the one in front. "At least have the balls to look a girl in the eye when you call her a bitch."

Another warning growl from Cale, his cat hovering close to the edge. That growl seriously hadn't been meant for her?

In front of them, the dragon who'd been eyeing her warily took a cautious step back. She would have considered the move a wise one and nothing more if not for the hatred she glimpsed in his eyes. Hatred barely masking his fear.

McKibben.

Chapter Seven

The damn dragon she'd gone looking for when she'd left Cale after that whole *I love you* fiasco—and now so wasn't the time to think about that—stood opposite them.

She strolled closer, ignoring the other three but speaking to them as she zeroed in on McKibben. "My fight is not with you."

One must have made a move toward her because Cale had him by the throat and pinned to the wall.

"If you shift, it's your funeral." Something in her tone must have given them pause, so she made herself perfectly clear. "I'm bound to track and eliminate any immortal who knowingly risks exposing us to humans."

"Huntress," one of them whispered.

"I suggest you three leave before you risk your scaly hides. Like your pal here."

One of the dragons cursed at McKibben.

"I think you can let that one go now." She nodded to indicate the dragon Cale had against the wall.

"In a minute." He gave the gargoyle, the same one who had been ready to shift earlier, a meaningful look. "Don't you have something to say to my mate?"

The dragon's eyes widened as though Cale had just said he was married to Medusa. Another squeeze of Cale's fingers and he choked out, "Sorry."

She rolled her eyes. Cale released the dragon and the three of them took off. McKibben was smart enough not to move as she spoke to Cale.

"Would you have been so quick to pin him if we'd been in Avalon?" Where the dragon could have shifted and used his sheer size as an advantage.

"If he had touched you, his throat would have been crushed before he had the chance to shift."

She didn't need to ask to know it would have been the cat and not the man doing the crushing. The violence she understood. That it stemmed from his need to protect her still took her by surprise, but didn't bother her half as much as she figured it would.

Cale looked at McKibben. "I've seen you before."

"Probably staking out the place before he made a move against your brother," Sorcha said. "He's after the dagger."

"My brother?"

"Our scaly friend here engaged a wraith to mark your brother's mate. He planned to trade her life for the dagger."

"Tristan never had it."

Hearing the guilt in his voice, she shook her head. "They handled it. And Kennedy looked more than fine to me." Men really needed to stop underestimating their female counterparts, mate or not.

"How do you know all this?"

McKibben's feet inched toward the right. Sorcha slammed her palm against the dragon's chest. "Don't move." She turned back to Cale. "I haven't exactly been sitting around keeping the home fires burning while you were gone. And you left to find a sorceress?"

Cale crossed his arms. "We need her to undo the curse."

She arched a brow. "And where exactly did you track her to?"

"First in Avalon, in the catacombs, then Korrigan territory. Then she crossed the veil and we lost her trail."

At least that explained why she hadn't been able to find him.

McKibben cursed. "Are you two done now? Or do you want to check his collar for lipstick too?"

Cale's lips twitched as though he too realized how mate-like she'd just sounded.

Scowling, she tightened her grip on McKibben. "Tell me why I shouldn't let the cat tear you into tiny bite-sized dragon bits for targeting his family."

"The dagger is the only way to guarantee Morgana will stay

off our lands."

"If the sorceress made that deal with you, you're a fool for believing her."

"We're out of options."

Call shook his head. "Why not ask the other gargoyle clans for help?"

McKibben laughed coldly. "I don't think so."

"So you'd sell us all out," he countered.

"Do you really think living under Morgana's reign will be any different than if Arthur rose again?"

"Yes," she and Cale answered in perfect unison.

"You're a goddess's flunky. I don't expect any different from you." McKibben glanced at Cale. "Our race was punished for Arthur's fall. What's to say Arthur won't seek vengeance against our clans if he awakes and reclaims Excalibur? We're better off taking our chances with Morgana."

"So it's true then," Sorcha mused. "Dragons do have brains the size of walnuts."

McKibben snarled at her but made no move to attack.

"So you figured you'd set Cale up as a traitor, then sweep in and collect the dagger when he was dead?"

The dragon frowned. "Traitor?"

"A representative from your clan had a meeting with Rhiannon—"

"You huntresses really are mad. Why would my clan involve Rhiannon when she might discover what the cat had in his possession?"

She and Cale exchanged glances.

"The dagger should have been mine anyway. I'd been tracking that sorceress for months before your brother swooped in and snatched it mere hours before me."

"That's not breaking our laws. You flew across the city," Sorcha reminded him.

Cale whistled.

McKibben paled. "The cat would have ripped me apart."

The cat being Tristan, she guessed. "Guess you shouldn't have targeted his mate."

A fresh wave of alarm crossed the dragon's face.

"Don't," she warned, anticipating a desperate move to get away from her.

Surprisingly, he obeyed.

Far from reassured by his compliance, she dug her phone from the pocket of her cargo pants and punched in Nessa's number. The other huntress answered on the first ring.

"I'm in the alley outside Pendragon's. I need a favor."

There wasn't time to mention the details before Nessa appeared in the alley.

Sorcha stuffed her phone back in her pocket as Nessa strolled up to them, her gaze sliding from Cale to McKibben.

"Is this Puff?"

McKibben gave her a blank look.

"As in Puff the Magic Dragon," she clarified, smirking.

"I need you to keep an eye on him for a bit."

"I suppose his limbs are off limits too?" Nessa sighed. "You're getting soft, Sorcha."

McKibben shot her a pleading look. "I flew one time. It won't happen again."

"That's what they all say, honey." Nessa patted his face, and then the pair vanished.

Cale relaxed a little. "Think he'll fight or flee?"

"Neither unless he wants to make his situation a lot worse."

"Sometimes we don't always have a choice in the matter."

Sensing he wasn't talking about McKibben's problems, she linked their fingers and flashed them to her villa. The moment she let go, Cale stumbled, forcing her to sweep both her arms around him.

"When the last time you became one with the stone, tiger?"

"You know I'm virtually indestructible that way, right?" At her arched brow, he added, "You've got that huntress look on your face. Figured I'd save you from ruining your sword trying to cut my head off when I'm stone."

Sorcha led the way down the hall, taking some of his weight as he leaned against her. "I'm not going to cut anything off."

"But you're thinking about it." He sat on the edge of the chair in the corner of her bedroom.

"Your tongue maybe." She lifted his shirt out of the way to check the wound.

Cale hissed. "Easy."

"Seeing as you faked your last injury, I'm not about to be

taken for a ride a second time."

He gripped her hips. "That's not the kind of ride I'm thinking about right now."

The suggestive comment succeeded in warming her blood, for a few seconds anyway. Nausea churned in her stomach at the sight of his wound, the makeshift bandage someone had applied hanging by the corner. "Shift."

His hand dropped to his buttons.

"I said shift, not strip."

Cale sighed. "Tease."

One look at the laughter in his eyes and she knew he'd heard correctly and was just screwing with her. "Cute," she drawled.

Despite the pain etched in the tight lines around his mouth, he grinned. "I was thinking more along the lines of irresistible, but cute works."

"Stop thinking and do your gargoyle thing before you get any more blood on my floor."

"Careful, you almost sound worried about me, mate."

"I'm worried about the bloodstains," she lied.

He stood, kissed her forehead, lingering there a moment. "I'm fine."

"Good to know," was the best she could come up with to mask the worry gnawing at her stomach. The sensation didn't last much past seeing him pitch his shirt and pants over his shoulder. "Cale."

He laughed, looking paler by the second. "Don't want them to rip."

A shimmer of color brightened the room. It wasn't the first time she'd witnessed a gargoyle shifting to their animal form, but it was the first time she'd reached out to catch the sparks that hovered on the air before fizzling out.

A large black cat stared up at her. "You're not going to lick me again, are you?"

He bumped her hand with his head.

"Smart call." She ran her palm down his back. "Though I guess I should have taken you to the roof or something."

He cocked his head, then turned and jumped on her bed.

"If you shed all over my silk comforter, I'll turn you into a throw rug."

He flopped down, but didn't close his eyes. The seconds ticked off as he watched her, waiting for something.

She sighed. "I'm not going anywhere."

Seemingly satisfied, he closed his eyes. Within seconds his fur lightened to a slate gray and he turned to stone before her eyes. She was still standing in the same position when Nessa appeared a short time later.

"Cool." Nessa rapped her knuckles on the cat's head. "Knock, knock." She grinned. "Guess nobody is home."

Sorcha snorted.

Nessa sat on the bed, one arm thrown companionably around the gargoyle's neck.

"Where's the dragon?"

Her friend cocked her head. "Do I detect a hint of annoyance in there somewhere? 'Cause if you don't want me snuggling with your stone kitty, just say so."

"He's not my—"

Nessa nodded to where Sorcha's hand had drifted closer to her knife. "Whatever you say."

Sorcha closed her eyes, cursed. "What is he doing to me?"

She spun on her heel, striding down the hall and into her favorite room in the house. Sunlight streamed through the wall of windows, caught by random prisms hung across the long panes. In the distance she could see the soft rolling hills of a neighboring vineyard.

Had she finally lost her mind? Nessa was her best friend, not some poaching enchantress, and yet she'd gotten possessive, nearly going for her knife when her friend had playfully touched him.

And it wasn't even really him, just the outer shell.

Turning back to her friend, who'd followed her, she held up her arm. "Did I ever tell you where I got this scar?" She pointed to the S-shaped mark.

"Is this really about a scar?"

"Yes!" Sorcha dropped onto the lounge in her favorite corner. "No." She closed her eyes, drew a deep breath, released it. "He's a target."

"Well it started out that way." Nessa sat next to her, bumping her arm, the gesture not one she expected when she'd nearly drawn a weapon on her friend.

"I shouldn't feel this way about him. It makes no sense."

Nessa held up two fingers.

"Peace?"

"No, two."

"Okay." Maybe Sorcha wasn't the only one suffering from temporary insanity.

"Two is the number of men you've let into your bed since your last cleanse."

"That you know of," Sorcha challenged, struggling to look like even either of those times had done much for her.

Nessa saw right through her. "Cale is the first guy to not take no for an answer. He's pursued you."

"He thinks—"

"Mate-schmate. It's not the same for us."

So why did it sound like Nessa was asking for confirmation then?

Her friend thankfully didn't wait for a response. "Our loyalty is to Rhiannon first and foremost. Right?" she added when Sorcha remained silent.

"Yeah."

"And how many times have I told you that you need to scratch the itch before the itch takes over?"

"Are you telling me sex will solve my problems?"

"Only if you're going to be open-minded."

"You do realize Cale—"

Again, Nessa cut her off. "Is just a target. It doesn't really matter what he thinks, right?"

A pit formed in the bottom of Sorcha's stomach.

"Think of it as a test," Nessa continued. "If some hot Italian stud can light your fire, then you'll know."

"Know what?"

"Whether or not you're totally screwed."

The icy stone broke away from Cale, the chunks disintegrating before they hit the ground. The scent of his mate filled his head, and he rolled to his side, stretching out across the blankets.

She wasn't next to him.

He lifted his head. She wasn't in the room either.

A pair of pants landed on the bed. He growled, baring his teeth at Sorcha's friend. He liked her even less than when she wanted to sever body parts.

She stood in the middle of the room, arms crossed. "You might want those." She picked up his shirt, gave him a disgusted look when she noticed the dried blood on it.

"Hang on a second." She vanished, returning moments later with a clean one.

He narrowed his eyes at her.

"Hey, if you want to be naked, your choice." She turned a bit, and he knew she either trusted him not to lunge at her back, or was confident he couldn't do any real damage if he tried. Probably the latter he decided, shifting back to human and pulling on the clothes.

Not once did he take his eyes off the other huntress. Certainly not when her fingers idly tapped the sword at her hip.

"Where's Sorcha?"

"Out."

Why didn't that surprise him? "How long has it been?"

"Since you got your stone on?" She smiled at her own humor. "About eighteen hours. Hungry?"

"About to offer me my last meal?"

She grinned over her shoulder. "Just trying to be nice."

He followed her at a cautious distance. "Like the kind of nice cannibals are when they fatten up the people they plan on eating?"

"As yummy as you might look naked and on a platter with an apple jammed in your mouth, Sorcha would—" she glanced at him quickly "—be annoyed if I denied her the kill. As good as your paws are between the sheets, Sorcha hasn't forgotten she has a job to do."

Cale perked up. "My paws are good between the sheets? Did she tell you that?"

Nessa rolled her eyes and led him down the hall and into the kitchen. "You seem like a decent cat—for a traitor. I'm just trying to be honest with you."

"And the point of you being so brutally honest is what exactly?"

She let out a breath. "This can only go down one of two

ways. You die or Sorcha comes up with a way to convince Rhiannon not to kill you. Either way, she stays one of us and you're still alone." She plucked an apple from the bowl on the table and took a bite. "Not exactly a win-win situation."

"Where exactly is Sorcha?"

"Whether you think you're her mate or not—"

"Where. Is. She?"

Nessa's eyes widened. "Does your voice always sound that sexy when you get all possessive? No wonder you've got Sorcha riled up."

Cale shook his head. He'd always found females in general to be confusing, but this one broke the mold. One minute she was talking about cutting off his hand and Sorcha killing him, and the next she was looking at him like he'd just landed the Sexiest Man Alive title.

If he hadn't just spent hours rebuilding his strength, he'd probably have a migraine by now.

"Tell me where to find her. Please."

"If you're really planning on being all cave-man like and dragging her home, you should know there is a dress code involved."

He felt like an idiot.

Cale set the empty champagne glass on a passing try.

An idiot for believing Nessa when she'd insisted he'd find Sorcha at an exclusive benefit of some kind. Hundreds of people were crammed among three floors. He could more easily imagine Sorcha sharpening her sword in Camelot's courtyard, waiting to call out Morgana, than chatting up any of the men and women circulating below.

He'd chosen a third-floor vantage point, leaning against the railing and scanning the crowd, and doing his best to ignore the surrounding people who'd tried more than once to coax him into conversation.

If Sorcha was here, he'd have caught her scent by now. Unless she was roaming the elaborate grounds, though he'd already checked the acres surrounding the mansion twice now.

Clearly he needed to face the fact Nessa was screwing with him. As far as he could tell, there wasn't even another immortal around that might have been of interest to Sorcha. With everything else, he doubted she'd come to support any causes.

Coming here had been a waste of time. He started to turn away, stopped first by Sorcha's tantalizing scent, then after a flash of rich dark hair. Hair piled up haphazardly, thick strands trailing across her bare shoulders and framing her face.

The cat growled softly at the edges of his mind, while the man leaned into the railing as the crowd parted and he got a glimpse of the strapless black dress clinging to every curve.

Sweet Avalon.

He'd barely begun to think of the dozens of ways he could get her out of that dress, depending on whether he wanted to start at the top or the bottom, when he noticed a human get close to her.

Close enough to drape an arm around her waist.

He dug his fingers into the railing. There was nothing friendly or accommodating about the hold the guy had on her. It radiated intimacy and possessiveness with the kind of cultured restraint Cale couldn't have exhibited on his best day.

Today wasn't even a mediocre day.

The bastard whispered something to Sorcha, and his mate smiled in response.

She was enjoying herself, it seemed, at least right up until awareness washed over her face, and she searched the crowd.

It took only a few moments for her to look up and lock onto him.

Nessa was an idiot, Sorcha thought. On the other hand, she was clearly a bigger idiot for letting her friend talk her into such a stupid idea.

And if the gargoyle striding along the third-floor balcony, moving quicker than he should and not caring who he nearly knocked over in the process, wasn't an indication of how freakin' stupid Nessa's idea was, Sorcha would give up her sword.

"Antonio," she murmured, keeping an eye on Cale's progress.

Antonio spared her a million-watt smile, but didn't break from the conversation with the guy next to him. Something about investments. Humans were way too obsessed with making money.

Cale vanished from view, and she craned her neck to spot him. "Antonio." Sharper this time, she managed to snag the attention of all the people in the immediate area.

She ignored the speculative glances, wondering as Antonio finally faced her what she'd been thinking when she had zeroed in on him earlier. So maybe he'd been one of the few men not to glance away when she made it clear she was sizing them up.

Antonio was smart, attractive, charming... Was that the problem? That she *noticed* his charm, like he had to work to keep her attention?

"*Sì?*"

"I have..." The rest of the words dried up on her tongue as she caught sight of Cale moving though the crowd in front of her.

She had only a second to take in the sex-in-a-suit impression he made before he came toe-to-toe with her.

Cale's blatant invasion of her personal space didn't go unnoticed by what's-his-name. She might have made an attempt at an introduction if she could have remembered buddy's name, and if her vocal chords cooperated.

Motionless, the seconds ticked off in her head. Cale's eyes bordered on feral. If she were smart, she'd move away from what's-his-name, or shove him out of the way before Cale took a swing at him. Or worse, a bite.

His lethal glare slid to the hand on her hip. He waited, jaw clenched for—Andy? Alex? Antonio!—to take a hint.

Her date made a sound in his throat, signaling Sorcha to say something. She didn't, couldn't, far too preoccupied noticing how Antonio's suit smoothed out the man's edges, while Cale's made his edges rawer, more primitive.

More exciting.

Antonio released her, offering his hand in greeting. Cale didn't look down, let alone take his eyes off Sorcha, his lips parting in a savage grin.

It was time to do something to stop Cale from making a scene, or worse, knocking Antonio out. So why wasn't she moving instead of getting caught up in the moment, wanting to see what came next as much as wanting to avoid it.

Or did she?

Her heart pounded, her breaths shallow and fast, a rush of adrenaline that had nothing to do with being in danger pushing through her bloodstream.

“Cale,” was all she managed before he made his move.

Instead of knocking Antonio clear off his feet, Cale caught her around the waist, and pulled her against him. Their knees bumped, and she braced one palm on his chest for balance. Not that it mattered when he swept his mouth across hers and knocked her whole world off its axis.

She heard the sudden ceasing of conversation around them. Felt the moment Cale’s need to stake a claim was overtaken by the hunger he never held back. The arm keeping her close tightened, his other hand sliding up, brushing her shoulder and finally cradling her jaw.

Someone close laughed, or maybe they were far away. The whole room could burst into mad giggles and she wouldn’t have cared. She was too busy melting into Cale, sinking her fingers into the crisp shirt as she angled her head, letting him deepen the kiss.

His tongue caressed hers in soft, teasing strokes, his mouth slowing things down until their lips were barely moving. For a moment everything around them came to a stop and they were alone in the vast room.

All at once the sensation evaporated and the real world poured back in. Voices, music and someone saying her name.

Nessa? No, Antonio.

Cale started to back away, but she caught his face between her hands, lingering for one more second.

Satisfaction and arousal glittered in Cale’s eyes when she finally drew back, but it was anger she heard when his lips brushed her ears.

“We need to talk.”

A shiver slid down her spine. From anticipation or dread? She didn’t even attempt to apologize or offer an explanation when he turned her around and maneuvered her through the crowd.

He growled something that sounded suspiciously like, “Unbelievable,” under his breath, and some of the heat building inside her fizzled out.

Sorcha planted her feet to the point one of her heels threatened to snap before Cale stopped. She opened her mouth.

"Did you find him here or come with him?"

"Does it matter? If you have your way I won't be leaving with him." Until right then she hadn't realized how dark his eyes could get.

"Is that what you came here for, to find someone to go home with?"

"It crossed my mind." Briefly. Though once she'd spotted Cale, she'd known she never would have stepped one foot out the door with Antonio or anyone else.

He nudged her down the hall and through the closest door, shutting it behind them. "We're mated. Does that mean nothing to you?"

"Do you really want to go there? Fine, then let's talk about your sex life or lack thereof. Because you've been completely celibate for the last eighty years, right?" she drawled.

Exasperated, he shook his head. "I thought you were dead."

"And I didn't even know you, how is that any different?"

"You know me now," he challenged.

"For days. Not years or months or even weeks. You might be able to slip back into the past, but it's not the same for me."

"You may not have the memories, but you feel what's between us."

"What I feel is—"

"All that matters," he finished for her. "You want to know what I think?"

"Not particularly." Not when it involved him propping one arm up as though keeping the door shut would give him some kind of advantage.

"I think you're feeling a whole lot more than you've been letting on."

She crossed her arms, did her best to look bored.

"I think I got you more worked up a minute ago with one kiss than Fabio could have done with a whole night."

"Full of yourself much?"

"Not really." He leaned in. "I was just right there with you. For every breath you drew, I took two. Every time you made that needy little whimper in your throat—" he nuzzled her there, "—mine got tighter and tighter.

"And let's not forget the most telling detail of all. That kiss made you wet, didn't it? I'll bet if I slipped my fingers under your dress, your panties would be damp."

Sorcha closed her eyes. "There's just one little hole in your theory. I'm not wearing any panties."

Chapter Eight

She heard rather than saw his jaw clench, and it took a good long minute before he finally drew back.

"Are you trying to provoke me, mate?"

"If by provoke you, you mean pointing out the obvious, then I guess so."

"It's been obvious you're not wearing anything under your dress?"

"I'm sure you would have figured it out by now if you stopped talking long enough to put your hands to better use than holding the door shut."

His eyes darkened, but he didn't move.

"If I wanted to leave, I wouldn't need to use the door. I'm not going anywhere, tiger, and I wouldn't have left with anyone tonight. Except you," she admitted, surprised by how true that was. She'd felt more alive in his arms in the middle of a party, surrounded by humans, than she did when hunting down her toughest adversaries.

And if she felt this way now, she could have—would have—before.

Cale snared her wrists and pinned them above her head.

"So now you don't trust me?"

"It's not you I'm struggling to trust." His gaze slid down to the deep V of her dress, then lower. He slowly released her hands. "Leave them there."

"Or?"

The promise of retribution flashed in his eyes. He gripped her hips, his thumbs idly massaging her.

She bit her lip, the warmth from his touch sinking through

the material to heat her skin.

Gathering the hem of her dress between his fingers, Cale tugged it up. He shook his head before she moved her hands an inch. "Don't."

"Are you about to play the dominate-male card again?"

A cocky smile curved his mouth. "Are you going to pretend you don't like it?" Cale didn't wait for her to answer before he slipped two fingers between her thighs and pushed up and inside her.

The gods help him, she was wet. And hot and tight and he wanted inside her, needed inside her.

Now.

In record time Cale had her dress to her waist and his pants undone. Catching her thigh, he opened her a little more, fitting the head of his cock against her slick center.

They both moaned, and then Sorcha rocked up on the balls of her feet, using the leverage to slide down his shaft.

His eyes nearly rolled back in his head. The sensation damn near short-circuited every last brain cell. Cupping her ass, Cale lifted her up, urging her legs around his waist a moment before he sank deep inside her.

Lust, thick and hot, licked up his spine. This wasn't exactly how he'd imagined the night playing out when he'd arrived, but he doubted it could get any better. Already she was gripping him so sweetly, rocking impatiently, demanding he move with those sultry little whimpers she made.

Buried to the hilt, he pumped his hips, sliding free and driving back into her. The hot walls of her sex closed around him, coaxing him to get as deep and snug as he could.

Sorcha cried out, gripping his shoulders so hard he wondered if her nails had ripped the suit. Not that he cared. He buried his face in her hair, fucking her against the door so hard it rattled.

She arched in his arms, clenched all those slick muscles.

Voices echoed in the hall, but he didn't back off, not even when whoever it was lingered outside the door.

"Don't stop," she murmured against his ear.

As if he could. Certainly not when she put her mouth on his neck and sucked so slow like that.

He slowed the rhythm, sliding soft and easy, so he didn't give them away. Sorcha flexed her hips, changing the angle just a bit. He growled low and deep, widening his stance.

Over and over he plunged his cock inside her, working deeper, faster.

"Cale," Sorcha whimpered, clinging to him even tighter.

Needing her in ways that scared even the cat in him, he nipped her jaw, snaring her attention. He'd been careful not to push her too hard, but tonight she'd pushed him and there was no softening the words he needed to say, no taming the savage instinct to make sure she understood him completely.

"You're my mate, Sorcha. I will not share you. *Ever.*"

Eyes dark with need, she silently held his gaze.

"Say it."

She averted her face, her eyes sliding shut.

"Sorcha." He bit her lip, thrust hard inside her. "Say it."

"I can't," she panted.

Already screwing her so slowly, it took the last threads of his concentration to take things down another notch. "Tell me. Tell me you're mine, Sorcha."

The denial came slower this time, softer. "I..."

He sealed his mouth over hers, sliding his tongue inside. If she needed proof he could do this all night, drag out the pleasure, until she admitted to the both of them—

"Cale," she begged. She squeezed her eyes shut tight. "I...we're mated. Sweet goddess, I'm yours. Always yours."

As much as he'd always believed they were incredible together, right then it was even better. Grateful and still a little bit desperate, he ground her harder against the door, getting all the way inside her and rocking fiercely.

Sorcha cried out, her sex clutching every inch of him as she came.

He caught her mouth in a wild kiss that almost matched the frantic finish as his own release roared through him moments later.

It took longer than he expected to catch his breath and lift his head off her shoulder. When he finally managed that much, Sorcha made a small sound of protest, so he didn't let go of her. He wasn't ready to anyway, and knowing she felt the same filled him with the kind of contentment he hadn't felt in decades.

She ran her fingers up his neck and into his hair, and both man and cat reveled in the light caress.

"Like that?"

He let the appreciative rumble that echoed in his chest speak for itself.

She laughed, and his goofy, insanely content smile widened. Gods, he loved the sound of her laughter. Loved her.

Cale leaned in for a quick kiss and ended up dragging it out until he felt himself get achingly hard all over again.

Which turned out wasn't nearly as much of a problem when their surroundings disappeared, both figuratively and literally. Not only were they back in Sorcha's villa, they were in her bed.

He wasn't sure if it was the method of travel or just how damn hot his mate was that left him a little dazed.

"It'll pass in a second," she whispered against his lips, sensing his disorientation.

He trapped her lip between his, indulging the cat's need to play. "Do you happen to have a very large, very hot tub by chance?"

She grinned. "Maybe."

He rolled to his feet, buttoning his pants so he didn't trip over them, then pulled her after him. His gaze fell to her throat and then lower still to the swell of cleavage.

He twirled his index finger. "Turn around."

"We should—"

"*We* shouldn't do anything, but you should indulge your mate."

Cale waited for that flash of denial to surface in her eyes, unsure of whether to be wary or relieved when she gave in without argument.

Brushing aside the hair that had fallen loose since he'd dragged her through the crowd, he pressed a soft kiss to the back of her shoulder. That was all it took to almost make him forget why he'd wanted her to turn around in the first place.

He indulged in another taste of her, another moment of drawing in her addictive scent until he forgot about hot tubs and running his hands down her slick skin, then finally reached back and unclasped the pendant Sorcha had given him long ago.

Sorcha shivered from the feather-light kiss, anticipating the next one before Cale's mouth left her skin. She glanced over her shoulder, but his arms were already coming around her.

Something cool brushed her cleavage and she recognized her brother's pendant.

Cale adjusted the thin strap, dropping another delicate kiss at the back of her neck. "It suits you."

She clasped the pendant in her hand and closed her eyes. "I didn't ask for it back." She hadn't asked for anything and yet he seemed to know just what she needed. A smile. A challenge. A kiss.

A piece of their history.

She hadn't wanted to ask for it back in the beginning, assumed she'd take it back when her job was complete. Thinking about it all had become hard, let alone wondering what would have possessed her to have parted with it in the beginning.

"Hey." Cale turned her around.

She ducked her head, but not before she was sure he'd seen the unshed tears in her eyes.

"Shit. I didn't think it would upset you." He wrapped his arms around her. "You'll remember me. When you least expect it, our past will come crashing back."

Of course the cat was just arrogant enough to think this was all about him.

But wasn't it? Wasn't it the whirlwind of emotion he invoked that made her actually *want* to remember him? That made everything so hard? She was drawn to him in ways that defied explanation. He should have been dead by now and yet from the start her instinct had been to get close to him.

Gods, she wanted to be with him, to relearn the ways to decipher his tone of voice, to gauge his moods. Wanted to find out how good he was with a sword and how fast he could run as a cat. Wanted him to teach her to swim and spend mornings tangled up in bed and mussing his hair so she could laugh at his bedhead later.

She wanted...forever.

Something in her heart broke a little. Because as crazy as it was to believe she could fall for someone so fast and hard, she knew it would never work. Not when it meant giving up who she was.

"No."

He frowned. "No what?"

"No, I won't remember." She moved out of reach, digging deep in search of the cool, practical woman she'd never had a problem being before.

"Won't remember, or don't want to?"

"I didn't die, Cale."

He shook his head, confused. "I'm aware of that."

"Then hasn't it crossed your mind that maybe I gave you my pendant for a reason. That maybe I knew I wasn't coming back."

Not until the words left her mouth did the truth of that sink in. She'd felt this way before and doubtlessly came to the same harsh conclusion. If he hadn't been a target when they'd crossed paths before she would have been able to lie to herself for a while. Tried to have the best of both worlds, loyal to both her mate and Rhiannon.

Until the time of her next cleanse had drawn closer.

"Slow down a second," he growled. "What do you mean, maybe you knew you weren't coming back?"

She shook her head. "It doesn't matter."

He caught her arm when she tried turning away. "The hell it doesn't."

The confusion on his face reminded her of the night she'd gone after him in the park. He'd been just as confused that night. Stunned.

Happy.

She'd remember that the most. The way he'd looked at her like she was the only thing that mattered.

Tears burned behind her eyes for the second time in a matter of minutes.

"Talk to me."

"There's no point." She touched his face, sweeping her thumb across his cheek.

"Sorcha?"

For the first time she saw fear in his eyes. Not once, not even with an arrow buried in his leg and her coming at him with her sword, had he looked nervous.

Rocking up, she brushed her lips across his, wishing they were still back at the party, before things had fallen apart so completely.

Cale groaned softly, pulling her against him, kissing her back with no restraint. Unchecked, untamed. As though the cat knew what was coming and struggled to hold on to her.

She ran her lips across his one more time, a slow soft slide that ripped her up inside, and then she backed up. "Good-bye Cale."

"Just wait a damn minute."

Running out of time, she shook her head. "We can't be together."

"We were together. We *are* together."

"No, we're not." She swallowed past the ache in her throat. "Don't you get it? I'll do it again."

"Do what? You're not making any sense."

"I didn't choose you." No matter how alive he made her feel, how cared for, protected, needed. She had turned her back on all of it.

"You think how we feel about each other is a completely conscious choice? That it's not also about recognizing something in each other and knowing we just fit. That we belong."

"It's not enough."

"Bullshit. Just—" he ran his hands through his hair, "—just try making sense. You know I'm right."

The desperate need to stop from losing any more of herself to him churned in her stomach. "I knew you'd be like this. Even then, I knew you'd pull this fated crap, didn't I?"

His eyes narrowed, more lethal feline than flesh and blood man. "So we've moved from you denying our bond to calling it crap? We're mated, Sorcha. You let me claim you, asked me to."

"No."

He stepped up behind her, ran his thumb along the back of her shoulder, close to her neck. "Right here. You might not see the mark, but it's there." He turned her around. "The same way I carry your mark here." He placed her hand over his heart.

She shook her head, determined not to let the cracks guarding her heart splinter into a thousand pieces.

"What is it that makes you so damn sure I'm wrong?"

For once she didn't have to lie to him or herself. "Because if we were really meant to be, I wouldn't have to choose."

"Choose what?"

"Between being me and being with you. You didn't see me die, Cale. I doubt I was even in any real danger." It was the only thing that made sense. "I wanted you to think I was dead."

Confusion gave way to disbelief until her words finally penetrated. "You what?" His hand fell away from her.

She should have been relieved but instead she had to force herself not to reach out and... And what, apologize? Ask him to forgive her? What would be the point? It wouldn't do either of them any good. It wouldn't take away the hurt clamping down on her chest, threatening to cut her in two. Wouldn't ease the pain she saw in his eyes.

They couldn't go back and they couldn't go forward. Not together.

She took another step back. He didn't reach for her this time.

It hurt to look at him and see the betrayal on his face knowing she'd caused it. She inflicted pain and death on countless immortals who'd crossed the line, but not once had she felt even a shred of the guilt twisting her stomach inside out now.

Damn him for making her feel this way. For making her want to be with him.

Damn her for knowing better.

"Watch your back." She meant it only as a warning if Rhiannon sent someone for him.

"Is that a threat, huntress?" The anger in his voice was sharper than any weapon.

"No." She couldn't explain beyond that, not when his gaze had turned accusing.

"Sorcha." The low growl carried just enough warning to make the next part a little easier.

Without another word, she flashed far away from her home.

Away from Cale.

"Who died?" Nessa asked, half joking, when Sorcha appeared in her friend's Manhattan apartment.

She'd taken the chance Nessa would be home, needing to know the truth. "Tell me."

Nessa sobered, her earlier humor quickly fading.

"I want to know."

The other huntress straightened. "Why now?"

It took her three tries to get it out. "I let him think I was dead, didn't I? I set the whole thing up. Nessa, please," she added when there was no response.

Her friend sighed. "You should have just let me cut off his hand and been done with it." She crossed her arms. "You made me promise not to tell you."

"Extenuating circumstances."

"Now or then?"

Sorcha shrugged. "Both."

Resigned, Nessa searched her face carefully. "You were crazy about him, though you kept your relationship with him even a secret from me for a while."

"Did I love him?"

"You don't need me to answer that," her friend said softly.

No, but it kept her from asking herself when facing the answer only made what she'd done so much harder to understand. "He wanted me."

"Cats are possessive that way."

"It's more than that." Feeling unusually contained by the surrounding walls, she started pacing, stopped. "He really thinks we belong together. At least that's what he thought before hating me."

Nessa frowned. "Wait. Hate you? Since when?"

"I chose to remain a huntress over sacrificing my abilities for a future with him." She glanced at Nessa, half expecting to find a *well, duh* look on her face.

Instead she found only concern mirrored in her friend's eyes. "And you told him that?"

"Am I wrong?"

"No. Your last cleanse was only a couple of months away. You knew he wouldn't willingly give you up, would have pursued you no matter what. You didn't think it was fair to either of you."

"I was afraid Rhiannon would kill him for interfering," she guessed.

Nessa shook her head. "No. You were afraid he would eventually make you change you mind."

"But letting him think I was dead?" The idea that she could do that to him pushed her back to pacing from one end of the room to the other. "If you would have seen the look on his face tonight." She closed her eyes, afraid to think about what she must have been feeling to make such an incredibly desperate and selfish decision.

Gods, how could she have done that to him?

"I should have talked you out of it. I had a Fae who owed me a favor and created the glamour."

"Guess that explains why he thought a wraith severed my head and kicked me into the fire pits." For a moment Sorcha put herself in his shoes, imagined him dying right in front of her.

"Where is Cale now?"

Once more Sorcha sank into the closest chair. "My place. I told him it wouldn't work between us."

"Before or after you told him about faking your death?"

"Before I think." She rubbed at the vicious ache at the back of her neck. "Maybe during, I don't know. He must hate me."

"Isn't that a good thing? If he hates you, he won't try to pursue you. That is what you want, right?" There wasn't time to answer before Nessa cursed. "Shit, you fell for him all over again, didn't you?"

Though she knew the truth, she had to voice the doubts. "How could I? We haven't been together long, and I've spent almost half that time trying to kill him or talk him into handing the dagger over."

"Just because you don't have any memories of him, doesn't mean your heart has forgotten him."

She arched a brow at her friend's uncharacteristic romantic sentiment.

Nessa shrugged. "Blame Sybil. She's got me hooked on these books..." She waved off the rest of whatever she'd been about to say. "That's not important. What are you going to do now?"

"The only thing I can." The only thing she knew how to do. "My job."

Hours. Hours without a fucking word from her. Cale didn't know whether to be relieved or furious.

Furious, he decided. At least whenever the cold ache in his chest let him feel anything at all. She'd lied to him, deceived him intentionally. The only thing worse than Sorcha dropping that bomb on him was her vanishing without filling in the rest of the blanks. And there were a lot of them.

Like why? Had she hated the idea of being with him so much she'd gone so far as to fake her death?

The vise stretched across his lungs clamped down a little harder.

Hell. He rubbed the heels of his hands against his eyes. It wasn't nearly enough to counteract the drilling pressure at his temples.

Angry and exhausted after prowling from one end of her house to the other, he dropped back on the edge of the bed.

There hadn't been a single thing on his mind earlier than getting his mate spectacularly naked, and in such a short space of time they'd done a complete one-eighty. He tried again to fully exhale, expecting some of the weight on his chest to ease, but in the seven hours and twelve fucking minutes she'd been gone, the sensation had only gotten worse.

She wasn't coming back.

The cat raked at the edge of his mind, more upset by that than the truth the man continued to grapple with. For eighty years she'd lied to him, let him think he'd lost her.

Damn, his head hurt.

She wasn't coming back. He'd seen it in her eyes in those last few seconds. Still he hadn't left, hoping, despite the fury keeping his blood pumping fast and hot that she'd realize...what?

He lay back on the bed, surrounded instantly by her unique scent. He fought the urge to roll and press his face into the blanket to breathe it in. How could she have done it to him, let him mourn her, ache for her?

And how could she have lied about getting her memory back? Or maybe it hadn't been gone at all. Maybe she'd played him from the start to get the dagger.

The cat snarled at the possibility.

"At least the place is still intact."

Cale cracked open one eye when he heard Nessa's voice. Part of him hoped she'd see him lying there as a disadvantage and make a move to attack him. He was looking for a fight just bad enough that the fact she was a huntress seemed more like a perk than a drawback.

Unfortunately she didn't move further than a few inches past the door.

Sitting up, he let the cat push as close to the surface as he dared, hoping it might provoke her.

Nessa rolled her eyes. "That's it? At least show me some of those sharp teeth if you expect me to even pretend to be worried."

She ran her gaze top to bottom, not even attempting to mask her horror. "Next time I hook you up with a suit like that, at least change before lying around like it's jeans and a wifebeater."

"If you're not here to tell me where she is, then you and I have nothing to say to each other."

Her eyes darkened. "Just because I'm not here to kill you, doesn't mean I'll listen to your crap."

He cocked his head. "What's stopping you?"

"Not you or any one of your little bitty claws, gargoyle. I would have killed you long ago if I thought it would spare Sorcha—"

"Spare Sorcha?" He laughed, the sound icy, bitter. "From what? The inconvenience of dealing with me?"

She gave him a bored look.

"Where is she?"

"She doesn't have anything to say to you."

"That's too damn bad."

"For you, yes." Nessa held her ground when he pushed to his feet and stalked toward her.

"Is acting part of your huntress training or do you all come by it naturally?" He circled her. "Maybe it's even a quality Rhiannon looks for when recruiting."

"That's right, I'm acting. Your big bad pussy cat impression is actually making me tremble in my boots."

"Was Sorcha?"

"Trembling?" She shrugged. "You were the one who got

frisky with her at the party."

"Acting," he corrected. "Or has it only been since she got her memory back?"

"Whoa. Back the litter box up, cat. Sorcha doesn't have her memory back. She never will." Her expression was almost sympathetic. "That's part of the deal we make. Our memories are wiped every hundred years."

"How convenient for all of you."

"Convenient would be killing you now. You have one week to use the dagger to free your brother and then she'll be coming for it."

"And if I don't hand it over?"

"She'll kill you."

Chapter Nine

"Let me get this straight," Tristan began, leaning against the bar. Pendragon's was empty, still closed for cleaning after the sprinkler incident. "We have a week to find the sorceress, who may or may not be in this realm, get the dagger from your super-secret hiding spot and free Cian before your amnesiac mate comes to kill you?"

Cale glanced at the empty shot glass in his hand, wishing that last one had burned as much as the others. "That about sums it up."

He reached for the bottle he'd been drinking from since Nessa had delivered him to the bar an hour ago. He hadn't quite figured out why she'd bothered. It would have slowed him down considerably if he'd needed to find his own way home from Sorcha's.

Cale met resistance and noticed Tristan's hand on the bottle.

"Is now really the time to drink yourself into oblivion?"

He glared at his brother. Tristan's eyes narrowed in turn.

A predatory grin caught Cale's mouth as he waited, daring his brother to give him an excuse.

"I think we could all use a drink." Their sister, Briana, took the bottle and filled four shot glasses.

Kennedy stood quietly behind her. He'd hired the bartender because she knew how to hold her own, never afraid to speak her mind. Yet tonight she said nothing. Considering the sympathy he read in her eyes, maybe that wasn't such a bad thing.

Cale moved a few feet from the bar, taking his shot with him. He lifted the glass to his lips, then pivoted and fired it across the room.

Fuck. He gripped the edge of the chair in front of him, breathing through his nose. The need to shift rippled under his skin, a fiery current with no way to discharge.

"What aren't you telling us?" Briana had moved closer but made no attempt to touch him, as though she knew he was struggling to contain the animal that only wanted Sorcha.

The man wasn't faring much better at curbing that urge. Except he wasn't sure how he'd handle a face-to-face meeting when her betrayal had cut open old wounds. By the gods, he'd mourned for her, for decades, and it was all a lie.

Briana touched his shoulder, but instead of lashing out, he dropped his head and closed his eyes.

"It'll work out."

Would it really? He wanted to ask but knew his sister didn't have any more answers than he did.

He loosened his grip on the chair, and sensing he wasn't in danger of throwing it and trashing the place, Briana rubbed his back a moment longer.

"We'll find the sorceress. You get the dagger."

"Nate and I—"

"Shouldn't have been tracking her alone in the first place," Tristan interrupted. His brother made it clear he wasn't happy he'd been left out of the loop on that one, even if he'd been preoccupied with his own mate at the time.

"Does she know who's looking for her?" Kennedy asked.

"I don't know. Nate and I were careful but by now..." Cale shrugged.

Kennedy finally spoke. "I could ask—"

Tristan growled. "Don't say it."

"Dolan for help," she finished.

Tristan sighed, and Cale recalled the numerous times his brother and the Fae regular had nearly come to blows.

"If he can help, then yes." Briana glared at Tristan when he started to protest. "Fae or not, we need the help. No offense," she added for Kennedy's benefit.

"None taken."

Cale just shook his head. Later he'd have to ask exactly what he'd missed when he'd gone looking for Sorcha in Avalon.

Trying and failing to be subtle, Briana returned the bottle

to the shelf behind the bar. "Will it take long to get the dagger?"

That was definitely the question of the hour. Until a few moments ago, he'd been so focused on what had happened with Sorcha, he hadn't stopped to consider the dagger.

"What?" Briana asked. "There's a problem, isn't there?"

"I hid the dagger at Sorcha's lair in Avalon."

Tristan exploded. "Are you crazy? She's been after the dagger from the start."

"Which made it the perfect place to hide it at the time." Now, not so much.

"And what if she'd killed you? We wouldn't have known where it was."

"She wouldn't have." The defense of his mate was instinctive even as he knew he deserved the fury in Tristan's voice. If he'd been wrong, he could have cost their brother his freedom.

"What about now?" Tristan challenged. "Because it sounds to me like you're next on her hit list."

According to Nessa anyway. But as much as Sorcha faking her death had stunned him, he struggled to understand how the woman who had come undone so completely in his arms was now planning to run him through with a sword. Then again, he would never have imagined the mate he'd argued with as passionately as he took her in bed, the mate he'd cherished—*loved*—would have been capable of betraying him.

Tristan crossed his arms. "How do you know she won't be there waiting for you?"

"Because she'd have to know that if I went looking for her, that's one of the first places I'd check."

"Unless she's counting on that." Tristan shook his head. "You can't go alone.

"If I don't go alone and she's there, she'll take it as a threat." He released the breath that lodged in his lungs at the thought of coming across her at all. "Besides, you need to find the sorceress."

Whatever Tristan had wanted to add, he changed his mind and headed for the office. Kennedy offered Cale an encouraging smile then trailed after her mate, leaving him alone with Briana.

"Do you think I'm as suicidal as he does?"

His sister shook her head, her dark hair pulled back in her

usual French braid. Of his three siblings, he'd always been most protective of her, and at the same time he knew she could be more deadly than either Tristan or Cian.

Her tracking skills were certainly superior. He'd been crazy not to seek out her help before, but there hadn't been time once he and Nate had caught the sorceress's trail.

"Where's your pendant?"

Not until Briana nodded at his chest did he realize he'd begun to adjust the strap out of habit.

"Sorcha has it."

"Did that happen before or after she went all Grim Reaper on you?"

"Before." He let out a breath. "She set it up, Briana. Her death. It wasn't real."

She was silent for a moment, then, "Why?"

"She didn't offer much of an explanation." Frustration swept through him in another choking wave, and he found himself telling Briana more than he'd planned, starting with Sorcha's revelation and everything Nessa had said about their memories being wiped.

"What are you going to do?"

"I don't know." He hadn't come close to figuring that part out. "Nothing if she had her way." That was the only thing he felt remotely confident about.

"You sure about that?"

At least he *had* been confident about that. "She decided for the two of us that things needed to end. No discussion, no warning." Not even a fucking hint.

"Then why give you her pendant? Why not sever all ties?"

"Maybe she wanted me to suffer even after she was gone?" She faked her death at least suspecting it would crush him. Doubtful she would have lost any sleep over leaving the pendant behind.

"Or," Briana suggested, "it wasn't meant for you, but for her. So if your paths ever crossed again, she'd know you meant something to her."

Cale.

Sorcha turned, feeling his presence as though he stood

directly behind her. She scanned the interior of her lair. How was it she'd gone so long oblivious to him and was now so finely attuned to him, she felt him even when he wasn't there?

Already here and gone, she decided. Recently.

Why? Had he come to fight her, or to fight for her? The thick tangling in her stomach made it impossible to tell which she feared most.

Drawn by a few cushions tossed aside in the room, her gaze turned critical. Next to the cushions, the second shelf of sturdy, bound volumes had been disturbed. A stack sat on the floor instead of tucked in with the others.

She crouched for closer inspection, wondering what her cat had been looking for. The books themselves were little more than exaggerated retellings of Rhiannon's huntresses. Nothing of much interest to a gargoyle, and yet he'd moved them.

A piece of paper jutted from the pages of one of the volumes, and she tugged it free.

Instead of reading the old language, she stared down at the English handwriting.

"Thanks for keeping it safe," she read aloud.

Unbelievable.

The dagger had been here the whole time? Her gaze fell to the post script at the bottom. "You'll have to kill me for it."

Did he provoke her intentionally to see if she was bluffing, or did he want to confront her? He could have retrieved the dagger and left without the note. Instead he wanted her to know how close she'd been to it.

She pushed to her feet. If the cat wanted to push buttons, she had no problem pushing back.

"Is the gargoyle dead?"

It took everything inside Sorcha not to react to Sybil's unexpected appearance. She was so focused on Cale, she wasn't paying attention to anything else.

"You forgot to knock." Sorcha glanced over her shoulder at the lanky redhead as though she hadn't been taken by surprise.

"Rhiannon is done waiting, Sorcha."

Which probably explained why Sybil was armed.

"If you're too busy—" she nodded to the book, "—reading, I'll handle it."

"I've got it under control." The lie rolled easily off her

tongue. Surprisingly easy when she'd had never before felt so far off her game.

Sybil looked about as convinced of that as Sorcha felt. "I'm to back you up if you're ready to finish this."

That rattled her more than Cale's break and enter. "Rhiannon doesn't trust me?"

"It's the gargoyle she doesn't trust. And his hold on you."

"I don't need help." Not the kind Sybil was offering.

Though exactly what she did need escaped her. Giving Cale the ultimatum certainly hadn't accomplished anything. Instead of cementing her resolve to do what Rhiannon demanded, she'd spent nearly every moment of their separation wondering where he was, what he was doing, if he hated her.

That ate at her almost as much as knowing she'd hurt him. But no matter how much she ached to be with him, to make it up to him for as long as it took, telling him the truth had been the right call.

Too bad the invisible fist squeezing her heart wasn't buying it. *She* barely was, and it was only thinking about the brief life they'd have if she turned her back on Rhiannon that kept her focused. Stripped of her powers, her mortal life would pass in a blink with her growing old and sick while he stayed young and strong. Immortal.

As much as she craved being with him, it would only hurt more to put off the inevitable. And if she couldn't find a way to compartmentalize the feelings he'd awakened, she only had to hold on until her next cleanse and the memories of him would be wiped out.

"I won't interfere," Sybil insisted. "The cat's head is yours."

Gee thanks, perched on Sorcha's tongue, trapped there by the lack of oxygen.

No one was touching Cale's head, unless it was her and involved running her fingers though his hair.

Yeah, that ultimatum had accomplished a lot.

Sorcha shrugged. "Fine. I've got to get some things together. Meet me outside his place in an hour and you can see for yourself I'm taking care of it."

Sybil hesitated. They might tease the other huntress about not being the sharpest sword in the armory, but tonight Sybil wasn't nearly as slow to catch on as Sorcha preferred.

Still, Sybil nodded and vanished.

Just what she needed, another headache. Arming herself, Sorcha flashed to the closest portal, and instead of waiting crossed the veil immediately.

Focusing, she concentrated on Cale's location and found herself in Pendragon's. She stood on the cat walk above the dance floor. Close by, a murmured voice went quiet and she heard what sounded like a cell phone snapping shut.

She turned, moving toward the open doorway.

Inside, Cale stood with his back to her in the middle of the room. One glance at his stiff shoulders, planted feet and one clenched fist and it was clear he knew she was there.

"I suppose you're armed," he drawled.

She grasped the hilt of her sword a little tighter.

"I'll presume that's a yes." Keeping his back to her as though she wasn't a threat, he moved to the small bar in the corner and poured himself a drink.

"I'm only going to ask once, Cale."

He took a leisurely sip. "I thought I was clear in my note." He said note like it was an inner-office memo letting her know the coffee maker was busted.

Cale set the glass down, his fingers lingering before a gentle push slid it away from him.

Just that fast she realized he wasn't dismissing her as threat at all. It was anger that kept his movements slow, controlled.

Was the cat so very close to the surface, ready to go for her jugular for betraying him? *Apparently*, she decided when he finally turned and his eyes were practically rabid.

"What happened to giving me a week?"

"You have no intention of handing it over at all so there's really no point in waiting."

"Fair enough."

She nearly gaped. Fair? What the hell was wrong with him? There was nothing fair about any of this. Not since he'd stood opposite her in the park, looking at her like she was a ghost.

Although that had to be preferable to the angry resignation on his face right now. It wasn't supposed to have turned out this way. He was supposed to use the damn dagger and hand it over, and if he was lucky, escape his death sentence, though how she hadn't worked out yet.

But no. He had to force her hand by refusing to give it to her at all. And now she had Sybil breathing down her neck. She'd been avoiding Rhiannon for so long, it shouldn't have surprised her that another huntress had been dispatched to assist.

"That's it then."

"Is it?" He took one purposeful step toward her. "Is it so easy to be the cold-hearted huntress again?"

Cold-hearted? Not judging by the heated rush that pushed into her bloodstream with every move that brought him closer. There was no mistaking the predatory gleam in his eyes or the way he looked ready to strike at any moment.

"Or," he continued, "was I a fool to believe you felt anything at all?"

She shook her head, willing herself to move, to react, something to stop him from getting closer. Her limbs refused to cooperate, her sword remaining lowered instead of blocking his access to her.

"So which is it?" he pressed, only inches separating them now. "Am I a fool or is it just that easy to pretend you feel nothing?"

Sensing his intention, she jerked her arm up, but not fast enough. He caught her wrist, his fingers closing around her skin, and everything inside her went still.

His hold lasted only a second, but that was all it took for their gazes to lock. Even if she'd had more time, she wouldn't have been able to mask how much his touch undid her on every level.

Surprise flashed across his face, followed by an arrogant satisfaction only the cat was capable of.

He knew.

The gods help her, he knew.

Just as she knew a moment later that they were no longer alone.

If she hadn't anticipated Sybil catching up with her, she might not have sensed the other huntress. It took Cale another few seconds to notice her outside the door.

"Job shadowing day?" he inquired, his voice cold and empty.

That should have made it easier to do what needed to be done. So why then did it feel like she was fighting everything inside her when she drew back and punched him.

Cale growled, catching his balance quickly.

"I didn't come here to play, tiger."

He drew his thumb across the blood from his split lip. "The dagger, right?" Wary now, he moved to counter the direction she circled. "Do you always whore yourself out to get what you want, or am I just special?"

Even if she deserved his anger, the words stung, and she lashed out, slashing down with her sword to catch him across his thigh.

Little more than a scratch, yet his gaze turned lethal. "You really want to do this."

She needed to do this, at least for Sybil's benefit, but she kept that to herself.

Snarling, he lunged and she flashed directly behind him, knocking his feet out from beneath him.

Like before, he recovered quickly, reaching back to catch her ankle.

Stumbling, Sorcha slammed into the desk. She had barely straightened when he tackled her, taking them both to the floor. Too easily she jammed her foot against his ribs, and pushed, flipping him over her head.

Somehow she managed not to wince when he crashed into the bar. Bottles shattered on impact, raining glass and alcohol across the floor.

He was bleeding in a couple more places when he got back on his feet.

"Stop fighting it." It was clear the cat wanted out. Cale's eyes were entirely feline, his teeth sharper looking, his claws out.

"So I should make it easy for you to kill me?" He shook his head. "If you want me dead, huntress, you'll have to look me in the eye when you do it."

"Don't make this harder than it needs to be."

"On who?" Glass crunched under his feet. "Unless you grew a conscience between your *death* and today?" Judging by his tone there was a bigger chance of an asteroid striking Earth.

"Hardly." She lunged for his right side and when he snarled

and moved to block, she flashed to his left, catching him again with her sword.

He hissed, his claws raking her shoulder in retaliation. She kicked out, dodging the next swing of his fist. He staggered under the force of her return attack, but stayed on his feet.

Even angry and bleeding, his clothing ripped, he was the best thing she'd ever laid eyes on. The best thing that had ever happened to her, and she was only hurting him more.

She didn't know whether to be grateful or frustrated that Sybil's presence kept her from tossing her sword aside and wrapping her arms around him.

"You never gave me a choice," he snapped, a thread of hurt buried beneath the anger. "You could have said something. We could have figured it out."

"What's done is done."

"Fuck that! You decided without giving me a say. What gave you the right to make that call? If you knew what losing you nearly did to me..." He broke off, his laugh chilling her to the bone. "You can't even remember if you felt the least bit guilty, can you?"

Worried Sybil would realize there was more to her and Cale's relationship than just their recent confrontation, she struck out, catching him in the chest.

She deliberately herded him away from the door and lowered her voice. "You know, tiger, even cubs know when to shut up."

Oblivious to how much he risked exposing everything, he pressed on. "But you know the one thing that doesn't add up?" He cringed when the next swing of her sword caught his shoulder. "Why not keep your pendant? Why leave it behind? Or did you just want history to repeat itself?"

She faltered, the significance of that hitting her nearly as hard as he did when he followed the comment with a blow that knocked her off her feet. She would have known that in leaving it behind, she risked recognizing it if they ever met again.

Had she hoped it would be different the next time around, that she'd find a way to have a future with him?

Sorcha wasn't sure who to be the most disappointed with. Her past self for hoping for the impossible or her present self for failing to find a way to make it happen.

But that wasn't what she said when she planted her hands

on the floor and pushed off, using the momentum to spring back to her feet.

"I actually try to learn from my mistakes." She said it loud, needing Sybil paying attention to her and not Cale.

Another trickle of awareness rolled down her spine. Nessa.

The other huntress leaned in the doorway. "Damn, if I'd known I was going to find a show, I'd have brought nachos and beer or something."

Cale snarled at Sorcha, ignoring the other two. "So killing is a spectator sport for you people?"

This time when they met, Sorcha twisted around to throw him, making sure he hit the wall hard enough to keep him down a little longer this time.

"It's under control."

Nessa's expression revealed only disinterest when she nodded to Sybil. "She's just gonna play with him now." She yawned. "Since I've got a serious craving for nachos all of a sudden, how about we hit that pub you're always raving about? Sorcha's got this."

Sybil slowly nodded, though Sorcha wasn't sure if it was because she was buying it, or simply wasn't about to push her to finish it then with Nessa there. Dissension in the ranks wasn't any more acceptable to Rhiannon than failing to complete an assignment.

By the time Cale started moving, the other two had vanished. Sorcha swore to herself she would never again complain about Nessa's habit of popping in at the most unexpected moments.

Relief spread through Sorcha, dulling her response time when Cale caught her ankle and yanked.

She landed hard on her back, pain flaring across her skull when her head hit. Cale was on her in a heartbeat, his grip on her arms crushing.

"Cale," she tried, but didn't get any further before his head slammed into hers, dazing her further. "Wait," she managed, getting one arm up and punching him in the side.

He flinched and his weight shifted, giving her just enough wiggle room to knock him off.

She scrambled to her feet, wincing at the pain that took a few moments to shake off. "I knew you were hard-headed." She rubbed her head. “But shit that hurt.”

Cale didn’t say anything and came at her again. The broken glass sabotaged both their footing, and they went down hard. He landed on top of her, his hand on her throat.

Neither of them moved, their breaths coming fast and hard.

“I’m not cold-hearted,” she whispered. “And you’re not an idiot, except for the last minute, maybe.”

His expression betrayed nothing.

She searched his eyes for the man beneath the animal. “I’m sorry.” She brought her hand up over his, but made no attempt to rip it away. “For everything.”

“Don’t,” he growled.

“Sorry for my choice, for what it did to you, for how I left things the other day. I’m sorry for all of it.”

He rested his forehead against hers. “Don’t.”

“Sorry.” She tipped her face up, grazed his lips. “So, so sorry.”

A rumble echoed in his chest, and she slowly opened her mouth over his, wishing an apology could even put a dent in the pain she’d caused him. Even if she could convince herself that she’d made the best decision at the time, it had hurt him more than she could stand to think about.

One soft kiss wasn’t nearly enough to prove just how sorry she was, but it became harder and harder to focus when he kissed her back, his lips sliding across hers.

His hand moved up from her throat to her nape as the kiss turned brutally possessive. She didn’t object when he sought to dominate her mouth, to punish her, to drive her out of her ever-loving mind.

Without warning, he broke away, putting a few feet between them before she’d even peeled her eyes open.

“I am an idiot. I just don’t know if it’s for believing nothing else mattered but our bond, or wanting to believe you now.”

Sorcha pushed herself up, the cuts on her hand from the glass already starting to heal. “It was just for show.”

He continued to watch her warily.

“They…Sybil…” She sighed. “I needed to show them…” Drained, she broke off. There really was no winning was there?

Regaining her feet, she crossed the room and picked up the sword she’d let go of at some point. Probably the moment he’d pinned her and she'd felt that explosive hunger tear through her.

"Drop it," Cale growled.

She arched a brow.

"Drop the sword, Sorcha." On his feet, he stood opposite her waiting, his arms crossed. There wasn't any warmth on his face, anything playful in his tone.

If he was trying to test her, expecting her to fight him on everything, all the time, he was in for some disappointment. She didn't hesitate, letting her sword hit the floor with a dull clank.

She'd come to depend on her weapons to keep her safe, strong. But with Cale she felt stronger, more powerful when it was just the two of them.

Nothing on his face betrayed his satisfaction that she'd obeyed him. "Your knife too."

Holding his gaze, she propped her foot on the edge of the couch they'd toppled over at some point, and drew out the blade tucked in her boot. "Feel better now?"

"Take off your boots."

"Worried I'm going to stab you with the heels?"

He only stared at her until she complied, keeping away from the broken glass once her bare feet rested on the floor.

"Pants too."

"It won't change anything, Cale." Fighting their attraction might be an exercise in futility, giving in might prove she didn't need to hide behind objects and agendas where he was concerned, but it wouldn't erase the obstacles between them and building a life together.

"Take. Them. Off."

She unsnapped her pants, worked them down over her hips.

Cale's heated gaze slid appreciatively down her body, pausing on the simple lace underwear. Letting his arms fall back to his sides, he approached her. Unlike before, it wasn't a threatening prowl, but the stealthy stalking of a hungry and skilled hunter.

He circled behind her. His lips brushed her ear. "Your shirt."

The seductive order made her nipples hard, and she bit her

lip when he brushed past her front, sending fiery currents racing across her skin. The hot ache building between her thighs jacked her internal temperature all the way up. Or maybe that was him. A steady warmth radiated between them, and she shifted closer.

"Are you purposely taking your time or do you need help?" He slipped his hand under her shirt and cupped her breast. His thumb teased her nipple, rubbing gently through her bra.

"No," she managed, catching the hem of her shirt and pulling it over her head. The least amount of fabric between his hand and her skin the better.

For a moment, she thought he was disappointed, then his gaze trailed down her throat, pausing on the swell of cleavage pushing against her bra.

He nipped her shoulder, then moved lower, covering the space between her neck and her breasts with slow sweeps of his tongue and teeth. His fingers traced the edge of her bra, dipping inside to torture her.

Finally, he bent and closed his lips over her, sucking hard. A whimper slid up her throat, trapped there as he tugged until she came free of his mouth, then laved the hard tip.

Overwhelmed by the intensity, she backed up. He didn't give her much space, sticking with her, thigh to thigh, chest to chest.

She sank her fingers into his hair, tugging when he pressed her against the end of the couch. The lopsided furniture didn't stop him from sliding his hands down to cup her ass beneath the elastic on her panties.

He pulled her up on her toes, grinding his shaft into her until they both moaned.

Sliding a hand between them, she worked his zipper down, slipped her hand inside. His sharp intake of breath only fueled the arousal simmering under her skin. She met and held his gaze, watching his eyes snap shut when she molded her palm to his cock, pumping softly.

More than anything, she hungered to push him to the edge, to watch his eyes go wild when his control slipped beyond his reach.

He didn't look away from her when she dropped to her knees in front of him and ran her tongue across the plump head, but the fierce sound he made in his throat was pure, satisfied male.

Wrapping her fingers around him, she traced him from base to tip, then greedily pulled him into her mouth.

Chapter Ten

Sweet Avalon.

The woman was going to take him out at the knees. The ones locked in place and keeping him agonizingly still as she licked her way up his cock.

"Sorcha," he breathed, burying his hands in her hair, twisting his fingers deeper as she pulled him harder between her lips.

Then he was moving with her, sinking into her mouth in short, smooth digs. Cale grit his teeth, thrusting just hard enough to satisfy the need rising inside him like a tidal wave, a need that only intensified as Sorcha traced the edges of his shaft with light, teasing strokes of her tongue.

All at once, her lips closed around him, and she sucked deeply. By the third—maybe fifth, tenth?—repetition, he was rocking his hips along with her, sliding into her mouth and cursing under his breath every time she stopped and started over.

Soft lips, hot tongue, slow suck.

He didn't have a clue how much she expected him to take. He only knew he was torn between making her stop so he could think for a minute, and begging her to drag out the pleasure as long as she could.

Suddenly desperate to be inside her, he pulled away, hooking an arm around her waist and turning her around as he sank down behind her.

On her hands and knees, Sorcha pushed back, brushing her ass against him. Slipping his hand between her legs and finding her already damp, he pushed two fingers inside her.

His mate's soft moan, combined with knowing she enjoyed

his touch, welcomed it, soothed both man and cat in ways he didn't think possible since she'd left him. He was no closer to understanding the choices she'd made or the ones she continued to try to make without him, but somewhere between his talk with Briana and his mate's appearance tonight, he knew that whatever happened, they'd deal with it together.

Gripping her hips, Cale fit his cock against her, inching inside just a little, then thrusting hard. Sorcha sucked in a deep breath, and arched her spine, sinking back on him before he could push inside her again.

Giving in to his animal nature, he pumped his hips, filling her up, and losing himself inside her. The rhythm was frantic, his need consuming him in slow degrees, creeping over his skin, they way she'd crept back into his heart as though he'd never lost her.

Sorcha looked back over her shoulder, watching him. Desire burned in her eyes. Locked inside her, he leaned down, catching her chin in his hand and taking sweet possession of her mouth.

Damn, but he needed to see more of her.

Growling, he flipped her over on her back, snaring one plump nipple between his lips. He tongued the tight nub, circling it before pulling her into his mouth.

"Cale!" She planted her heels and flexed her hips, brushing her slick center along the side of his cock.

All at once he surged forward, sliding deep.

Unbelievably perfect.

Cale didn't move for a long moment, gazing down at her. He didn't care that she couldn't remember their past. It didn't seem nearly as important as right now, as finding a way to be together.

Sorcha cried out again, her breathy little whimpers coming faster, closer together, melting with his own ragged moans until he couldn't tell where her sounds of pleasure began and his ended. Her nails raked his back, her body moving to meet his, her sex so slick and tight.

Every thrust he made inched them farther across the floor. His office was half destroyed. Hell, the world could be falling down around their heads, and he wouldn't have given up one moment that he spent watching the pleasure race across her face.

"Cale," she breathed. The velvet-edged plea struck both man and animal in the heart, and he bent to capture her lips.

The kiss was slow, their bodies instinctively easing down to match the drugging pace. Although barely plunging inside her, he knew the moment he hit all the right places.

She locked her legs around his waist, tipping up.

"I..." She thrashed around, trying to get away from him one second and clinging to him the next.

"I know." Eyes squeezed shut, he felt their connection—their bond—in the deepest places, where she was and would always be a part of him. No matter their past, no matter their future.

"I love you," she whispered against his lips, her tongue sliding inside to stroke his. She lifted her ass, and he knew the second he was losing any ability to speak, think or even breathe.

His need for her trumped everything else.

Spurred by the need to give his mate everything, he rocked them both, fucking her harder. Faster, and faster.

She moaned loud and long against his lips, her sex clenching him tight as she came. Her release triggered his own, the deep waves of it ripping down his spine as he continued to thrust inside her until he had nothing left.

Spent, he collapsed next her and pulled her close. He wasn't sure how long they laid there, limbs roped around each other, their hearts slowly calming.

"How did we meet?"

He waited until she finally looked at him, sensing she was as afraid as he was of knowing it wouldn't live up to her expectations. "You were fishing actually."

Her frown melted away, a smile playing at her lips. "What?"

"Well, that's what you always insisted anyway." Even with his office ripped apart and the two of them lying on the hard floor, Cale was more content than he'd been in decades.

Sorcha rolled to her stomach, rested her chin on his chest. "At the lagoon?"

Cale nodded.

"I don't swim, but I fish?" Her skeptical expression was laced with amusement. "But you don't think I was fishing that day, do you?"

"Nope."

She cocked her head, poked him in the side when he remained silent. "So what was I doing?"

Still a little sore from their fight—and he planned on getting the full story on that very soon—he stretched and folded one arm under his head. "Checking me out."

"Uh huh. And what were you doing at the lagoon?"

He rolled to his side, nudging her on her back. "I happened to be minding my own business and taking a swim."

"And I happened to be what, spying on you?"

He wrapped a strand of her hair around his finger, tugging playfully. "I didn't say it."

She laughed. "So you've always been so full of yourself." She rubbed her cheek against his shoulder, and he waited for her to ask whatever else was on her mind. "When did you know?"

Guessing what she meant, he caught her hand. "That we were mated?"

She nodded, slowly raising her gaze to meet his. Gods, she was stunning.

Finding it impossible not to, he ran his thumb along her jaw. "Not until the third time we met, which took me about two weeks to arrange. You were stubborn then too."

"Two weeks of skinny dipping? It must have been all that pruned and wrinkled skin that finally wore me down."

Growling, he rolled until he had her trapped fully beneath him. "You love to provoke me, don't you?"

Sorcha laughed. "No more than you love trying to dominate me."

He bent his head until their noses touched, then slid down to take her mouth slow and soft. "If I thought you would be happy with someone who would never test or push you, then I would be that man."

"So it's my fault—"

Cale nipped her bottom lip, silencing her. "Whatever you need to be happy, I'll give you. If you need me to have your back, I will. If you need me to give you space, I will. If you need someone to crawl across Avalon on their hands and knees—"

"And then have to listen to you whine and lick your wounds all the time?" She shuddered. "Let's skip the last one."

"Cats do *not* whine."

"Whatever. Meow." Her smile faded, her face vulnerable as she cupped his cheek. "You're already more than I ever imagined I would have in my life. I don't want you to change for me or anyone else."

Chest tight, he touched his forehead to hers. "Then stay with me. We'll figure out a way to make it work, Sorcha. Together. It doesn't have to be right now, or tomorrow, or even before your memories are wiped out again. If it takes keeping after you and reminding you every hundred years what we are to each other, then that's what I'll do."

She opened her mouth to reply, and seeing the doubt in her gaze, he quickly added, "Just promise me no more decisions without talking to me, no more leaving without a word, okay?"

"Okay."

A rumble echoed between them, and he glanced down. "Was that your stomach?"

She punched him in the shoulder. "I'm a little hungry. What do you have to eat around here anyway?"

"Peanuts. Maybe a bottle of maraschino cherries in the fridge behind the bar."

"Wow, nuts and garnishes. You really know how to appeal to a woman's appetite."

He ducked his head, nuzzling her throat. "If it's any consolation, I'm very, very good at satisfying some appetites more than others. Carnal ones happen to be my specialty, actually."

"Food first, then we'll talk about your specialty."

Sitting up, Cale grabbed his pants and jerked them on. He dropped a quick kiss on her head, then strode for the door. "I'll be right back."

Smiling to himself, he jogged down the steps and crossed to the main bar. The hair on the back of his neck rose, and he pivoted around.

Something struck the back of his head before he could shift, knocking him into the wall.

"Cale?"

It was a wonder he could hear Sorcha through the ringing in his head. He scrambled up, the cat in him snarling to get loose, but unable to. Panic swept over him as he faced his attacker.

Few creatures could completely contain his animal half, and the one opposite him, cloaked head to foot in black, was apparently one of them.

An invisible hand closed around his throat, cutting off his air, pinning him. He saw Sorcha step out of the office, saw the sword in her hand.

"No."

She ignored him at the same moment his attacker's sword slashed down in a deadly arc. Between one second at the next, Sorcha was in front of him, but he knew it was too late. There wasn't enough time to get them both out of there unharmed, and the regret and acceptance in her eyes told him she knew it too.

His hand closed over her nape in vain to shield the neck she'd exposed to protect him.

Pendragon's disappeared as she fell against him, her body going limp.

Cale fell back, landed on an unfamiliar floor. "Sorcha!" He rolled, cradling his mate against him.

Her eyes drifted open, and the moment awareness sank in, she jerked her hand back to touch her neck.

"He missed." Relief crashed through him.

She shook her head.

"He missed." Cale pulled his own hand from her neck. "No blood. You're fine."

Sorcha sat up. "She wouldn't have missed."

"Who?" He watched the indecision flash across her face, and gripped her shoulders. "Was this supposed to be another trick? Were you going to fake your death again?" His chest turned to ice at the thought.

"No." She moved to her knees, coming up to eye level. "I wouldn't do that."

He never would have believed she was capable of it at all if not for their past. As much as he wanted to have faith that they'd work things out, he knew she was holding back something. "Who was it? You know, don't you?"

"Cale." She touched his face, the caress. "I'm not leaving you. I swear it."

Closing his hand over hers—maybe a little too hard—he

struggled to set aside the doubt that wanted to take hold. "You put yourself in the path of the sword." Anger finally cut through his shock. He'd come so close to losing her again.

"And you would have done the same for me."

"Damn it, Sorcha—"

"I get that you will always want to protect me, but you told me we're in this together, equals. Or has that changed?"

Sensing his answer was important, he didn't hesitate. "No."

She nodded, looking relieved. "I might not always be as strong or as quick as you, but that won't stop me from fighting for you. If you can't handle that, then it will never work between us."

He shook his head, increasingly confused, but not enough to keep him from answering. "I've never tried to change you. I'm not about to now." And he meant that. As much as she pushed him, driving both man and animal crazy with the risks she took, he couldn't imagine her any other way.

"I'll never get those memories back, you know."

He pushed her hair back from her face. "We'll make new ones." Another unwavering truth. Wanting her to remember their past wasn't nearly as important as proving to her that they deserved a future.

A slow smile spread across her face, and he knew they'd be okay. Better than okay.

"There's something I have to do."

He shook his head. "It works both ways, you know. You want me to deal with your independence, you need to deal with the fact I'll always want to protect you. You fight for me, I fight for you." He waited, expecting her to vanish on him, knowing there would be no way to stop her.

Sorcha was right. If he couldn't show he trusted her to handle herself, then it would end up hurting them both down the road. Though it went against his most primitive instincts, he let go of her. Let his hand fall back to his side, his fingers curling into a fist so he wouldn't reach out to sweep her back into his arms.

Her lips parted in surprise, then she snagged his shirt and drew him forward. Every inch of her fit against him as she rocked up to catch his mouth with hers.

The kiss was almost over before it began, but in the

possessive tangle of lips and tongue—so damn hot a few of his brains cells were liquefied—he felt his mate staking a claim.

"Okay," she murmured against his lips. She laced her fingers through his. "Just try not to get your furry ass killed by a goddess."

Sorcha knew the second Cale understood, watched the shimmer of colors as he shifted to his cat form. She laid her hand on his back and returned them to Pendragon's.

"Rhiannon?"

The cloaked figure with her back to them turned, lowering her hood.

Seeing the goddess's face confirmed Sorcha's suspicions. The familiar sound she'd heard before she'd anticipated the slash of the sword had been the braided gold chain Rhiannon wore at her waist.

Stunned by the anger that pushed through her, Sorcha didn't trust herself to speak right away. She'd been loyal for centuries, learning from Rhiannon, trusting her judgment, and she'd been set up from the start.

"You never suspected Cale of being a traitor. You knew he was in possession of the dagger from the start."

Rhiannon nodded.

"What if I had killed him the very first day?" What if she hadn't hesitated and had done her job as she had every other time? "I would have lost my chance."

"Chance at what? You're a huntress."

"I love him." Without reservation, without weakness. Men had been underestimating her potential most of her existence. Her father, even the brother who'd adored her had always fought her battles for her. Few of the rogues she hunted down had considered her a threat until she'd more than proven how lethal she could be.

But not Cale. The cat wanted to keep her safe, yes, and though he'd been reluctant to let her face Rhiannon on her own, he'd been prepared to let her go. He had faith in her, had trusted her from the moment in the park, certain she would recognize the bond that existed between them.

They were mated.

Rhiannon cocked her head. "You would sacrifice all I have given you to have one mortal lifetime with him?"

"No."

Something akin to disappointment blinked across the goddess's face.

Sorcha continued, "No more than I suspect you're willing to sacrifice finding Excalibur to punish me for wanting a future with my mate."

Not surprising, the cat had to communicate his satisfaction hearing her call him that, and gently snapped his tail across her ass.

Amused, Rhiannon flicked her gaze to Cale before returning to Sorcha. "You seek to bargain? With me?"

She shook her head. "I'm merely asking you to consider that I deserve to keep my immortality as a reward for my centuries of loyalty and service."

"And I suppose if I went along with that, you'd immediately hand over the dagger?"

"Not exactly," Sorcha hedged.

Rhiannon's expression revealed nothing, then she laughed. "You've never ceased to surprise me, Sorcha." Almost relieved, she slipped into the closest chair. "I had to be sure."

"That he had the dagger?"

"That you would die for him," the goddess said softly. "How else would I know that releasing you from my service would be the right decision?"

"Release me?"

Rhiannon nodded. "Of course I hadn't anticipated you threatening me." She waved her hand before Sorcha could voice any objection to that. "You're not the first huntress to bond with another immortal, and certainly not the first to try keeping her relationship from me."

"You've released other huntresses before?"

The goddess nodded. "I had every intention of releasing you before, but you surprised me then too. You gave him up." She glanced at Cale. "He might look at it like a betrayal, but to me it was noble. Few huntresses have ever been able to make such a sacrifice. I couldn't make that sacrifice."

For the first time the ancient goddess looked vulnerable. "If I had, Arthur's mortal father might still be alive."

Sorcha shook her head, needing to be honest with both herself and Rhiannon. "My choice wasn't noble, it was selfish."

"And it wouldn't have been selfish to choose him over protecting our world, our way of life? How many immortals would have exposed us, sabotaged our ability to move unnoticed in the human world if not for you and the others?"

"And choosing him now—"

"Comes with a price," Rhiannon interrupted.

The cat growled.

Rhiannon glared at him, more annoyed than threatened. "You will retain your abilities with the exception of traveling by mere thought alone. That I cannot allow when it could be used against me."

"And in exchange for that?" Sorcha prompted, sinking her fingers into Cale's thick fur to keep him from reacting to whatever the goddess might demand of her.

"You will both vow to hunt down the four remaining daggers and bring them to me as soon as they're found."

Most of the tension in Sorcha's spine uncoiled. "Done."

"Good. Now, how about you explain what you meant by 'not exactly' handing the dagger over."

One week later

Cale brushed her hair aside, his mouth hot on her neck. "You still take too many risks."

Sorcha had to force herself to reply, guessing he'd deliberately waited to say that until his lips slid down to the curve of her shoulder, distracting her. "And it wasn't a risk when you pounced on that Korrigan?"

He snorted. "Cubs pounce."

Laughing, she looped her arms around her mate's neck, threading her fingers through his hair. "I hope you don't think that you'll be able to pounce on me when I'll no longer be able to flash out of the way."

"Aside from the fact that you love it when I pounce—" he nipped her shoulder, "—I wouldn't dream of taking advantage of you that way." His tone gave him away a heartbeat before he hooked an arm around her.

Dropping to the ground, she planted her foot in his

stomach and flipped him over her head. Landing on his back, he hadn't even caught his breath before she straddled him.

"How about I take advantage of you then?" She leaned down, grazed her lips across his.

Cale gripped her hips and rocked up, rubbing against her. "I have absolutely no problem with that."

"Things could get rough. I might scratch—" she trailed her nail across his jaw, "—bite—" she caught his bottom lip between her teeth, "—suck."

He moaned when she did exactly that, pulling him into her mouth. "Yes. Please. And I sure as hell hope so."

Grinning, Sorcha reached between them.

An impatient sound came from the sack next to them, reminding Sorcha that they weren't alone. Neither were they really in any shape to be going at it on the floor, but that hadn't stopped them before.

Beneath her, she watched Cale finger the singed hole in her shirt, his gaze turning feral when he studied the twitching sack. "She's lucky you're fast."

The sorceress's hit-and-miss ability to manipulate fire hadn't been Sorcha's biggest concern when they'd finally caught up with her. She found the way the sorceress had given up the moment she realized why they were there was more of a red flag.

Sorcha nodded in the direction of their prisoner. "Think she'll be enough to get the job done?"

"For my brother's sake, I hope so. You sure those chains will hold her long enough to undo the curse?"

"She's not going anywhere." Strangely enough, the sorceress didn't seem to *want* to go anywhere.

Cale shifted under her, pulling her attention back to him. "Now," she murmured, leaning over once more and linking their fingers together. "Where were we?"

Laughing, he scooped her up, regaining his footing effortlessly. "I believe you were about to take advantage of me."

She wrapped her legs around him. "Right." She waited until they'd cleared the basement door in Cale's mansion, watching as he keyed in the lock. The chains would prevent the sorceress from escaping by magical means and the security system would take care of the rest.

As he negotiated the stairs, she reacquainted herself with that tempting hollow at the base of his throat.

He groaned, one hand sliding under her bottom even if he already had a solid grip on her. "We could get there faster, you know."

"You mean your room?" She licked at his skin, breathing in his scent.

"Any room will do right now."

Laughing, she kissed her way up to his jaw. "I think I need to get used to traveling the good old fashioned way, don't you?" She could easily imagine herself getting used to him carrying her around like this.

At the top of the stairs he pressed her against the wall. Lethally seductive, he slanted his mouth across hers, pushing deep with his tongue until she moaned.

Slowly, he drew back, his grin cocky. "What's the matter, huntress? Cat got your tongue?"

She shook her head, willing him to see right into her soul and know he was the center of *her* world. "It's worse than that actually. He's got my whole heart."

About the Author

A born and raised Maritimer, Sydney Somers fell in love with writing at the age of eight. Since finishing her first book in 2002, Sydney has written over twenty-five romances—one of which will forever remain hidden under her bed.

When she's not tracking down remote controls, chasing after three very energetic children or exterminating rogue dust bunnies, Sydney can be found curled up with a good book or working on her next sexy, paranormal romance. She loves to hear from readers and invites them to e-mail her (sydney@sydneysomers.com) or drop by her website (www.sydneysomers.com) any time.

LaVergne, TN USA
03 January 2011
210885LV00002B/148/P